In

She sprang.

And tripped flat on her face, twisted in her own skirts.

"Oh, suds!" she grumbled as she freed herself. Quickly, she hurried across the street . . .

Harsh music spilled around the corner from the Purple Fox, and the Silver Dollar and several others down the way. Piano music and laughter. Someone singing.

"Come out of there!" she called, her pistol raised. Damn those blasted skirts, anyway. "Come out, you coward!"

She couldn't hear a thing over the sounds from the saloons. Then suddenly, the sound of boots, of running feet. One man. She gave chase, holding her skirts in one hand and the Colt in the other, but by the time she reached the end, the culprit wasn't in sight.

Disgusted, Maggie dropped the Colt back into her pocket and turned around. And nearly ran headlong into a cowhand who'd had about two drinks too many, by the looks of him.

"Baby!" he cried happily, and clamped a hand on each of her upper arms.

"Wrong!" she replied just as heartily, and kneed him in the groin . . .

MORE MYSTERIES FROM THE BERKLEY PUBLISHING GROUP...

SISTER FREVISSE MYSTERIES: Medieval mystery in the tradition of Ellis Peters...

by Margaret Frazer

PENNYFOOT HOTEL MYSTERIES: In Edwardian England, death takes a seaside holiday...

by Kate Kingsbury

GLYNIS TRYON MYSTERIES: The highly acclaimed series set in the early days of the women's rights movement..."Historically accurate and telling." —Sara Paretsky

by Miriam Grace Monfredo

MARK TWAIN MYSTERIES: "Adventurous . . . Replete with genuine tall tales from the great man himself."—*Mostly Murder*

by Peter J. Heck

MURDER
AT BENT
ELBOW

KATE BRYAN

BERKLEY PRIME CRIME, NEW YORK

MURDER AT BENT ELBOW

A Berkley Prime Crime Book / published by arrangement with
the author

PRINTING HISTORY
Berkley Prime Crime mass-market edition / February 1998

The Putnam Berkley World Wide Web site address is
http://www.berkley.com

ISBN: 0-425-16194-3

Berkley Prime Crime Books are published
by The Berkley Publishing Group,
a member of Penguin Putnam Inc.,
200 Madison Avenue, New York, NY 10016.
The name BERKLEY PRIME CRIME and the BERKLEY PRIME CRIME
design are trademarks belonging to Berkley Publishing Corporation.

PRINTED IN THE UNITED STATES OF AMERICA

10 9 8 7 6 5 4 3 2 1

JUNE
CENTRAL NEVADA

THE HOWLING WIND PELTED THE LITTLE GIRL'S FACE
and whipped her pinafore, stinging her eyes and nose
and narrow legs. "Mama, no!" she cried against the
wind's shriek, against the frantic shouts of men calling to circle the wagons, and the eager, savage whoops coming from
the horizon, growing louder with every second, sounding like
the end of the world.

"Mama, please!" she cried again, and tried, monkeylike, to
climb back up into the wagon.

But her mother, wild-eyed, pushed her down again, shoved
a metal box into her hands, and shouted against the wind,
"You go! You bury that! You don't and you'll burn in hell!
The Lake of Fire, Daddy'll see to it!"

"But—"

"Harriet! Do as I say or God will strike you down! Bury
it!"

Just then an arrow dug in the wagon only a foot above the
child's head, and she turned and ran through the blowing grit,
the crying wind, clutching the box in her arms.

She ran and ran, and finally dropped to her knees beside a
tall upthrust of yellow stone, turning her back on the wagons,
trying not to hear the human screams that were already carried
on the wind, mingling with its cry.

And she dug. She dug through the hard dry clay as if her
very soul depended on it, worming her small fingers into the
caliche, pawing madly at stones. She dug until the hole was

big enough, and then she dropped the metal box into it and covered it, shaking, with bleeding fingers.

The dust, caught in her tear tracks, scratched her when she rubbed her face, but she barely noticed. The screams were farther apart now, as the Indians leisurely finished off the last of their victims. She realized this on some level, and suddenly she froze, like a panicked rabbit. If she was still, if she was very, very still . . .

And then, from out of the blowing grit, a hand seized the back of her dress and lifted her high up, high enough that she was suddenly face to face with a mounted brave. His face was terrible, leathery and painted and scowling and wild, and blood spattered his hands and naked chest.

He was the devil.

Harriet began to scream.

ONE

MAGGIE WAS BARELY THIRTEEN, AND THE CARNIVAL'S current trick rider was teaching her how to vault a galloping horse.

"No, no, no, the left—" was the last thing she remembered Pablo shouting at her, and when she woke up she had two black eyes, a broken nose, and a very disgruntled father.

"General" Custus Maguire had stood over her, that thick shock of gray hair tipping over his brow, his broad hands set akimbo on the hips of his full dress uniform. "Next, I suppose it'll be sword-swallowing. Fire-eating. Biting the heads off live chickens!"

"Sorry, Papa," Maggie replied, wincing when her nose hurt. Behind him, she saw the doorway of their caravan crammed with carnies, each fighting for a better position. She was their pet. "No chickens, I promise."

Ernesto, the geek, looked crestfallen. She caught his eye and said, "Sorry, Ernesto."

Her father had shooed away the carnies and closed the door on the New Mexico landscape, and then he'd sat down next to her—adjusting the samurai sword that hung at his hip—and taken her hand.

"Ah, Magdalena," he'd said with a sigh. "So much like your sweet mother, God rest her, with your pretty face. Shaped like my heart, it is. And those big brown calf eyes. Promise me you won't kill yourself before you're fourteen?"

"I promise, Papa," she'd said, holding her face very serious. "I won't kill myself. Not until I'm fifteen, at the very least. Can we go to the river tomorrow?"

Then he'd laughed, tousling her long hair. "Swimming good for a broken nose, is it? Well, we'll see." Then he'd brought up a bowl. "Queen Athena made you some broth. Eat it, or her feelings will be hurt, and if her feelings are hurt, she'll be careless with Sylvester."

Maggie ate. You couldn't have a careless snake handler, now could you?

Maggie Maguire grew up, in her father's words, "on the road," and some might say she grew up wild. Some might also say she was destined to be, for lack of a better word, original. On her father's side, she was of Irish, English, Scotch, and Dutch blood; on her mother's side, she was mostly French, Spanish, Portuguese, and Irish, with a dash of Mandan Indian.

She was descended from Spanish pirates and the men of the Dutch East India Company, fur trappers and whiskey traders; deportees and survivors of shipwrecks, shanty and lace-curtain Irishmen; bishops and charwomen, patriots of England and France, cutpurses and rogues, and an Indian girl who stayed too long in the bushes one afternoon.

There are those who say that America was founded by the worst and the best, and nothing in between: the deported chaff of Europe, the prostitutes and swindlers, felons and riffraff; and the clergy, the reformers, those who swore the Puritan ethic. In Maggie, like so many others, the best and the worst had married many times over and produced a curious hybrid— in Maggie's case, a girl who couldn't stay away from trouble, and who then insisted on making it right.

Her mother, Yvette, was taken by diphtheria when Maggie was two, and so she was raised by her eccentric huckster father, Custus Maguire.

Custus had the benefit of a university education (although the identity of this university changed continually) and wore a general's uniform dripping with gold braid and medals (although the country of origin was shrouded in mystery). He was the sole proprietor of a traveling carnival, and this carnival's name changed with the seasons, likely to avoid process servers. The acts changed as quickly as the carnival's name, due to injury or better offers, but its mainstay was the tonic Custus brewed in the back of the caravan and sold for a dollar a bottle in good times, three for a dollar in poor.

Custus traveled the West, never venturing east of the Mississippi, staying to the territories and the wild country. He told Maggie it was because the far Westerners were in greater need of entertainment. Or because the weather suited him better there. Or because back-East people made him nervous.

She didn't believe him for a minute, of course, for even as a young girl, she was quite precocious. And imaginative. From time to time she made up stories to explain her father's wanderlust—that he was a notorious cat burglar, for instance, retired to safe country (well, relatively safe) to raise his child. Or that Mandarin thugs were chasing him for acts against the tong, or that he was really a secret agent scouting trouble in the West, and reporting directly to the president.

Whatever the reason, Custus raised a singularly happy child. Her days were spent scooting under camels and elephants— well, elephant, singular—and riding horses and throwing knives and walking the wire, all under the tutelage of her father's acts.

She learned rudimentary martial arts (not to mention how to keep four balls in the air at once) from a Chinese tumbler and juggler, the Amazing Hong Fu. Flipping people was hard for her at first—she was only a child, after all—but Hong Fu persevered, and in no time she was upending the strong man and flinging people over her shoulders to beat the band. Maggie often wondered if Hong Fu regretted teaching her, although he seemed hale enough—despite a broken collarbone— when they waved good-bye to him in Council Bluffs.

A Mexican trick roper, Pablo DeGarza, taught her crude Spanish (as well as he could—he was a Scotsman), and how to use a lariat and vault a galloping horse. And although Custus Maguire held him responsible for Maggie's broken nose, Maggie always knew it was because she'd stepped right when she should have stepped left. From that time on she paid strict attention.

Mesmo the Magnificent schooled her in the art and science of mesmerism. "Fix them, child!" he'd intone. "Fix them with your eye and lull them to sleep. A stroke of the mind, a gentle suggestion is all it takes."

At first, all she could manage was livestock. Her father would come out of his caravan wagon in the morning, his medals clanking as he stretched his arms and yawned. And then he'd stop, casting his eye over the small white feathery heaps of drowsing, spellbound fowl that dotted the dusty yard of wherever it was they had camped.

"Ducks!" he'd thunder. "Ducks and chickens asleep all over the place! *Magdalena!*"

Much to her father's relief, she graduated from feathered victims, and soon could drop almost any subject—usually willing—into a deep trance. "You're a natural, child," Mesmo had said. "Keep this up, and you'll put me out of business."

She passed up sword-swallowing and fire-eating and biting the heads off live chickens, but Tandalowe the Magnificent taught her the art of knife-throwing: By the time he left the caravan, she could throw a perfect circle around the long-suffering Mrs. Tandalowe. Or anyone else, for that matter.

And so she was instructed in all of life's finer things by Chinese jugglers, pseudo-Mexican trick riders, Siamese elephant handlers, German contortionists, knife throwers of unknown origin, *ad nauseam.* And in between, she was schooled in more pedestrian matters by her father.

"I won't have you running round like a wild Indian, Magdalena," he'd said, pretending to be cross. "You're eight years old, and it's time you knew the capitals of Europe. Now, once again. Iceland?"

She knew the capitals of the world (and jujitsu) by the time she was nine, could do long division and fractions (and hypnotize her father) at ten. At eleven she could draw you a map of South America, complete with topographical details, quote selected passages from Shakespeare, file a horse's molars, and juggle eggs while doing a backbend. At twelve she could swim a mile upstream, skip rope in a spinning loop on horseback with a monkey on her shoulder, and chart the inner workings of a frog. And at thirteen she could say the Lord's Prayer in Gaelic and in German, play "Camptown Races" on the calliope, and tell you more than you ever wanted to know about the Trojan Wars.

It was an eclectic education, but then, Maggie was an eclectic girl.

Most of the time they traveled, going from Texas to Colorado to Wyoming and back again with stops in New Mexico and Kansas and the Dakotas—anywhere there wasn't too much Indian trouble, anywhere people were hungry for the excitement of a carnival (and thirsty for "the remedy"), and anywhere her papa hadn't been thrown out of.

"Where are we going this time, Papa?" she'd ask as they set out again, over green and virgin plains or dry and dusty hills or fields deep in clover.

"Someplace new," her father would reply, as always, with a grin, "someplace adventurous." Then he'd settle his pipe in his mouth and gather his reins, and call back over the wagons, "Hup hup! Wagons, ho!"

Custus Maguire liked to brag that his daughter never performed, and it's true that she never ate fire or danced with elephants for money. But three times a day, when they were camped and set up for business, she'd crook up her leg or her arm into some impossible position—it helped that she was double-jointed—or flop her head on her shoulder and cross her eyes, and a few minutes later, she'd be miraculously cured by Dr. Entwhistle's Miracle Balm. Or Amazing Kickapoo Juice, the Cure-All from Our Indian Brethren, or Hargrove's Secret Remedy, or whatever snake oil Custus was selling at the moment.

It didn't much matter. He brewed it up, tea-colored and smelling like tar and lemons and one hundred and twenty proof—the same every time—in a tub in the back of the caravan. The labels changed over the years, but not the recipe.

"Passed from my father's father to him, and then to me," he'd say, "and I'd pass it along to you, Maggie darlin', except it's so terrible bitter. Plus, I expect you to do grand things with your life." Then he'd take a spoon from the vat to his lips, and then grimace, drawing air through his teeth.

Then, "Perfect! Care for a wee nip?"

She'd make a face and run from the caravan, with her father laughing and leaning out the door, calling, "Are you sure, Magdalena?"

It was a ritual. If he'd ever found her sampling the recipe, he would have skinned her alive.

TWO

THE CARNIES HAD TAUGHT HER A GOOD MANY THINGS, but her father had taught her to shoot and fish, to swim underwater and waltz and value books. She had loved him best. She had loved him unconditionally.

She had loved him even when he sent her away, when she was fifteen and a half, to New Jersey, to Miss Sophia Beckmyer's Academy for Young Ladies of Good Breeding and Refinement. That was after what she looked back on as the Claude DuBois Incident, in capital letters.

Maggie was growing into a handsome girl. Not a classic beauty, but comely enough, with glossy dark brown hair and a heart-shaped face that framed long-lashed, dark brown eyes. Claude DuBois, the Prince of Prestidigitation, had joined the carnival when she was fifteen, and just coming into herself.

A tall, handsome, mysterious fellow with a mustache she found intriguing for reasons she couldn't remember (or perhaps had blocked out), he taught her all sorts of interesting things. For instance, how to pull an ace from anywhere at will and shave a deck and cheat at cards.

This last bit of business entailed very sensitive fingertips and a great deal of practice. It also entailed, according to Claude, sensitizing her whole body—her aura, he called it— "so that it might be in tune with the cards, my dainty flower."

Her papa had caught them while Claude was "manipulating her aura," and she was packed up and steaming her way over the rails to New Jersey before she knew what had hit her.

She was good and angry with him, until she realized that

her sister students at Miss Beckmyer's had never so much as
heard of three-card monte or the old thimble game, bless their
blushing, naive, monied little hearts.

She made quite a killing.

So she stayed at Miss Sophia Beckmyer's Academy, balancing books on her head and parsing sentences and taking
up smoking. For which offense she was forced to write
"Young ladies of good breeding do not smoke" on the black-
board five hundred times.

And discovering detective novels. ("Young ladies of good
breeding do not read popular fiction"—one hundred times.)

And studying mathematics and elocution and china painting
and chemistry. ("Young ladies of good breeding do not set
fire to the dean's office"—a record one thousand times.)

By the time she had reached the advanced age of seventeen,
she'd had enough of the Academy's dank halls, not to mention
Miss Beckmyer's determined admonitions that she was fit for
nothing but the scullery. She was about to run off to Chicago
to join the Pinkertons—an idea she'd picked up from her dime
novels—and had, as a matter of fact, concocted a splendid
little bomb with which to blow up the big marble bathtub in
the staff washroom. Or at the very least, she thought, make a
loud *boom* in it. She was just putting the finishing touches on
it when the telegram came.

Her father had died in Wichita, it seemed. A heart attack.
There was no money, no carnival. No papa.

Miss Beckmyer was ghoulishly gleeful, Maggie thought as
she sat in her room, bleary-eyed, watching the headmistress's
narrow, black-skirted rump as she cheerfully packed Maggie's
bags and announced she had secured a position for her as a
second upstairs maid with a local family.

"More than you deserve, my dear," she'd said as she fas-
tened the last strap on the last bag with a happy yank. "Nothing but trouble since the day you arrived. You leave in the
morning."

But Maggie didn't leave in the morning. She left that night,
after placing her bomb and then standing outside, at the edge
of the long green skirt of a lawn, while the explosion blasted

out the window and part of the brickwork and sent a wash-basin rocketing toward the trees.

It made quite a fabulous show, she thought cheerfully, as she turned her back—the sparks still flying and the bricks still falling—and walked down the road to catch the streetcar that would take her to the train depot. Quite a show, indeed. Perhaps just a tad too much fulminate of mercury.

The last thing she heard, as the horses stopped and she wrestled her bags aboard, was Miss Beckmyer's distant shout of "Magdalena!"

By the time she got to Chicago and Allan Pinkerton's office, Maggie had twenty-three cents to her name. Pinkerton wouldn't see her, but she persevered. For three days she sat in the outer office, by night camping on the stoop outside, until she finally passed out from hunger. He had his secretary see that she was fed, and then he reluctantly sent her on a trial assignment—acting as matron in the transport of one "Cactus Rose" Magee from Lincoln, Nebraska, to Chicago. And then he hired her.

Maggie was delighted! A Pinkerton at last! Her papa, God rest him, would have been so proud! She polished up her identification card—the all-seeing eye was engraved upon it, along with the printed legend "We Never Sleep."

But being a Pinkerton, at least a lady Pinkerton, wasn't all it was cracked up to be. The months crept on and turned into years, and Maggie was wasting her considerable talents. She saw male Pinkertons get all the plum assignments, while she was stuck gallivanting to unheard-of towns to transport the likes of Molly "Big Foot" Rosenberg or "Cherry Nose" Ruth Sykes to jail or to trial.

How could a girl use her martial arts or knife-tossing or lariat-twirling skills when the quarry was already caught and hogtied? A person couldn't haul off and fling them over her shoulder and to the ground just because she was bored. People objected. It wasn't sporting.

She couldn't even complain to Allan Pinkerton, because he was hardly in the office anymore, being consumed with the James gang down in Missouri. When Pinkerton and a few of his men bombed the James house, killing Jesse's feebleminded brother and blowing away his mother's arm, Maggie said, "Enough."

Bombs were all well and good when they were concussing somebody's empty bathtub, but when you used them to maim an old woman and exterminate a simpleminded child, you had gone too far.

She'd drawn her pay and climbed aboard another train, this time headed for San Francisco and her as yet unmet cousin Grady, to make a fresh start. She'd been not yet twenty years old, but she knew what she wanted to do: open her own agency.

THREE

MARCH 1875
SAN FRANCISCO

>─┤─◆─❯─○─❮─◆─├─◄

GRADY HAD BEEN IN THE TANK, A DISGUSTING PLACE, full of vomiting drunks, and in had walked this little slip of a girl. What was she? Eighteen? Twenty at most. Although if you asked his cousin Maggie now, she'd probably say she was twelve. Vain wench, but she had a right. She'd been lovely then, and had remained so.

She'd walked in—walked right up to him, in fact—and said through the bars, "You're Grady Maguire." No question, just a statement of fact. Actually, almost an accusation. "I'm your cousin Maggie and you're all I have in the world and I'm all you've got, too. If I pay your fine, will you come to work with me?"

He'd agreed, of course, no questions asked. He would have agreed to masquerade as a milkmaid to get out of that place.

"Pickpocketing?" she'd asked later, over a beer at Limey Joe's.

He'd shrugged. "It's a living." Even then, she'd made him anxious. A young lady, going in a place like that! He'd tried to stop her, but he'd learned right away that you didn't stop Maggie Maguire once she got her head set on something. He was sure they'd be shanghaied and sold into white slavery and forcibly vanished into the fog forever before they finished their beers.

He was used to the rougher elements, of course, for he made the larger share of his living on the Barbary Coast. Bilking greenhorns—and some not so green—shoulder to shoulder with the jayhawkers and the con men and the whores, he knew

his way around the cribs and opium dens and dance halls and
deadfalls. Maybe he didn't like it so much, but he knew his
way around. He could stay out of trouble (mostly), for he was
wise to the situation, if not always up to it. And while he was
most certainly up to watching his own backside in a rowdy
establishment like this, he wasn't up to watching Maggie's,
too.

But she hadn't even looked nervous. She'd said, "You're
on the game, Grady. You're twenty-three years old, by my
calculation, and you're smart, but you've got nothing on the
horizon except lifting purses and loading dice, and you're not
very good at it."

When he started to protest, she'd just looked at him flatly
and said, "You got caught, didn't you?"

He couldn't answer that.

He'd started to ask her if she had anything in mind besides
insulting him, when a tough from the crowd behind her made
a grab for her purse. Before Grady could jump to her rescue
(somewhat reluctantly, he admitted—the fellow was enormous), she brought up one arm and grabbed the man's ear
while she slapped the other hand on his wrist, and all of a
sudden the tough was on the floor, moaning, and Maggie was
picking up her beer and saying why didn't they find another
table, because this one was too noisy.

He'd been flabbergasted. But impressed.

So he'd gone into the detective business with her, out of
boredom more than anything else. Well, curiosity, too. And
also because he was afraid she'd crack him like a nut if he
said no. After all, she was putting up the money.

They'd rented the loft (well, Maggie called it a loft, he
called it a dingy attic) over Hammacher's Toys in a less than
illustrious part of the city—a rock's throw from the Barbary
Coast. The first thing she'd done was have a small brass name-
plate engraved and installed on the downstairs street door. "M.
Maguire & Co.," it read. "Discreet Inquiries."

And then they set to cleaning.

About halfway through that first gritty, gruesome day—the
first of many—Grady thought he heard pounding. He waved

a hand at Maggie, motioning at her to stop. "Listen!" he said, once he had her attention.

Sure enough, there was a dull, irregular thump. He went to the door and looked down the stairs, but there was no one there. Furthermore, the sound wasn't coming from that direction. He couldn't tell *where* it was coming from.

"Grady?" said Maggie, over in the far corner, the place where they planned the partitions for his rooms. "Grady, come here." She was staring at the floor.

By the time he got there (what with having to scoot around several sawhorses and battle his way through cobwebs and kill three spiders and a roach), she was bending down, wiping at something on the floor. And then she smiled and said, "Hello!"

Not to him. Not to anyone. To the floor.

Well, this was it. She'd cracked, gone round the bend. As he neared, he tried to decide the best way to handle this. Pleasing tones? Stern, perhaps. He supposed she'd best see a doctor.

Except that when he reached her side, he saw that she'd been cleaning glass—window glass!—and that there was a face staring up at her.

"You push!" she shouted to the man in the floor—he could see now that there was a door, set down flush with the floorboards—and she began to tug at the knob.

It came open with a *whoosh* and a great deal of dust, and through this cloud rose a white, shaggy head and a ruddy, muttonchopped face, the bulbous nose holding up a tiny pair of gold-rimmed half glasses. The jowly head looked first at Maggie, then at Grady, and then announced, in a thick German accent, "You people put through my ceiling a lot of dust."

Maggie held down a hand and led him the rest of the way up the stairs (for there was a narrow staircase beneath the door). She brushed at his shirt and said, "Sorry if we've inconvenienced you. I'm Maggie Maguire, and this is my cousin Grady Maguire." She added, rather proudly, "We're detectives."

The old German, unimpressed, regarded her. "And you think maybe you solve a big mystery in my attic?"

"No," she said, still smiling, "I think I'm going to put my office here."

The old man arched a brow. "So. We got now a lady detective? America. Some country this is, eh?"

He introduced himself, while everyone was dusting off, as Otto Obermyer, a retired toymaker who now served as night watchman—with residence on the premises—for Hammacher Toys. Grady figured he served as "grouch in residence," too. But he liked Otto. He especially liked him after he learned that the old man was a tinker.

He made things, wonderful things, which he showed Grady when he accompanied him downstairs. His rooms were a warren of gadgets and whatsits, wires and pumps, cogs and wheels, and things that bumped or thumped or whirred when you least expected it.

"Grady?" Otto said, and Grady banged his head on the inside of the melodian he had it stuck in. "I think," Otto continued, once Grady was standing upright again and rubbing the bump on his head, "that we gonna get long fine. A little dust, I can always clean up."

"This will never work," Grady said to Maggie two days later. He was covered in dirt and cobwebs, and had a handkerchief tied over his nose. He was also surrounded by gray boards and dirty glass and far too many spiders, living and dead. "This is a terrible place. Even if you can manage to get that big window clean, which I doubt, you can't see the ocean. It faces the wrong way! And nobody'll ever come to this part of town. They won't climb the hill, for one thing! And if they do climb the hill, they'll be too exhausted to climb the stairs. Even if they do—which, once again, I doubt—this rat trap will never in a million years—"

He stopped, his face suddenly covered by a wet rag, which Maggie had thrown from across the room with unerring accuracy. Otto, pushing a broom in the far corner, chuckled softly.

"Yes, they'll come. And yes, it'll be right. It'll be wonderful," she said, and once he peeled the rag off his eyes, he saw that she was smiling at him. Smiling!

Well, she saw something that he didn't, that was for certain.

"*Ja,* you just wait," said Otto knowingly.

Grady was about to reply that no one had asked him, when there came a tentative rap on the upstairs door. It opened a bit, and a head, attached to a very prim, nervous-looking woman, poked through. She looked at the mess, looked from Maggie to Grady and back again, and then said in a timorous voice, "M. Maguire? Inquiries?"

Maggie said, "Do come in. I hope you'll excuse our mess," and smiled confidently as she stepped around a rather large hole in the floor and made her way toward the door. And as she passed Grady, she whispered, "Told you so."

The first case financed an interior door and two shelves, the second two missing windowpanes and some flooring, and so on. By the end of the first year, Grady—dutifully keeping the books and fronting when need be and repairing the woodwork and sifting through newspapers or the town records while Maggie was out doing the real work—had decided that maybe, just maybe, they could make a go of it.

Just in case, though, he kept in practice. A fellow never knew when he might have to lift a purse.

FOUR

THE PRESENT: MID-MAY 1883
SAN FRANCISCO

"**W**HO?" MAGGIE ASKED.

She was sitting in Quincy Applegate's office, a large corner affair on the third floor of the Western Mutual Specialties Building. Rain pattered softly at the windows, dulling the afternoon light, turning Quincy's view of the bay into misty watercolor, and painting shifting moiré designs over the room and the furnishings. And Quincy.

"Harriet Hogg," Quincy repeated, leaning back in his leather chair. "Daughter of the late Horace Hogg. Ever heard of him?"

The name seemed somewhat familiar. She frowned for a moment, trying to concentrate more on the matter at hand and less on Quincy's jawline and then said, "Timber?"

Quincy nodded. He was really quite attractive, and she would have described him as "tall, dark, and handsome" if only that didn't sound so trite.

"The Washington Timber King, to be precise," he continued. "Left a sizable estate to Harriet. The only trouble is, Harriet was captured by Indians . . ." He shuffled the papers on his desk until he found what he was looking for. "Yes. Captured by the Shoshone in 1869. Six years old then, about twenty now. She and her mother were going West to meet up with Horace when their wagon train was attacked. Harriet was the only survivor. Maggie?"

She sighed. "I was just thinking that in 1869 I was busy learning to trick ride. Where was the attack, anyway?"

"Central Nevada. About eight or ten miles from where Sky

Butte is now, to be exact. It's on the railroad line. You learned to trick ride?''

Maggie fingered her handbag, ignoring the question. "She's more than likely dead, you know. Probably been dead for a long time."

Quincy shook his head. "No. We found her."

Maggie furrowed her brow. "Well, then why—"

"We found where she *was*," Quincy said quickly, cutting her off. "Three years ago, she was liberated by troops out of Fort Lowell. She'd been—"

"Three years ago?" Maggie interrupted. "Why didn't Horace collect her then?"

"Mr. Hogg suffered a stroke six years ago—three years before Harriet was liberated. I take it that up until that time, he was actively seeking Harriet. Well, 'actively' is putting it mildly. He dumped a lot of cash into it, but no one ever came up with anything concrete. Because, as I was about to tell you, the girl had been traded or sold several times. They found her with the Chiricahua Apache in Arizona. We wouldn't have known to look for her at all, except that his will—for which dear old Western Mutual has the dubious honor of serving as executor—was old. It names her as his heir."

Maggie forced herself to ignore the blue of his eyes and think about business. "And so you put out the standard inquiries, figuring nothing would come of it. But something did, and now you want me to track her down. Correct?"

"Correct. There's just one problem."

"Just one?"

Quincy smiled. "Besides the obvious. Horace's will specifies that his daughter be found—and I quote—of sound mind and will, untouched by liquor or spirits, and unblemished by savage hands.' "

Maggie groaned audibly. How Horace figured she'd escape a little sullying was beyond her. He should have settled for "breathing, with most of her bodily parts intact."

She said, "Quincy. That's impossible."

Quincy shrugged. "Terms of the will. Of course," he said, leaning forward and folding his hands on the desk, "I suppose I could be a bit lenient about that. You can put Grady to work on her before she meets me officially, like that. Of course, I didn't say any of this. Do you still do it?''

Maggie had leaned toward him without thinking, and she suddenly jerked herself erect. ''Do what?''

''Trick ride.''

Her eyes narrowed with a smile. ''Don't start, Quin. This is business.''

He grinned, and, as always, the mischievousness of it took her by surprise. In the office, he was always terribly businesslike. Well, almost always.

He unfolded himself from the chair, eyes still twinkling, and stood up. ''I almost didn't ask you, Maggie. It seemed such a tedious case. I won't blame you if you turn it down. But before you say no, I think there's someone you ought to meet. The someone who inherits everything if you—that is, we—can't flush Harriet out of the weeds.''

He turned and walked over the carpets to the door, and she was thinking that she'd pass on this case. It could take weeks to track down the girl, and what would she find, if she found anything at all? A savage, probably. Besides, she didn't like to be gone from San Francisco for too long. Her plants would die. (They always died anyway, but that was beside the point.)

Quincy leaned out the door, then straightened and came back in, followed by a small, absolutely repugnant man. It hit her immediately and hard. Only later did she take in the sticklike wrists poking from the worn cuffs of his cheap suit, the furtive, watery blue eyes, and the tight lips that twitched from side to side beneath a sparse mustache. All she knew, in that first second, was that she didn't like him. And that was an understatement.

She could practically hear her papa warning her about similar types wandering the crowds back at the carnival. ''You see a feller with eyes like that, Magdalena, you holler, 'Hey, Rube.' And for the love'a Mike, don't go tryin' that judo stuff on him!''

Dear Papa. Always afraid she'd hurt somebody.

Quincy said, ''Miss Maguire, may I introduce Ralph Scaggs? He was Mr. Hogg's third cousin, and was with him in his last days.''

"Just call me Ralphie, hon," he said. "I'll have a cup'a coffee, plenty of sugar," he added, pumping his eyebrows up and down twice before he turned to Quincy. "What's the holdup, Applegate? I been down here three times since the old geezer croaked, and—"

"*Mister* Scaggs," Maggie said to his back, through clenched teeth, "I do not work here. And even if I did, I certainly would not get you coffee."

"Miss Maguire is a private investigator," Quincy broke in. "It is the company's hope that she'll find Harriet and return her to us."

Just-Call-Me-Ralphie turned, his jaw gaping open, then just as fast he barked out a laugh. "You're sending a *female* to find Harriet, Applegate?" He moved toward Maggie, looking her up and down, and stopped three feet away. "Why, I reckon I can start spendin' that money now!"

"Miss Maguire does quite a bit of work for the company, Scaggs," Quincy said, full of umbrage. "If anyone can find Harriet Hogg, she's the one."

"Now, hon," he said, ignoring Quincy and coming near enough that she could smell him, "what's a pretty thing like you doin' in the detecting business?" And before she knew it, he had pinched her backside with those bony fingers.

Her immediate impulse was to just haul off and flip him out the window. A three-story drop would do him wonders. But she didn't. Suddenly she found herself filled with resolve to find Harriet and bring her back and let Quincy shower her with her father's money—and let Ralphie crawl back to whatever sewer he'd slithered out of.

Slither back to it and drown in it, hopefully.

No, the window wouldn't do at all. Instead, she moved away from him, toward Quincy, and as she did, she stepped down hard on Ralphie's instep with her heel.

"Oh, my!" she said, hand to her mouth as he let out a shriek and hopped on one foot. "Did I do that?" Then to Quincy, "Is this the file?"

Quincy whispered an amused "Magdalena!" and nodded that yes, it was, and then turned his head away, smirking—a smirk that said, "I knew you couldn't resist."

While Ralph Scaggs hopped to a chair, cursing under his breath, she scooped up the folder from the desktop and tucked it under her arm. "Standard rate?"

"Plus a bonus, if you find her."

"I'll find her," she said, stepping toward the door. "You can rely on it."

FIVE

>———+—<>—○—<>—+———<

"**T**HAT'S THE WAY, MR. FESTING," SAID CHAUNCEY Garrett. "Let your eyelids drift, drift, drift, down, down, down. So tired, so tired. So pleasant to let the body relax, so very pleasant."

Festing mumbled something through slackening lips, and then his head lolled back in his chair. Good.

"That's it, Tom. May I call you Tom? Such a nice, deep, soothing sleep. You can hear only my voice, can't you, Tom?"

"Yes." A whisper.

"Now, Tom, in about three or four days, a couple of fellows are going to come in here looking for Harriet Hogg." Festing looked puzzled, and the man added, "I believe you call her Swivel Hips Hattie."

"Hattie. Yes."

"These men are going to take Harriet away, Tom. And you won't interfere. You'll keep quiet and not call in the sheriff, and let her go. You're not to make any trouble. Do you understand?"

"No trouble," Festing repeated groggily.

"That's good, Tom," said the man. "That's very good. In return, my employer is making a very generous donation to your campaign fund." He perched on the edge of the desk and opened the sterling cigar box. "You want to run for sheriff, don't you?"

Festing, his eyes closed, smiled. "Sheriff."

"You'll have enough money to run for governor, Tom, not sheriff. Wouldn't that be nice, to run the whole shebang? If you do your part, my employer is going to come into a very great deal of money." He chose a cigar and bit off the end. "And he has empowered me to offer you fifteen percent of the proceeds for your services. In case you're wondering, that's more than fifty thousand dollars."

Festing twitched. "Fif—fif—"

The man lit his cigar and said, "Don't stutter, Tom." He looked around the office, at the framed sporting prints and the duck decoys and the shelf filled with leatherbound books, and rolled his eyes. Only trappings, if he was any judge. Just a surface show, the slick on the oil, the oil being this run-down saloon. The trappings of a man who hoped for more.

The whole thing was a big waste of time, if you asked him. Why offer Festing the moon? Why not just trance him and get him to do what you wanted, and then give him exactly nothing? He wouldn't remember the service, let alone the fee.

But Ralphie boy had insisted.

Personally, he was beginning to think Ralph Scaggs didn't know dirt about mesmerism. Or mathematics, for that matter. Just how many people had he offered 15 percent to, anyhow?

He rolled off his ash on the sole of his boot and said, "Now, Tom, I'm going to have to be away about a week or so. Got a show to do up in Denver. And when I get back, I want to find that you've been good. I want to find Harriet missing, understand? I don't care if you have to leave town, or stay and shoot somebody, but I want to find her gone. Otherwise, something bad might happen to you. Extremely bad. Understand?"

Festing, eyes still closed, head still lolled back, had broken out into a light sweat. "Yes."

"I'm glad we understand each other, Tom," the man said, taking his feet. "Now I'm going to leave. When you hear the door close behind me, you'll wake up, and you'll remember what you're supposed to do, but the details of my visit will be fuzzy. In fact, you can't remember what I look like at all, can you?"

Festing looked puzzled. "No," he said at last.

Garrett smiled. He thought about having Harriet or one of the others before he left, but decided against it. Why take a chance on fetching up a case of Cupid's Itch? No, he'd wait to see what was on the stagecoach. Might be a nice plum, ripe for the picking.

There'd been a girl, a pretty girl, on the stage out here. You dropped them in a trance, and they'd do anything you wanted, and they didn't remember a thing afterward. It was almost too easy.

Absently, he said, "You might think about getting some acts in here, Tommy boy. The entertainment's pretty tame." There was a place he went, sometimes, a place on the Barbary Coast, where you could watch a naked woman do it with a mastiff in a spiked collar or even a burro, and the woman wasn't even mesmerized. Now, that was entertainment! The mastiff was his favorite. He said, "Maybe you ought to get a trained dog."

Festing mumbled, "Dog?"

Garrett chuckled softly, and checked his watch again. Almost time for the stage. And then he took one last look at Tom Festing, whoremonger and candidate for the office of high sheriff. More than $50,000! Well, perhaps, once the job was done, he'd have another little chat with Ralphie Scaggs. Tom Festing didn't deserve all that money. Why, it was as much as he was being paid, and he was actually doing some work! Maybe he'd knock off the private investigator Ralphie had hired, too, and the men he'd paid to kidnap Harriet, and the . . . How many had he hired, anyway? Old Ralph was just too goddamned free with his money.

Don't cut any throats yet, he reminded himself. Perhaps after he mesmerized the girl. Perhaps after she told him whatever it was that Ralphie wanted to hear—something about when she was six, Ralphie had said, something about the time just before the Indians made off with her. After, he could decide what course to take.

But what in the cross-eyed world could this girl know that was more important to Ralph Scaggs than $350,000? It must be very big, very big indeed.

He checked his watch again and saw his time was growing short. Denver, and the Happy Higgins Theater, awaited. Lord, but he hated the provinces. Settling the bowler hat back on his head and dropping a cigar ash onto Tom Festing's floor, he said, "See you around, Tommy."

He walked out of the office, slamming the door behind him.

A few minutes later, Tom Festing emerged from his office. Business was slow—just four miners and a couple of cow-pokes sipping beer and playing cards—and two of the girls, both pale blond, both tiny, were slouched at a table in the rear, a bottle of whiskey between them. "Hattie! Corinne!" he snapped, angry for no reason he could remember. "Get busy."

Hattie was passed out by the looks of it, but Corinne lifted her head and regarded him sullenly. "Ain't nothin' to do."

"Well, find something. You can haul Hattie upstairs, for starters. And put on something besides your underwear. You look cheap."

Corinne wrapped Hattie's arm around her neck and strug-gled toward the stairs. "Can't help it if I look cheap. I *am* cheap."

The girl grumbling behind him, Festing went to the bar. There was something he had to do. Now, what was it? He motioned to the bartender.

"I have to be gone for a few days, Will."

The bartender, a big, balding men, ran his polishing rag over the bar top out of habit and said, "Where to, Mr. Festing?"

Blankly, Festing stared at the mirrored backbar a moment and then said, "Carson City. I suppose." He turned abruptly, heading for the rear exit, and as he left he said, "Get us a dog, Will."

"A dog?" The bartender's brows shot up. "What kind of dog you want?"

"Damned if I know. One that'll jump through a hoop, I guess."

SUNDAY, JUNE 3

>─┼─◆◆─○─◆─┼─◆

THE HARD WOODEN STAGECOACH SEAT BOUNCED MAG-
gie into the air, only to meet her sitting parts again with
an audible crack. There was no relief. Bustles didn't
help, they only pushed you forward. Extra petticoats didn't
help, they only made you hot. Even pillows were useless, because you kept bouncing off them. Plus which, all the other
passengers were sure you had piles.

Holding her hat down, she leaned out the window and
shouted against the gritty wind, "Think you hit that rut hard
enough?" just as the stage bounced over another pothole—
and she cracked her head against the window frame.

She sat down hard (was there any other way?) in the seat,
rubbing her skull and wishing she'd never heard of Miss Harriet Hogg or Western Mutual Specialties Insurance; and especially that she hadn't spent these past three and a half weeks
bumping and thumping her backside over every rut and chuck-
hole in Arizona and Nevada, looking for the aforementioned
Miss Hogg.

"Are you all right, Miss Maguire?" asked the matronly
woman across the way. She'd introduced herself as Cora Trimble at Tree Line Station, which had been about a hundred ruts
and a million swiftly passing tree trunks ago. In the close
confines of the stage, she smelled like dust and lemon verbena.

"Fine, Mrs. Trimble." Maggie jealously eyed the woman's
hips. All that padding! "Just—whoops!—fine," she added, as
the stage bounced her into the air again. She landed a good
foot to the side, and muttering a "Pardon me" to the drummer
next to her, scooted back to her side of the coach.

The drummer was an average enough man—average height,

average build—but he had a distinctly ferrety look and a las-
civious face. He also had a small case filled with his wares at
his side, and the body scent of old sweat and bay rum. It was
not the most aromatic of mixtures.

He smiled and said, "No trouble, I assure you. No trouble
at all." He said it to her bosom. He'd boarded at Tree Line
Station, too, and hadn't offered his name. He also hadn't
looked at her face once.

"Where are you headed?" He asked the question, so far as
she could tell, of her left breast. "Will you be stopping over
at Blandings Station?"

She said, "No. I'm getting off at Bent Elbow." He just
kept staring at her chest. An annoying habit, outstandingly
rude. She said, "They don't talk, you know. I'm up here,
Mister . . . ?"

"What? Oh. Corcoran. Silas Corcoran. You traveling on
business or pleasure?"

"I said, I'm up here. If you wouldn't mind." Exasperated,
she ducked down and at last met the line of his gaze. "A little
of both, Mr. Corcoran. You see, I travel the countryside in
search of men who ogle young women's bosoms, and then I
strangle them."

It worked. Corcoran colored, and his eyes followed hers as
slowly, she sat up. She leaned closer, saying cheerfully, "I'm
equipped to do it, you see. As a young girl, I was instructed
in the martial arts by the Amazing Hong Fu. Have you ever
heard of him, Mr. Corcoran?"

He put a finger under his collar, and just as quickly pulled
it out to steady himself when the stage jolted to one side. "I
. . . I can't say that I—"

"He taught me how to fend off attackers and throw men
twice my size to the ground," Maggie said, bracing herself
between the seat and the window. She was enjoying the dis-
traction.

"He also taught me the ancient oriental art of strangulation.
Not just any strangulation, but *oriental*." She drew out the
word, giving it (she hoped) a tantalizing and deadly air. "With
a garrote. Agonizingly slow. And how to paralyze my oppo-
nent so that there is no escape, no crying out for help." She

et her voice drop theatrically. "And no pleading for mercy."

She sat back in her seat, cocked her head, and gave him a blinding smile. "Just a hobby, you understand."

He fumbled for a handkerchief, finally found it, and mopped at his forehead. "Yes," he said, and his voice was a little shaky. "Most interesting."

The stage was slowing, and when she lifted her eyes from those of Mr. Corcoran, she saw that they had left the trees behind and were out on the flatlands, and they were coming into a town. Well, sort of a town. If you used a very loose description.

"Is this—"

"Bent Elbow!" came the stage driver's shout as the stage lurched to a stop.

Whispering, "Thank God," she picked up her handbag and opened the door.

Mrs. Trimble smiled at her as she got out—gave her a wink, in fact. "Bully!" she whispered as Maggie climbed past her and down to mercifully solid ground. "Bully for you, Miss Maguire!"

Maggie smiled back, despite the freight raining down almost on top of her, and found her valise. "Nice meeting you," she said, and then louder, "That's right, Mrs. Trimble. A good big knot in the cord."

Mr. Corcoran scrambled out the other side of the coach and scuttled for the safety of the stage line office.

Maggie started down the dusty street, looking for a hotel or the Purple Fox Saloon, whichever came first, and was relieved when it was the hotel. Well, *a* hotel anyway, called the Famous West.

She signed the register as Magdalena Maguire, out of San Francisco—no need for a false name on this case—and, ignoring the young desk clerk's wiggling eyebrows, trudged upstairs to the second floor.

The Famous West Hotel was clean, although shabby, but she supposed she should be grateful for small favors. The hotel in Abelard had had bedbugs, and she'd slept on the floor. The hotel in Consequence had been crammed full, and she'd had to share a room with three other women. Moldy River hadn't

had a hotel, and she'd had to sleep—furtively—on the bench
at the stage office. And in those towns, and four others, she'd
followed the trail of Miss Harriet Hogg.

For somebody who'd been "liberated" from the Apaches
for only three years, Harriet had been busy. Maggie had traced
her from Fort Lowell to a "rehabilitation residence" for freed
but unclaimed Indian captives and run by Mexican nuns—
God's filthy work camp was more like it, if you asked her
opinion—to a saloon in Rusty Hinge, Arizona. And since then
it had been one saloon after another. Harriet, it seemed, had
found her niche.

It was a good thing Horace Hogg had passed on to wherever
tight-laced, buttoned-up, diehard Baptists went. He'd never
stopped looking for his daughter—or preaching the wages of
sin, or swatting at invisible insects—until the stroke hit him.
He was quiet as a felled tree afterward (though Maggie understood he'd managed to babble a bit at the end). Quincy's
dossier on him was at the same time laughable and frightening.

She thought about unpacking her suitcase, then decided
against it. If Harriet had moved on—again—then she'd be
moving on, too. She'd move on as many times as it took to
find Harriet; she'd said so from the beginning.

She thought she'd caught sight of Ralphie in Abelard, gave
chase, and couldn't find him, which led her to believe that she
was seeing things. But still, she had an itchy feeling that she
was being followed, and those itchy feelings were usually
right.

Three more towns, she decided. She'd give it three more,
and then she'd quit and take her bruised fanny home. Of
course, she'd said that four towns ago, too. She'd probably go
on three-towning herself after some rube or other until she
keeled over, a dried-up, crotchety old maid. It wasn't quite the
future she'd conjured for herself when she left Chicago eight
long years ago.

She washed her face, then straightened her hat and tucked
in a few stray wisps of dark brown hair. Actually, she didn't
look too bad, she thought as she studied herself in the mirror,
for somebody who'd just taken the devil's carriage ride down

rom the mountains. Dusty—she batted at her collar—but not
oo bad. She still had her looks. Sort of. Heart-shaped face,
rown eyes, no freckles, no gray in the hair yet. Reasonably
ttractive.

She leaned closer to the mirror, inspecting a new line that
urned out to be a smear of dirt. "Vanity, vanity," she grum-
led, turning away. "Thy name is Maggie Maguire. How's
hat for a mixed metaphor? Or something . . ." She gave her
odice a tug, then locked her room behind her and went down
he stairs.

The desk clerk jumped to his feet. His eyebrows seemed to
ave a life of their own. "Help you, miss?" he said, his voice
reaking. What was he—seventeen? Eighteen at the most.

"Yes, you can. Where could I find the Purple Fox?"

"It's um . . . um . . ." His Adam's apple bobbled up and
own.

"Just point."

His hands, poking from too-big cuffs, stayed on the counter,
vhere they twisted excitedly. "It's um . . . Are you workin'
here? I mean, you gonna be?" he squeaked at last, his voice
ull of adolescent hope.

She eyed him, saw that this whole conversation was going
owhere in a hurry, and picked up the letter opener from the
ountertop. It was sharp enough. If Grady were here, he'd
nake that face and tell her she was showing off, and she'd
ell him to shut up, she was in a hurry; but he'd be mostly
ight. As usual. That was what was annoying about Grady.
'Mind if I borrow this?" she asked sweetly.

"Anything you want," the boy replied dreamily.

"Fine," she said. And expertly flung the letter opener to-
vard the back wall, where it stuck, just beneath a framed,
ellowed newspaper clipping whose title read "Kid Concho
)isappears," and above another with the headline "Silver
ound!" A short throw, but then, she didn't trust the letter
pener much farther. Lousy balance.

She smiled, and leaned an elbow on the desk. "The Purple
ox?"

Open-mouthed, the boy stared at the blade, which was em-

bedded in the pine paneling and still quivering with a lo
thrumming sound. Slowly he turned toward her, swallowe
once, and said, ''D-down the street a half block and tur
right.''

SIX

>━┼━◆━◯━◆━┼━<

ALL CONVERSATION HALTED WHEN SHE WALKED through the swinging, peeling doors of the Purple Fox Saloon. Not that there was much to stop—four men playing cards at a rickety table propped, under one leg, by a tattered copy of *Lorna Doone*. Another three men were slouched against the bar. As one, they all turned to stare her up and down.

It was always the same. She frowned and said, "At ease, gentlemen," and walked to the bar, trying to seem nonchalant and thinking how much easier this would have been if she'd just sent Grady.

"Excuse me? I'm looking for Miss Harriet Hogg."

The bartender—a big, balding man, who was busy trying to teach a small, scruffy-looking terrier mix, seated atop the bar, to sit up—looked at her flatly, then turned his attention back to the dog. "You want work, see Tom Festing. Sit up, Chico. Sit up, damn it!"

"I'm not looking for work," she said. Behind her, someone let out a low whistle followed by a laugh, but she ignored it. "I'm trying to locate Miss Harriet Hogg."

"Never heard of her."

The other men went back to their cards and liquor, except for one lanky blond cowpoke, who looked away nervously when she glanced in his direction.

Maggie pursed her lips, then with a resigned sigh dug into her bag for her change purse. She snapped a five-dollar gold piece on the scarred bartop. The bartender looked up from the dog.

"She's five-foot-one. Blond hair, blue eyes. She doesn't speak English very well, but she talks fluent Apache," Maggie said, using up most of the sparse information she'd been given in the previous towns. "They told me at the Happy Skunk, down in Moldy River, that she was headed here. You'll have better luck with the pooch if you use boiled liver."

Just tell me where she went, she thought, *and you'll get me out of what's left of your hair.*

"Stay, Chico." The bartender stepped down the bar as the dog lay down on it. His gaze dropped from her eyes to the coin, then came back up again. At least he didn't stop at her chest.

"Why you lookin' for her?" he asked, his voice low, his brows bunched. "She in trouble?"

Good. He knew who she was. "Nothing like that," said Maggie.

"As long as she ain't in trouble," the bartender said, and reached for the coin.

Maggie put her finger on it before he could snatch it away. "Where is she?" she asked, expecting him to utter the name of another ridiculous town, like Possum's Butt or Goat Dump or Cracked Monkey.

"Upstairs," he said, to her amazement. "Second door on your left."

Maggie let go of the coin, and he grabbed it. Upstairs! Finally! She started for the steps, congratulating herself.

"I'd knock first if I was you," the bartender called after her. "She's got a customer." Then he called to someone, "Mick! Run to the Kid Concho Café and get me some boiled-up liver!"

Maggie rapped on the splintery door. There was no answer, and she knocked again, louder this time. Nothing.

"Miss Hogg?" she called. "Miss Hogg, are you in there? Hello?" No answer.

She tried the latch. The door swung in to reveal a claustrophobically small room, barely big enough to contain a cot and a chair. Ragged curtains fluttered in the open window. The bedclothes were mussed, but the room was empty.

She went back out into the hall. It was the second door on the left, all right. She was about to go back down and have further words with the bartender, when she heard snores coming from the next room. She knocked and called out, and when there was no response, opened the door.

The room was the same as the first she'd tried—claustrophobic—but sprawled on the cot like a rag doll, loose-armed and floppy-legged, was a small blond woman. Her resemblance to the photograph supplied by Quincy Applegate, even though it had been taken when she was only a child of six, was unmistakable. Harriet Hogg.

Lord have mercy.

Maggie stepped sideways between the wall and the bed and shook the girl's shoulder. "Harriet? Wake up, Harriet."

Harriet Hogg, heir to the Hogg timber fortune, gave a thick, nasal snort and rolled over, exposing a quart bottle of Old Backwash. Empty.

Maggie gingerly picked up the whiskey bottle and set it on the floor. Why couldn't Harriet have been sober? Why couldn't she have been all done up in a pressed pinafore and said, "Me? Really? How marvelous!" and raced to pack? Why couldn't she at least have been *clean*?

Nothing was ever easy, not even giving people a fortune.

Maggie gave her another shake, more firmly this time. "Harriet!"

The girl flipped on her back suddenly, swinging an arm that nearly clipped Maggie in the face.

"Me no Harry," she said, the words slurred and guttural. She didn't bother to open her eyes. "Me Hattie. Pay downstairs."

Maggie stood up, hands on her slim hips, thinking. The first thing to do was to get this girl sober, and she certainly couldn't do that in this place. She'd have to get her back to the hotel, and she'd worry about the rest later.

She bent once again to try to heave the girl up, when she heard someone clear his throat. It was the blond cowpuncher from downstairs. He stood in the doorway, a worried expression on his face. His hat was in his hands, and his fingers nervously twisted the stained brim.

Maggie said, "She doesn't work here anymore."

The fellow just stood there like a brick. A big, dumb, blond, droopy-mustached brick. He wore a leather vest, studded with silver conchos, that must have been made from a bull hide, it was so thick and stiff.

"Make yourself useful, then," said Maggie at last, standing up and letting go of Harriet, who flopped back to the thin mattress with a loud snore. "Help me get her up."

Wordlessly, the cowboy stumbled forward and scooped Harriet up, then stood staring at Maggie.

"Follow me," she said, and led him from the room and down the stairs. She slapped her card on the bar, saying, "I'm staying at the Famous West. If she has things, send them over," and gave the bartender another five-dollar gold piece. She felt generous. She was spending Quincy's money. Or Western Mutual Specialties'. Same thing.

The bartender, who had the terrier under his arm by this time, snatched up the coin quickly enough, then studied the card. " 'Discreet Inquiries'?" he said, looking up. "What's that supposed to mean?"

She shot him a pained expression.

One of the card players looked up, his eyebrows cocked with amusement. "Whatcha got there, Biscuit?"

The blond cowboy blushed.

"That your name?" she asked. "Biscuit?"

"T-they calls me B-biscuit Pete, ma'am," he replied slowly, and flushed more deeply.

"All right, Biscuit Pete," she said, feeling a little like she was addressing the menu. "Follow me."

After a brief discussion with the young hotel clerk, who scrambled to change her room to a double down the hall and just about *yes, ma'am*ed her to death, she had Biscuit Pete put Harriet on one of the beds. Reminding herself to write down all these expenses, she fished a ten-cent piece out of her purse and handed it to him.

"For your trouble," she said.

But Biscuit Pete had his hat off again, and was twisting the brim with long, grimy fingers. He stepped back from her hand, as if the dime contained hoof and mouth disease, and haltingly said, "What . . . what you gonna do to Hattie?"

Maggie frowned. "I'm not going to do anything to her. I'm going to sober her up and take her to San Francisco." She wiggled the dime. "Here. Take this."

Biscuit Pete shook his head and backed from the room. Sighing, Maggie watched him move away down the hall, tripping over his own feet, then down the stairs, and she thought how amazing it was that he should be so clumsy on his own. He'd carried Harriet as if she were an egg.

She snorted. He could have thrown Harriet in a water trough and she wouldn't have noticed.

She closed the door and studied her new burden. *Of sound mind and will untouched by liquor or spirits, and unblemished by savage hands.*

Good gravy. Harriet looked to be failing on all accounts.

Lank, greasy blond hair, raggedly cut, hung across a face that might have been pretty if it had been acquainted with a little more soap and water and a great deal less Old Backwash. Smeared rouge sagged down one cheek and wandered around the rims of her lips. She wore a low-cut red spangled dress that had definitely seen better days (although few of them wash days), a cheap necklace studded with glass baubles, and cardboard shoes that were falling apart.

"All right, Harriet or Hattie or whatever you want to be called," Maggie said to the limp, soiled form currently dirtying the worn counterpane, "first, we get you cleaned up."

She began with the girl's face, and started to scrub. The face was done, and then the neck, and she was just rising to get a better angle on Harriet's fingernails—when somebody fired a gun, down on the street. At the same instant she heard the shot, something burned her ear, and the wall across from her popped with splinters.

She put her hand up to her ear, touched it and found it intact, then brought her hand down and saw the blood on her fingers.

"Suds!" she breathed. "I've been shot!"

SEVEN

>─┼─◆─┼─◯─┼─◆─┼─<

"I TELL YOU, SHERIFF SEERSUCKER, SOMEONE SHOT AT
me." They were in her hotel room with the young desk
clerk, whose name was Eddie, and Harriet, who snored
blissfully in the bed at Maggie's back.

"The name's Sopsucher." He was a big, well-worn man of
about fifty, with callused hands and dark brown hair that was
more gray than brown. "And like I been tellin' you, honey,
some yahoo shoots off a gun every five minutes in Bent Elbow."

Maggie ground her teeth. "I'll call you by your right name
when you stop calling me 'honey.' And darlin'. And sweet
pea. I am a private investigator," she said for the third time.

Her right hand was clamped to her head, holding a compress
on her ear, but in her left she held up the bullet, which she'd
dug out of the wall. "I'm not a hysterical female, Sheriff.
Somebody shot at me. Or Harriet. A slug doesn't just travel
up to a second-story window all by itself and nip the top of a
person's ear."

"Now, little lady," Sheriff Sopsucher said with the sort of
patient tone usually reserved for the elderly and the insane,
"don't go gettin' your petticoats in a bunch."

"Listen, Sheriff Toesucker or Sodbuster or whatever it is,
let's leave my petticoats out of this, shall we?"

"Sopsucher," he said again, wearily. Maggie thought he
had the tired look of a man who'd fought in one too many
Indian campaigns. Probably took an arrow to the head and
hadn't noticed it.

"I want you to do something about this," she went on, before he could call her "little darlin' " again. "I've told you I believe I know who's responsible. I expect you to—"

"An' I told you, honey, there ain't nobody by the name'a Ralph Scaggs in town." Sopsucher leaned elbows on his knees, his hat dangling loosely from his wide-knuckled hands. "I know everybody in town. And I don't know any Ralph Scaggs."

"He's probably using an alias!" she said in exasperation.

Slowly, Sopsucher got to his feet. She could hear his knees pop from where she was sitting. "Nobody by that description, either," he said. "Ain't nobody in this town mad enough to start sniperin' you, lady. Yet. Although I'm gettin' close. And ain't nobody gonna draw down on ol' Swivel Hips Hattie, there. Why, a town can't have enough good whores."

He settled his hat back on his head. "Like I told you, it's just some'a the fellers cuttin' up. Them boys was prob'ly aiming for the hotel sign, that's all. They get drunk enough and can't none of 'em hit the wall with a handful 'a beans."

Maggie opened her mouth, but he beat her to it, saying, "I don't know what's exactly legal here. I don't know if I should be lettin' you haul ol' Hattie off and sober her up. Seems to me there oughta be a law about interferin' with a body. But you showed me your papers, and I'm inclined to give you the benefit. Just don't go pushin' me, shortcake. And don't go imaginin' assassins round every corner."

He turned his back and walked out the door, the desk clerk dogging his heels. "She's dangerous, Sheriff," she heard the boy whisper as they turned down the stairs.

"Shut up, Eddie."

"But I'm tellin' you, she threw a knife at me!"

"Well, she missed you, didn't she?" was the last thing she heard the sheriff say.

She closed the door and plopped on the spare bed. Maybe the sheriff was right. Maybe it was nothing but drunks. Maybe not.

Of course, the smart thing to do would be to load Harriet on a stage and get her to the first available train depot. Shove her into a compartment, take her by rail to San Francisco, and squirrel her away at the office until she was sober enough to comply with the terms of the will. And if sobriety didn't do the trick, coach her until she was able.

On the other hand, if Just-Call-Me-Ralphie was dogging her trail, Harriet might not make it to the train. After all, her dead papa's fortune was considerable.

Night was falling, and her ear had stopped bleeding. Lighting a lamp to the sound of Harriet's ragged snores, Maggie inspected it in the mirror. It was just a little nick, right at the top. She didn't think it would be noticeable once it scabbed over and healed. Too bad her nose hadn't fared as well. Well, it wasn't much of a bump. Just something to remind her that when you were supposed to step left, you stepped left, not right.

Across the room, Harriet made a loud snorkeling sound in reply and opened one eye. The eye swiveled in its socket, traveling up and around and across, seeming to take in the whole room, and then Harriet looked at her and belched.

The eye closed.

The snoring resumed.

So much for the exciting life of a private investigator.

Having convinced herself that Sheriff Sodbuster or Sapsucker (or whatever his name was) had probably been right—that Just-Call-Me-Ralphie had been a figment of her imagination and that the shooting had been a random act of drunkenness—she scribbled a quick wire to Grady and went downstairs.

The boy was still on the front desk, and he tensed when he saw her coming.

She slid the message onto the countertop. She smiled. She said, "Can you send a wire for me, Eddie?"

The boy swallowed. "You're not gonna throw knives, are you?"

"Not as long as I have your attention," she said sweetly. "The wire?"

Outside, a gun barked twice. She jumped to the side, landing behind an upholstered chair, and Eddie ducked down behind the desk. After a pause, someone outside hollered, "Goldurn it, Arnie, you winged my goat!"

Both Maggie and Eddie slowly rose out of hiding. Eddie cleared his throat and picked up the paper. "Anything else?"

Maggie gave a surreptitious glimpse toward the darkened street before she turned back to him. "Is there a decent restaurant in town?"

The boy nodded nervously. "Don't know what you'd call decent. But the Kid Concho Café is just down the street. Maizie's a pretty fair cook."

Kid Concho? She glanced at the newspaper clipping on the back wall. This town was certainly fixated on a dead outlaw. Shaking her head, she clicked three dollars down on the counter. "Eddie, I'm not going to hurl any more knives at you, I promise. Be a nice boy and send that wire, and then scurry your tail over to Maizie's and get me some dinner. Some part of a steer, preferably not scorched, all right? And a glass of beer. And Eddie?"

"Ma'am?"

"Make sure that goat's all right, will you?"

EIGHT

>─┤─◆─○─◆─┤─<

I N A LESS-THAN-FASHIONABLE SAN FRANCISCO NEIGHBOR-
hood, a well-lubricated Grady Maguire stepped down from
the cab in front of Hammacher's Toys—not the store
(which was in a much nicer, more upscale part of town) but
the warehouse—and tossed the driver a coin. As the cab
clipped away, disappearing quickly around the gaslit corner,
he walked back down the hill a few steps to the left-hand side
of the storefront—just under the H in Hammacher's—to a
door with a small brass placard that read:

M. MAGUIRE & CO.
DISCREET INQUIRIES

He fumbled for his keys to the tune of "Tip-Top Susie Ain't
No Floozie," which he hummed in a vacant, happily off-key
way, and at last managed to open the door.

"Ah!" he exclaimed, scooping a white envelope from the
floor of the foyer and cramming it in his pocket.

"Too late for mail," he said as if this were a great revelation, and groped his way up the darkened stairs because if
he turned on the gaslight, he'd only have to come down again
to turn it off. "Must be a tele . . . must be a tele . . . must be
a wire!"

At the top of the stairs he unlocked another door after several tries, and let himself into the dark office. Soft moonlight
made its way through the other warehouses and factories lining
Brumstead Street to stream in through the enormous semicir-

cular window—taller than a man at its highest point—that faced it. The moonlight washed over the polished oak floor and the oriental carpet, picked out glints of brass and the shadowy outlines of potted ferns, and part of the slope of a sofa.

It was the sofa he headed for, feeling his way toward the wash of hazy blue light. And he found it, tripping only twice—once (abortively) over an ottoman and once (full out) over the cat.

"Blast you, Ozzie," he grumbled into a leather cushion, face-side down and backside up over the arm of the couch. A rather mocking meow answered from the far side of the room.

The fall sobered him to a degree, and he wiggled himself erect on the sofa, lighting the lamp behind the couch and turning up the wick. As he shook out the match, the room eased into view.

It was large: The main part of a loft, it had been sectioned off and turned to the work of a reception room/office. The furnishings were comfortable—dark leather and mahogany and teak and cherrywood—and much more upscale than the address would have led one to believe.

The brass fittings and spittoons were polished. The potted ferns were—well, the potted ferns were dying. Maybe he'd watered them too much. He never could quite get the hang of that. But all in all, it was quite a grand surrounding for an old—well, not *old*, exactly, in fact not old at all, not even middle-aged!—pickpocket like himself to call home.

"We've come up in the world, Maggie, old girl," he said to no one in particular. To think that Maggie bailing him out of jail so long ago would lead to all this. And now, eight years later, here he was: the bookkeeper, nursemaid, and picker-upper-after; the message taker and occasional front man; the legwork man, data gatherer, and errand boy, the 40 end of a 60/40 split of the proceeds.

Other than the split, he liked it fine. Maggie did the part she loved best, and so did he. And his association with the detective business had brought him respectability.

Sort of.

There were still people in the world who looked down their long, snooty noses at private investigators.

But, he thought happily, relaxing into the cushions, seeing Miriam Cosgrove's champagne-flushed face and her bee-stung lips and her slightly mussed blond hair in his mind's eye, there were those who thought it a rather exciting profession. He hadn't the heart to tell Miriam that he spent most of his time in the office and it was Maggie who did the real work: Maggie, who over the years had turned this loft from a shabby, dusty, forgotten storeroom into the paneled and polished bastion of respectability it was today.

And Maggie, who kept ruining the paneling with her damn knives. "How many times do I have to tell you," he said aloud, frowning at the vacant wing chair beside him, "that knives belong outside? Preferably in another state."

But no, every time she was stumped on a case or thinking or just bored, for God's sake, out would come the knives, and thump, thump, thump, she'd throw them at the paneling. At least she was good at it. At least she always kept the pattern small. At least she always—well, most always—did it in her rooms.

He craned his head toward the door at the far side of the office, the door with the small, softly glinting brass plate that would have read *PRIVATE* if only he'd thought to turn up the gaslights before he stumbled to the middle of the room. If only he could have seen that far in his present condition.

He went to dig out the telegram, which he'd just remembered, and found that the cat had somehow materialized on his lap.

"Ozymandias," he said. The cat, the lone one of Maggie's constant stream of strays who'd managed to stay on, clamped his eyes closed and began to purr.

"Ozzie, it's not working." The cat purred louder and began to knead.

The Siamese mix had large feet for a cat his size. Maggie said that when Ozzie kneaded, his paws didn't go from small to big to small to big, they went from medium to huge. And right now they were going huge right through Grady's pants leg.

Grady let out a weak "Oo-oo-oo" and peeled the cat off his opera trousers, brushing the hair away, and looking for signs of blood. Finding none—and ignoring Ozzie, who jumped to the low table in front of the sofa and sat beside the humidor, licking his shoulder—Grady dug the telegram out of his pocket and neatly tore open the envelope. Well, *someone* had to be neat, didn't they?

It was from Maggie, from some godforsaken hamlet called Bent Elbow, Nevada. When had she gone to Nevada? She'd set off for Arizona, as if that wasn't bad enough. The telegram read:

QUARRY FOUND **STOP** NEEDS URGENT TOUCH
OF PYGMALION **STOP** COME SOON FAMOUS
WEST HOTEL **STOP** GET OTTO FOR OZZIE
STOP MAGGIE

An urgent touch of Pygmalion? He shuddered. The old Greek sculptor and his maid of stone. Maggie was on Quincy Applegate's insurance case. If he remembered the details correctly, she had probably found the girl dirty and barely literate, and needed him to chisel her into shape.

He'd never doubted she'd find Hortense—no, he reminded himself, it was Harriet, Harriet Hogg, a singularly unfortunate name. He had hoped, however, that she'd find the girl in better shape. At least, in good enough condition that she could be brought here, to San Francisco, where they could polish her up in comfort.

But no. Maggie always had to do things the hard way. Maggie had to throw knives at the wall. Although sometimes she did juggle to clear her head. . . . He reminded himself to stock up on apples, nice big round ones. A bowl in every room to distract her, that was the ticket.

He stood up, weaving slightly, and went to his desk. Taking a pen from the stand, he dipped it into the well and wrote, on a clean piece of thick vellum notepaper in a clear, strong hand, "Apples," then blotted it. Then he wiped the nib fastidiously and replaced it, and stabbed the note on his spindle.

He didn't rise, though. Lovingly, he took out his handkerchief and flicked a speck of dust from his new telephone. It was a beauty. Black and shiny, its trim candlestick design smacking of the future, it held sway over the desktop. Of course, Otto had wanted to take it apart, first thing.

He had said no (even though he was perishing to see the guts of the contraption), because there existed a slim possibility that once they took it apart, they wouldn't be able to get it back together again. And *then* what would he say to the phone company?

"Bah," Otto had responded, frowning, his half glasses low on his nose. "Coward."

He might be a coward, but he was a coward with phone service, and he intended to take advantage of it tomorrow. First a call to Miss Angelique LaBeau down at the travel service. He sighed. The lovely Angelique. He wondered if she could find Bent Elbow—ghastly name, that—on her charts.

Then Western Union, to reply to Maggie's wire. Then Miriam Cosgrove, she of the champagne blush and the toppling blond curls, to cancel their engagement for this coming Saturday night.

He sighed. It couldn't be helped. But then again, maybe this was a good thing. A private investigator, called away on urgent business? It might be just the ticket, when he got back, to carry Miriam into his arms. He didn't have to say he'd been playing schoolmarm and Lady Etiquette to some grubby timber heiress. He'd just shake his head seriously and say, "Sorry, my dear Miriam, but I must respect my client's confidence. You understand, I'm sure."

He smiled, picturing Miriam's giddy response to that.

Miriam was worth the journey. Plus, he'd get to use the telephone three separate times, and legitimately—not just calling the operator and asking her to test the line.

They were beginning to get crabby about it.

Ozymandias had appeared on the end of the desk sometime during his love affair with the telephone. Giving the phone a last swipe, he scooped up the cat, one-handed, and walked to his door, which was at the opposite end of the office from Maggie's, near the landing.

He turned up the gaslight in the little sitting room, walked past his bedroom, and into what Maggie referred to as "the tinker's lair."

Humph.

He threaded his way past worktables piled with bits of wire and glass and leather and springs, past boxes flowing over with hammers and pincers and awls and needle-nose pliers, nails and bolts and scraps of copper and tin and lead. Past stacks of spare wall panels (to replace those that Maggie's knives ruined), and past walls hung with blueprints and diagrams and sketches that bordered on the fantastic, he walked to the rear of the room.

For all that was in it, it was not a large room. It took him exactly five steps to cross it.

There in the floor was a door, painted so many times it was lumpy. The latest coat was green. It was set down flat, its cut-glass knob sticking up like a tiny beacon, its glass upper panel looking for all the world like the floor of a glass-bottomed boat. Except instead of the wonders of the sea, what he saw through the glass was a set of steep, narrow stairs.

Transferring Ozzie to the other arm and wobbling slightly, he bent and turned the knob, and lifted the door back on its hinges.

"Otto?" he called. He sat down on the top step. "Otto, you there?"

Heavy footsteps and a light neared the base of the stairs, and then a red nightshirt-clad Otto Obermyer appeared. "Grady?" he said, craning his red-cheeked face upward, adjusting his half glasses. "What the H-E-double you doing awake, and in dem fancy clothes?" Then he saw Ozymandias and smiled wide. "Hello, little schnitzel!"

The cat mewed.

Grady said, "Maggie wired. I've got a customer for you."

"Well, what you waiting for?" Otto said, setting down his lamp and then holding up his heavy arms, a rare beatific look on his ruddy features.

"You know," said Grady, as he handed down the cat—or rather, as the cat leapt from his arms to Otto's—"I never noticed it before."

"What you haven't noticed?" said Otto, distracted as an ecstatic Ozzie burrowed into his muttonchops.

Grady cocked his head. "You look like Santa Claus."

Monday, June 4

>─┤─◆─┤─◯─┤─◆─┤─<

S HE WAS DREAMING OF QUINCY APPLEGATE. MORE TO the point, she was dreaming about his chest, about putting her head on it and his arm coming around her. And he smelled so nice, of pipe tobacco and something else— strawberries, maybe—and then he was kissing her and yes, it was strawberries, and someone was shooting at them.

Shooting at them?

"Quin?" she said in the dream, and then his chest turned into her pillow but the shooting didn't stop, and she rolled off the bed and under it before she remembered where she was, and that the gunshots weren't directed at her. On purpose, anyway.

The shooting stopped, and she crawled from beneath the bed, pulling herself up to sit on it, yawning before she groped for the bed table and her watch pin. Six-thirty and barely light. They started early here. She hoped they hadn't blasted that poor goat again. Last night they'd creased his tail.

She stood, her hands in the small of her back, stretching and bidding the last wisps of Quincy good-bye. She said, "Harriet? You awake? Miss Hogg?"

Other than a small wet stain of yellow vomit, the spare bed was empty, the covers thrown back.

Cursing under her breath, Maggie ran to the door, then remembered she was in her nightgown. She grabbed a robe, threw it on, and dashed into the hall. "Harriet!" she called, trotting toward the staircase, bundling herself against prying eyes as best she could. "Harriet!"

She raced down the stairs—and ran directly into Eddie, who knocked her flat.

"What do you do, work every shift?" she muttered, climbing up from the floor and shaking her robe.

He didn't offer to help her up. His back against the wall of the landing, he was too busy trying to keep the swaying stack of towels, balanced before him, from toppling. "My daddy owns the place," he explained sheepishly. The top four towels fell to the side, and Maggie caught them.

She eyed them before she reached up and settled them back on the stack. "I never got any of those. Not nice ones."

"Yes, ma'am. Sorry, ma'am." He started to go around her.

She stuck out an arm. "You been on duty all night?"

The top four towels dropped again, and landed on the floor. Eddie clamped his chin on the rest of the stack and bent his knees, feeling for the strays. "Yeah. All night."

"Did Harriet come past here?" She frowned. "Oh, stand up, Eddie. You look stupid." She swept up the towels and put them in his arms again.

"Thanks," he mumbled from behind the stack. "I didn't see her, but I been in the back sometimes." He paused a moment, then added guiltily, "Well, a feller can't stay awake *all* the time!"

"Good gravy," said Maggie with a snort, not so much at Eddie, but at the circumstance. She crossed the small, deserted lobby and peered through the front door glass. It was cheap, and through it the town looked wobbly, almost as wobbly as Harriet. It was fitting, truly fitting. She could have vacated the premises at any time and gone anywhere. Wonderful.

But she wouldn't have gone far, Maggie reasoned, once she passed the first sharp bit of panic. She'd be sick. She'd want whiskey. She'd probably go no farther than the Purple Fox and the closest bottle of Old Backwash. Well, Maggie Maguire wasn't going to walk into any saloon in her nightclothes—not if she could help it, anyway. She turned on her heel and started for the landing, where Eddie was still standing.

"Give me a few of those," she said, swiping three off the top as she climbed past him. The pile swayed.

And then she heard something. She stopped. She heard it again. A weak groan, coming from behind the desk.

"Harriet?" she called, and turned around, brushing past Eddie on her way back down.

It was Harriet, all right. Harriet, lying in a pool of sick, curled into a ball on the floor behind the counter. She was shaking. Her teeth chattered. Perspiration drenched her brow.

Maggie bent to her, doing her best not to vomit at the stench of the contents of Harriet's stomach—not to mention Harriet herself, whose gamey smell seemed to have transcended new heights during the night. She managed to sit her up. "Harriet?" she said softly. "Harriet, can you hear me?"

The girl's hands went to her ears, and she began to sniffle. "Mama, Mama, don't make me go out there!" she said in perfect English, then her head turned abruptly. Her eyes opened, she looked straight at Maggie and whimpered, "Why you all the time shouting?" in her familiar pidgin English.

The sniffling turned into full-fledged wailing. Harriet's nose began to run, down her cheek and onto Maggie's sleeve. Maggie did her best to ignore it.

"Hattie want whiskey. Give Hattie Backwash."

"No," said Maggie, and heaved her to her feet. The woman wasn't heavy—ninety or ninety-five pounds at the most—but she was deadweight. Steadying herself against the desk, Maggie managed to get Harriet's arm around her neck, and her own arm around Harriet's shoulders. To the sound of Harriet, who now seemed to be chanting an Apache song of some sort, she began to half-drag, half-carry her toward the stairs.

"Backwash now!" Harriet said suddenly, in English, as Maggie got her up on the landing. "Drink!" she wailed as they started past Eddie, who seemed to have been mesmerized by the whole process.

"Step up, Harriet," said Maggie, growling through clenched teeth, shooting Eddie a sidelong glance.

Harriet at last noticed Eddie, not two feet away, peeking out from behind his burden of towels. "Hey, cowboy!" she said, suddenly brightening. "You buy Hattie whiskey?" she asked. "Take ride?"

She gave an exaggerated wink, then an abrupt shake of her hips, a shake that was supposed to be an alluring sort of come-hither shimmy, Maggie supposed. But the shake ended in a spasm, and Maggie lost her grip on the girl.

Harriet went down to her knees with a flailing *thump,* which pushed Eddie off his balance and sent him reeling backward, and sent the towels flying across the lobby.

He landed against the wall, and slowly skidded down into a crouch, one towel clutched in his hands.

Harriet, oblivious to the chaos she'd just instigated, turned her head toward him and said, through strings of greasy hair, "So, you want go make thumpy-thump or not?"

Maggie stood above it all, hands on her hips, robe half off and hanging open, exposing her white cotton nightdress. She was too exasperated to care.

She muttered, "This is going to be harder than I thought." Then louder, "Well, don't just sit there, Eddie. Help me get her upstairs."

By noon, Harriet was screaming. Not just random screams, but wails and guttural curses and weepy pleas: half in pidgin English, half in Apache, and judging by the tone and substance of the English parts, Maggie didn't care to have the Apache half translated.

She'd tied her to the bed by that time, bathing her forehead and giving her liquids and pausing occasionally to answer the door and apologize to another hotel guest for the noise.

Eddie had been sent to scour the town for oranges—her papa had always recommended oranges for a hangover—but had turned up only four poor specimens, scrawny and puckered. Maggie peeled them anyway and thumbed out the seeds, and every time Harriet opened her mouth, she'd stick in a section.

"Chew," she'd said over Apache curses and threats and the terror of hallucinations. "Yum, yum. Chew, goddamn it."

By midafternoon she was almost as bedraggled as the girl on the bed. At least Harriet was finally sleeping—sleeping fitfully, to be sure, but sleeping. Maggie was sprawled on her own bed, staring at the ceiling, fighting off sleep. Once she got Harriet sobered up—and Grady arrived in town—they'd set to the work of getting her presentable enough for the insurance company.

A girl like that, getting all that money! It staggered the imagination. Not so badly as the thought of Just-Call-Me-Ralphie making off with it, but still . . .

She sat up, pinning a few errant wisps of hair back into place and taking three deep breaths. "Three deep breaths to clear the mind, Magdalena," Papa had said before each performance. And then she'd hobbled out onstage ready to be "cured" by Papa's 120-proof remedy, branded with the label of the moment. Which was, in her case, tea.

Not that she couldn't hold her liquor. During her years in Chicago, a certain young man had tried to get her drunk, and she'd decided to take him up on it. And much to her surprise, after eight beers and four whiskeys, he was under the table and she was still standing. She'd poured him into a cab and sent him clopping home, and then she'd had three more beers just to test this new gift.

Sober as a judge. Well, almost as sober. But sober enough to walk herself home and buy a bottle of whiskey on the way, sober enough to put the key in the latch on the first try and then put away half of that bottle until she couldn't stand the taste anymore, and sober enough to realize that this might be useful someday.

It caught up with her the next morning. She was so sensitized that she could feel every hair on her head, every finger- and toenail, every tooth, every pore, every flake of skin, and they all hurt with indescribable agony.

Just her luck, she'd thought, once she could think again without wincing. None of the sport of liquor, but all of the pain.

She had a certain amount of sympathy for Harriet.

She picked up Grady's telegram again, brought up around noon by Eddie's father (who, it seemed, was finally on duty), and went to the window. She held it to the sunlight.

CAN'T YOU DO ANYTHING BY YOURSELF
STOP ARRIVE TUESDAY **STOP** FURBALL
CRISIS AVERTED **STOP** GRADY

She smiled. Everything was a crisis with Grady, even sweet little blue-eyed Ozymandias.

Actually, she was amazed that Grady was coming at all, that he'd leave behind his new pride and joy. Ever since they'd had a telephone installed, he hovered over it, flicking away specks of dust, waiting for it to ring.

Well, she supposed they had to keep up. Had to "get wired" like everybody else, as Grady would say.

Absently, Maggie turned from the window. Tuesday was tomorrow. Leave it to Grady Maguire to get the best travel connections. Wining and dining that Miss LaWhatsis at Stoner's Travel didn't hurt anything, either. Grady was—

The first shot sang past her head, and Maggie hit the floor even as it was burying itself in the wall. The next three came quickly, and burrowed themselves into the wood in a five-inch spread from the first slug.

Harriet woke up, slurring, "Hey, cowboy, you buy Hattie whiskey?" then suddenly covered her face, shrieking, "Bats!"

"Shut up," barked Maggie from the floor. At least Harriet was tied down and couldn't sit up into the line of fire.

"Whiskey! Hattie need Backwash! Bugs, bugs!"

This was too much for coincidence. Ignoring Harriet, who had now lapsed into Apache, Maggie crept to the window and peeked over the sill. It was business as usual on the street. The goat who had been winged yesterday was tied to a rail across the street. He stood between two dozing horses, blithely chewing his rope, a bandage the size of a cigar box fixed to his twitching tail.

"Doesn't anyone in this town have a nerve in his body?" Maggie said under her breath, and barking at Harriet to be quiet, went to the door and hollered, "*Eddie!* Get the sheriff again!"

Then she opened her suitcase and rummaged through the underclothes and the stockings and the pair of emergency trousers to the panel at the bottom. Feeling for the catch, she released it, and fumbled through a sea of knives and cards and wax key molds and blackjacks and a hide-out rig, to pull out a well-tended Colt Peacemaker.

Slowly shaking her head with a *tsk, tsk, tsk,* she began to load it.

NINE

TURNING FROM HER SECOND-FLOOR WINDOW AT BENT Elbow's Kid Concho Hotel and secreting a derringer into the folds of her skirts, Cora Trimble answered the knock on her door. "Oh," she said, opening it wider to admit the young man, and slipping the gun into her pocket. "Come in. Did you do it?"

Jim Caulder nodded. "He quit his job and took off for Arizona. Seemed there was a family emergency. Facilitated by my hundred dollars, that is."

Cora indicated a chair, and he sat down. "Good," she said. "It's always so much nicer when they take the money and vacate the premises of their own free will." She sat down opposite him, smoothing her skirts thoughtfully. Youngsters were always so eager. "And the rest?"

"The bartender asked me if I was a mind reader. Said the night man had just up and quit a half hour ago. Family emergency." He smiled. "Hired me on the spot. I start tonight."

"Fine. That's fine, Jim. Sooner or later, those idiots are going to figure out they've got the wrong girl. And they'll check the saloon. I'm curious to see if they'll check with Mr. Festing."

"Cora?"

"What?"

"I don't see . . . that is, why don't we just go up the street and get her? We know where she is. Why don't—"

Cora held up her hand. "We know where she is, but what good would it do us to have her now? Let Miss Maguire do the dirty work. Get her sobered up. Get her talking. Get her remembering. If we play our cards right, she'll lead us straight to it. And if she doesn't remember?'' She shrugged, then patted his knee. ''Well, we'll just have to think of something else, won't we?''

TEN

>━┼━♦━◦━♦━┼━<

IT WAS AFTER DARK BEFORE SHERIFF SOPSUCHER DEIGNED
to visit Maggie. By now, the Kid Concho Café was sending
over three meals a day without being asked, and she'd already finished hers. And she had actually gotten some apple-
sauce down Harriet's craw.

Eddie had helped her to move Harriet's bed, but with two
of them in an already crowded room there wasn't much place
to go, and she'd be damned if she'd share with Harriet. She'd
still have to cross in front of the window, but she could do
that on hands and knees for the time being. The main thing
was to hold out till tomorrow, when Grady would get here,
when she could leave this room and do a little snooping on
the street.

Until then, she was stuck baby-sitting Harriet, and stuck
with this fool of a sheriff.

"Like I been tellin' you, missy, it's just a whatchacall, a
coincidence," he was saying. This time he hadn't bothered to
take his hat off. "Why, I'll bet them boys don't shoot up this
hotel twice in the same week more often than ever' half year
or so. I reckon you got this month's share, and June's, too."

"Sheriff Sapsucker—"

"It's Sidewinder!" he said in an angry burst. "I mean Sopsucher. Aw, hell."

"Hattie's lost!" came a weak voice from the bed. "Where
you take Hattie?"

They both ignored her. Maggie said, "Good. Maybe you'll
call me by name instead of those ridiculous endearments."

He stared at her blankly.

"It's Miss Maguire. Miss Magdalena Maguire."

"Mag-wire?" came the voice from the bed. "Mag-wire let Hattie go now? Hattie go see nice cowboy, nice miner-man, get whiskey."

The sheriff's eyes flicked toward the bed, then back, and letting loose an enormous, overly dramatic sigh, said, "*Miss* Maguire. I got a whole lot better things to do than runnin' up here three times a day and six on Sunday on nuisance calls. I got me two stole horses to worry about, then there's Sass Becker's chicken thief, and a missin' whore, and—"

"Stop." Maggie held up a hand. "Who's missing?"

He shot her a long-suffering look. "Another one'a Tom Festing's gals. One from the saloon."

"Festing love Hattie," Harriet muttered belligerently. "Hattie good whore." She brightened. "Festing give Hattie whiskey, give Hattie Backwash whiskey."

"From the saloon?" Maggie asked.

"Oh, he keeps the best gals over to the Purple Fox. Has a row of cribs over on Perch Street for the others."

Harriet was one of Festing's "best gals"? Before Maggie could think of a thing to say, he lowered his voice and said, "I imagine he'll be up here lookin' to put ol' Hattie back in the traces. You just happened to haul her outta there when he was away, over to Carson City. But he's comin' back in a day or two, and he ain't gonna be pleased, I can tell you that right now."

Harriet mumbled, "Hattie work good for Festing. Hattie work real hard."

Maggie craned her head to look at the girl. "I'll just bet you did, Harriet. I'll bet you worked very hard indeed."

Wearily, the sheriff said, "Well now, missy—dagnabit, I meant Miss Maguire—"

She held up a hand. "I'll deal with this Mr. Festing, Sheriff Sopsucher."

He closed his eyes for a second, probably thanking the lord that she'd used his right name. She bit at her lips to hold the smile in. He was really sort of cute, in a bumbling, grandfatherly sort of way. Too bad he was in a position of power.

"About this girl that's gone missing," she said. "I wonder if you could tell me—"

Sopsucher yanked her down to the floor as a bullet sped through the open window, embedding itself in the wall fewer than two inches from the holes left by the previous volley.

Maggie yanked her arm free and got to her feet, away from the window. "I was already ducking," she said testily, brushing at her skirts.

But Sopsucher wasn't listening. From the floor, he said, "Goldangit! If that don't beat everything! You better get back down here, little lady, 'fore they get to rowdy-dowin' again."

They were back to "little lady." With a sigh, she crossed her arms over her chest and stared down at him. "It *always* comes through that window! And I'm over here. Don't you think you should get down on the street and do something about this . . . rowdy-dow?"

She had absolute faith that he'd do absolutely nothing, and he didn't disappoint her. They heard another shot—with the resultant splat of splinters in the wall, right on target. Whoever was out there knew what he was doing, all right. Who he was or why he was doing it remained to be seen. But she could do something in the meantime.

She slid her pistol off the dresser.

Taking a giant step over the sheriff—who made a grab for her, presumably to pull her to safety, but missed—she marched out into the hall, to the next room. She heard another shot as she tried the latch, then banged her fist on the door. It was immediately opened by a middle-aged man, stripped to his suspenders. His face was half covered in lather, and there was a razor in his hand.

With a cursory "Excuse me," she pushed past him and crossed the room to stand next to his window. "Come on," she whispered. "Take another potshot. Let me see you."

The room's tenant, hastily wiping the lather from his face in light of this surprise bonus offered by the hotel management, said, "Miss? I'd get back, if I was you. Why don't you come over here by the bed?" He patted the covers. "Somebody's having a little fun out in the street, and—"

Another shot. And this time she saw something, just a flash

across the way—the flash from a gun at the edge of the alley. Quickly, she crawled out the window, the man behind her calling, "Miss? Lady! Hey, what you doing?" as she skidded down the overhanging roof and dropped the ten feet to the sidewalk.

She landed, crouching, her blood pumping. Now, this was fun! Pablo DeGarza would've been proud to see the way she landed. The alley was in sight. She reached into her pocket and freed the Colt, heavy and cool in her hand. An old friend.

Spring and rush to the opening of the alley, that was the ticket. Spring and rush, just to the side, then call for whoever it was to come out.

She sprang.

And tripped flat on her face, twisted in her own skirts.

Maybe Pablo wouldn't have been so proud of her, after all.

"Oh, suds!" she grumbled as she freed herself. Quickly, she felt her nose to make sure she hadn't broken it again, and hurried across the street. She flattened herself against the rough board wall, inches from the alley.

Harsh music, softened by distance, spilled around the corner from the Purple Fox, and the Silver Dollar, and several others down the way. Piano music and laughter. Someone singing.

"Come out of there!" she called, her pistol raised. Damn those blasted skirts, anyway. "Come out, you coward!"

She couldn't hear a thing over the sounds from the saloons. No breathing, not the scuff of a boot.

"I said, come out. I won't say it again."

Nothing.

Then suddenly, the sound of boots, of running feet. One man. She whipped around the corner, into the mouth of the alley, just in time to see a figure dash around the corner at the far end.

She gave chase, holding her skirts in one hand and the Colt in the other, but by the time she reached the end, the culprit wasn't in sight. Well, he might have been. Several places were open for business. Cowhands and miners lounged on the rails out front, half-clad girls moved in and out of the doorways of red-lantern-lit cribs.

Disgusted, Maggie dropped the Colt back into her pocket

and turned around. And nearly ran headlong into a cowhand who'd had about two drinks too many, by the looks of him.

"Baby!" he cried happily, and clamped a hand on each of her upper arms.

"Wrong!" she replied just as heartily, and kneed him in the groin.

As she marched back up the alley, the luckless cowboy groaning to his feet behind her, she could just hear Grady. *You've got to stop busting these boys in their goodies, Maggie,* he'd say. *One of them might turn out to be marriage material.*

"Oh, shut up," she grumbled aloud, and walked into the hotel lobby. She found Eddie behind the desk, reading the newspaper. He snapped to attention when he heard her come in.

"Miz Maguire?" he said, puzzled. "When did you go out?"

"Just now."

"But I was here and—"

"Never mind. The sheriff still around?"

"Nope. Somebody come up from the Silver Dollar. Said there was a fistfight over a card game."

"And he *went*?"

Eddie's grin was lopsided. "No, ma'am. I think he had urgent business, cleanin' spittoons down to the jail or some-such."

Maggie grinned back at him.

"Don't be too hard on Sheriff Sopsucher, Miz Maguire. I reckon he's a good enough man. He was a real fast gun in his time."

She'd never heard of any shootist named Sopsucher, but she didn't say so.

Eddie continued, "Pa says they just keep votin' him in for old times' sake. Next election, though, he's apt to get voted out. Tom Festing's runnin' against him, and he can hire more votes than Sopsucher can get the regular way. Anyway, probably more than he could hire, on his salary."

Tom Festing again. A girl's best friend.

"Eddie?"

"Yes'm?"

"I hate to ask, but could you move me again? Maybe to a bigger room." She added hopefully, "With no windows?"

"Ain't got a room like that," Eddie replied, all seriousness. "Most folks like the air. And I ain't got nothin' bigger. You're already in the presidential suite."

Maggie closed her eyes. The presidential suite? Good gravy. President Chester A. Arthur was going to be in for a shock if he ever visited Bent Elbow. She opened her eyes again. "Something without a clear shot from the street."

"That I can do," he said, and produced a key from behind the desk. "I can give you the Doc Holliday suite. Doc and Kate Elder used to come to town every once in a while and use it. Well, Doc only came once. But Kate ain't been here for three, four years, now. It ain't the biggest, but there's no way anybody could take a potshot at you unless they wanted to climb straight up and hang from your windowsill."

"Sold," said Maggie. "Lead on."

A half hour later, she was chewing on a pencil and perched in a rocking chair. The rocker was crammed between two narrow beds in the Doc Holliday suite, which was a good deal smaller than her old room, and slightly shabbier, if that were possible. But it had the distinct advantage of facing the blind wall of the building next door.

Hattie was asleep already, snoring softly on her bed. Maggie figured the worst was over, at least as far as her physical condition went. Eddie had been glad to hear it. The woman who did the hotel's laundry had threatened to quit.

She discarded the pencil—filthy habit, she really should give it up—and picked up the book she'd brought, a romance that bore the title *Samantha and the Seafaring Salt*. There was a drawing on the cover of a sweet-faced, dimpled, blond girl wearing a sailor's cap at a jaunty angle.

Maggie tipped her head in imitation of the cover model. She struck a pose, beaming, with the tips of her forefingers digging into her cheeks where the dimples should have been.

Balderdash.

With a resigned sigh, she tossed the book on the bed and began to rock. She was too nervous to read. Too hopped up on gunshots and Tom Festing and lousy sheriffs and chases down alleys and missing ladies of the night. And Harriet. Poor Harriet. There was certainly a lot of work to do there.

Well, she'd let Grady worry about that part.

A soft knock rattled the door. She looked up. "Eddie?"

"Yes'm," came the reply, and she went to the door and opened it.

"I did like you asked. Went to the saloon, I mean."

"And?"

"I just caught Will goin' off duty. Will's the bartender. They got a brand-new fella for the night shift, name of Jim."

"Get to the point, Eddie," she said.

"Oh. Well, the girl what got took was named Corinne Gish. Will said there was a couple fellers in there 'bout a half hour before you showed up, askin' about Hattie, an' they went upstairs. He said he told you to knock on account of he hadn't seen them come back down yet."

Maggie said, "Did he say if they came down later?"

"No, ma'am. But he's always workin' that bar. I reckon they could have come down without his seeing; 'course, he coulda been foolin' with that dog he's got now. . . ."

Or they could have gone out the window, Maggie thought. They'd taken the girl in the second room on the left, but it hadn't been Harriet. They'd gotten Corinne instead.

"I don't suppose he said what they looked like?"

Eddie straightened. "Well, as a matter fact, he did say they was kind of odd."

"Odd?"

"Said they looked like they just come from the general store. On account of all their clothes was so new. Oh. And speaking of the general store, I got 'em." Eddie handed her a paper sack. "Just like you said, 'cept they only had the three. But if you don't mind me askin'—"

"I mind," she said with a smile. "Dime enough?"

"Fifteen cents."

"They've gone up," she said, tucking the sack under her arm excitedly. Slickers. City slickers had been in the bar, and they'd kidnapped Corinne because they thought she was Harriet, because she'd been in the wrong room, probably passed out. She smelled Ralphie's hand in this. She handed Eddie twenty cents, the extra nickel for his trouble, then closed the door.

"Now!" she said to no one in particular as she reached into the bag. "Now I can think!"

Casting the crumpled sack to the floor, she began to juggle three black and shiny India rubber balls.

TUESDAY, JUNE 5

>─┤─◆─•─○─•─◆─├─<

I T WAS DARK WHEN, RUMPLED AND TIRED AND DUSTY, Grady Maguire stepped down from the Sky Butte to Bent Elbow stage. He gave his backside a rub. After six hours on the coach, even with two rest stops to change horses, his rear end felt like pounded steak.

He wondered, for the sixth or eighth time, why Maggie couldn't have found the girl in, say, Denver. Or better yet, Sacramento. He knew a girl in Sacramento.

Well, actually, three girls. The Mulrooney triplets—Siobhan, Sinead, and Shannon. Delightful young ladies, all redheads, and—

"Heads up!"

He ducked out of the way, narrowly avoiding decapitation by a trunk the driver tossed down like so much chaff. That would teach him to daydream, he thought as he rescued his valise—an alligator Gladstone with shiny nickel locks and trim that had been unscratched (up until this minute)—from the growing pile on the ground. He removed himself to the safety of the boardwalk.

Disgustedly banging the dirt from his valise, he asked directions to the Famous West Hotel.

Filthy town, he thought as he made his way down the covered sidewalk. A mix of cowhands and miners and far too few women, and most of those looked like tarts. The storefronts appeared as though some of them had been standing—barely—for twenty years, and the rest looked like they'd been haphazardly nailed up within the past few months. Some of them hadn't even been painted yet.

It was a typical boomtown, silver being the culprit in this

case. Well, it wouldn't last long. They'd dig it all up and move on. They always did. Easy come, easy go.

He stopped in front of the hotel. Two stories of weathered boards, a peeling sign, dirty windows. There had to be a better place to stay than this! Leave it to Maggie to pick the first establishment she came to, blind to the possibilities. Prepared for the worst, he walked through the front doorway—the lobby was a dark, dingy abomination, just as he expected—and up to the desk.

He was greeted by a muttonchopped, blondish man who leaned over the desk. A wall centered by a key rack and mail slots, and otherwise covered in framed newspaper clippings, loomed behind him. He closed the book he'd been reading, looked up, and smiled. "Can I help you, sir?"

At last, a touch of civility. Why, this might well be the cultural epicenter of the entire town! "Indeed you can, my good man," Grady replied brightly. "Maggie Maguire, please?"

The man's smile collapsed. He picked up the book again—it was, of all things, *Little Women*—and snapped it open irritably. "She's in number twelve. Today."

So much for civility. Grady said, "Thank you," the man grunted, and Grady started up the stairs, eyeing the frayed runner-rug beneath his feet. The stairs creaked. And they were dark, not to mention narrow.

Perfect.

He came to number twelve and raised his hand to knock, then paused. He put his ear to the wood. From inside, he heard Maggie's voice.

"Good day, Mr. Applegate," she was saying, the words emphasized and drawn out theatrically. "Good day, Mr. Applegate." Then, "Damn it, Harriet, say it! Good day, Mr. Applegate!"

"Hattie no want no goddamn Mr. Apple! Hattie want food! Hattie want whiskey, Mag-wire! Why you no get Hattie Backwash?"

"You can have a bite of potatoes if you say, 'Good day, Mr. Applegate.' Yum, yum, potatoes."

There was a crash that sounded suspiciously like china. His

mouth twisting to hold back the grin, Grady knocked.

Maggie answered the door almost immediately. Her hair hung down in thin, damp loops from her usually tidy bun, her face was cranky and flushed, and there was a long smear of gravy on her bodice. A clump of mashed potatoes dripped from her hem to the floor.

"Hard at work, I see," he said with a straight face.

She grabbed the front of his suit and pulled him into the room. "Finally!" she said. Then, without preamble, turned him toward the far bed. "Grady, meet Harriet."

Harriet, having already tossed her plate, threw Maggie's.

He ducked down and it hit the wall behind him, leaving, as it slid to the floor, a trail of green beans and mashed potatoes and what he thought was meat loaf, although he couldn't be sure because he was back out in the hall so fast.

Maggie was out there with him, her back pressed hard against the door. She ran fingers over her throat, wiping away the sweat, and said, "She's a little . . . nervous."

Grady pursed his lips. "Do tell. And by the way, lovely to see you, too."

"Oh," she said. "Sorry. But you were supposed to be here three hours ago." She picked at something on his sleeve. "Cat hair," she said.

"The train was late. Missed my connection. And stop fussing." There was another crash from inside the room, but Maggie ignored it, so he did, too. "I had to wait for the next stage. Charming girl, by the way."

Maggie muttered, "Oh, shut up," and wiped potatoes off her forehead.

ELEVEN

AMAZING, MAGGIE THOUGHT. SIMPLY AMAZING WHAT a man's voice could do. It could permeate a thick female skull, at least.

Across the room, Harriet was slowly repeating, "Good day, Mister Applegate. It is a pleasing to meet you."

"Pleasure," Grady prompted. "It is a pleasure to meet you."

"It is a please—pleasure to meet you." Then, "Give Hattie drink now, Grady?"

Grady patted her hand. "Now, now. What did we say about the whiskey?"

Harriet, pouting, said, "If Hattie talk good, she take train ride. If Hattie take train ride, Hattie get all Backwash in world. That a very much lot of whiskey, Grady?"

"That is very much indeed an enormous amount of whiskey. And not just all the whiskey, Harriet. You can have anything you want. Anything that money can buy. Lovely clothes. A nice house. You might even decide you don't want the whiskey."

"Hattie want whiskey," she repeated stubbornly.

The girl certainly looked better, Maggie had to admit. She'd washed Harriet's hair that morning, and while it still looked like it had been last cut by a madman with pinking shears, the shampoo had washed away several layers of dirt to expose pale, ash-blond hair that was softly textured, with a bit of a wave to it. Maggie had pinned it up and back to keep it from falling into Harriet's wide blue eyes.

She was actually rather pretty. Given a good dressmaker and six or eight months to grow her hair out and lose the rest of that tan, she might even be beautiful.

"Good day, Mr. Applegate. It is a pleasure to meet you. Okay? Hattie have drink now?"

Grady squeezed her hand. At least Maggie thought it was Harriet's hand he was squeezing. She picked up the India rubber balls. Just two. Now, where had the third gone?

"No, Harriet," Grady said patiently. "First you have to learn to speak correctly. And then we'll take a nice trip on a train to see Mr. Applegate. And if Hattie is very, very good, then Mr. Applegate will give her the money."

Harriet scratched her neck thoughtfully. "Why this Mr. Applegate give Hattie money? Hattie no give him ride."

"No more rides, Harriet. You have to stop offering," Grady said. "And Mr. Applegate works for the insurance company."

Maggie thought, *Good luck explaining that,* at the same moment that Harriet said, "Insurant's company?"

Smirking, Maggie got down on her knees and reached under the bed, groping for the lost ball. After a few sweeps of her hand, she found it and pulled it out, covered with lint and dust. Eddie had said that Kate Elder hadn't been here for two or three years, and neither had anybody else, it seemed, the maid included.

Grady was all tangled up in the insurance company, trying to explain actuarial tables.

"It's like a tribe, Harriet," Maggie cut in, wiping the dusty ball on her skirts. "A tribe of white men who hold money. You give them money, and when you die, they give it to your, um, children."

She started the balls moving in the air. "Honestly, Grady. Stop trying to explain long-term benefits and group risk. You have to be rudimentary about these things."

"But Hattie no die!" the girl cried. "Why this tribe want Hattie's money, Grady?"

Through the balls she was juggling, Maggie saw Grady gently push Harriet back in the bed. "They don't want your money, Harriet," he explained, shooting Maggie a dirty look.

"They want to give you your father's money. He's the one that died."

Harriet's face screwed up in concentration. After a pause, she said, "Hattie's father?"

Grady leaned toward Maggie. "Didn't you tell her *anything*?"

Maggie gave a shrug of her shoulders, pleased that it didn't disturb her rhythm. "Didn't think she was in much shape to retain it. We've been having a very interesting time these past couple of days, what with the shakes and the sweats and the throwing up and the diarrhea, and somebody shooting at us and all. Yes, interesting." She wished that she'd gotten four balls instead of three. Maybe tomorrow.

"Somebody shot at you?" Grady said, ignoring the more colorful bits that went before it.

Harriet tugged at his sleeve. "What about Hattie's father? Hattie have father?"

"There's more," Maggie said. "One of the other, uh, *ladies* from the saloon is missing. A little blond thing named Corinne Gish. I found that much out from the kid downstairs. Taken about the time I showed up in town, as I understand, and taken by mistake. They thought she was Harriet." Maybe five balls would be better. She thought she could handle five.

"Yes, Harriet," Grady said. "He loved you very much. He died." He stared at Maggie. "And?"

"That's it. Except the bartender says they were slickers. Just-Call-Me-Ralphie's got a hand in this, I'll stake my reputation on it."

"Who?"

Maggie snorted. "Scaggs. Ralph Scaggs. You know, He-Who-Will-Inherit-if-There's-No-Harriet. Skinny little bottom-pinching, bottom-feeding, Barbary Coast trash."

The corner of Grady's mouth quirked up. "So what don't you like about him?"

Maggie slid a glance his way, but his cocky expression convinced her it wouldn't be expedient to pursue that line. She said, "I haven't been able to get out of this blasted hotel room, what with Princess Hiawatha trying to duck out every fifteen minutes and crawl into the nearest whiskey keg. And the sheriff's a waste of time.''

Harriet pouted on the bed. ''They not burn Hattie's father's things?'' she said peevishly. ''Apache burn things of the dead.''

Grady said, ''Hattie's father was a white man, not Apache. An extremely powerful . . .'' He sighed. ''He was a big chief, Hattie. Up north. He left you a very fine house and lots of money, which you're never going to get if you don't stop referring to yourself in the third person.''

''Hattie not understand.''

''Say *I*, Harriet. Say *I* don't understand.''

''You neither?''

''Can I turn around yet?''

Maggie tucked her shirttails in, then bloused the worn work shirt out and gave a pull to the tattered cuffs. ''Yes,'' she said softly, so as not to wake Harriet. She turned sideways in front of the mirror, smiling in approval. If she didn't stand up straight, a person would hardly know she had breasts at all. Suddenly, she frowned. This was a thing to be happy about? Sighing, she said, ''I believe I'm decent.''

Grady turned around, looked her up and down, and shook his head in exasperation. ''You're crazy, you know.''

Grady always made her feel better. He was so . . . well, so Grady. She winked at him. ''Yes, dear.''

Securely bound, she knotted her hair, then pulled the old hat Eddie had given her down over her ears, careful to cover the one with the wounded tip. Next, she smudged her face with cork. Not too much, just enough to make her appear reasonably dirty. Reasonably boyish. Reasonably invisible.

''I could go down there just as well, you know,'' Grady said, arms crossed. He was being peevish.

''No, you couldn't.'' Maggie fussed with the hat, tried the brim up, then down, then up again, then decided down was best, then caught sight of her chest in the mirror—bound down but still bumpy, damnit—and reminded herself to stoop. She said, ''You'd stick out like a sore thumb.''

''Gosh, that's original.'' He slumped into the rocking chair, then jumped up straightaway, removing Maggie's juggling balls from the seat. He held them out accusingly. "Will you *ever* learn to put things away?"

"No," she said. She gave herself a last check in the mirror. She liked disguises. They always gave her, well, sort of a lift. It was fun being somebody else for a while. Not as much fun as jumping out of windows or throwing some villain flat on his face—What was?—but almost.

Setting an old bent pair of glasses on her nose and giving the hat one last tug, she stepped to the door and pulled it open, saying gruffly, in a deeper-than-normal voice, "Don't wait up for me."

She heard a ball bounce off the door behind her, and walked down the hall, whistling.

TWELVE

>──!──◆──◯──◆──!──<

MAGGIE STOOD AT THE END OF THE BAR IN THE DIMLY lit Purple Fox, nursing her second beer, feigning indifference to the gunshots coming from down the street. Nobody else was ducking, so why should she? She'd gone back to a corner table when she first came in, carrying her beer with her, but there wasn't much going on back there besides poker, and eventually she wandered up front again.

The bartender was a different man than she'd spoken to about Harriet. This one was younger, with a big handlebar mustache, and he seemed even more bored with the job than the previous fellow. The only congress she'd had with him was his indifferent, " 'Nother beer, sonny?'' She drained that one, and when she motioned at him for another and plunked down her coin, he drew one and slid it to her, foaming and sloshing, without a second look.

It was a good thing Grady hadn't come, she thought. He would have been all over the place, handing out coasters.

Nobody had attempted to strike up a conversation with her—tried very hard, that was. After all, she was just a grimy boy at the end of the bar. She just acted antisocial and stupid, and pretty soon they got bored and went away.

The only man she recognized wandered in halfway through the third beer. He was the fellow who'd carried Harriet to the hotel the first day. Biscuit Pete, that was it, the cowhand with the fancy vest.

From the corner of her eye, she watched him saunter over

to one of the poker games and slide out a chair. He sat down with his back to her. Nothing going on there.

She supposed she might as well fold her tent and go back to the hotel. Coming down here tonight had been a dead end, unless you were the absent Tom Festing and could count what she'd paid for three watery beers as a boon. Even the girls—well, girl, singular—hadn't been any help. Every time she'd come down the stairs, looking more bedraggled each time, to shove another grinning, sated cowhand or miner on his way, another would go right back up with her. There had been seven just since Maggie came in.

It was a rough way to make a living.

She was just lifting the beer to her lips with the intention of draining it, when she noticed the bartender leaning over the bar slightly. Since his normal manner, as she'd observed it, had been to stand back a couple of feet, it caught her attention.

He was talking to a man. A man wearing range clothes, but range clothes fresh from the mercantile's shelf. Even his hat was so new that he hadn't bothered to put a crease in it. A surge of adrenaline shot through her when she first spied him. *Ralphie!* she thought, springing to attention on tiptoes. But then he turned so that his face was in the light, and she sagged back to her heels. Not Ralphie.

After a quick conversation with the bartender, the only part of which she caught was "Festing" and "late," he turned and went into what she assumed was the back office, leaving his whiskey on the bar. A small dog—the one she'd seen on the bar—appeared in the open doorway and scurried away from the new man. He closed the door behind him.

Now, that was interesting. She drained her beer and ordered another, thinking to wait him out.

Had Festing come back into town? It was certainly possible. He must be annoyed, coming back to find two of his girls gone. And who was late? Festing, or the slicker, or somebody else?

She'd barely got her beer when the door opened again and the slicker came out. She took a look at his boots as he walked past. They were new, too, with hardly a scuff.

Leaving the beer untouched, she wandered out of the Purple

Fox and turned left, as he had done, trying to decide between throwing him to the ground and demanding the return of Corinne, or just watching to see where he went.

She decided that while the first option was more satisfying, the second was the wiser.

She didn't follow him long. She shuffled past him, feigning drunkenness, as he clumsily untied his horse from the rail in front of Kid Concho Feed & Grain. After an abortive first try, he mounted and jogged down the street, out of town.

He wasn't much of a horseman. Bad seat, terrible hands. Of course, that didn't mean anything, not really. Out here, there weren't any streetcars or hansom cabs. You rode whether you could ride or not. But even if he was a naturally poor rider, he just didn't move around a horse as if he was at all used to them.

He rode like a city boy.

Come to think of it, he rode like Grady. Well, like Grady would, if she could ever get him on a horse.

"I should have knocked him down," she grumbled. She started to turn, to go up the street and back to the hotel, but something caught her eye. Behind her, a figure slipped out of the Purple Fox, slipped across the street. White sleeves, green garters, handlebar mustache. The bartender.

He hurried down the walk, Maggie following at a safe distance, and ducked inside the Kid Concho Hotel. She caught him up and peered through the glass just in time to see him breaking off a conversation—who with, she couldn't see, for just as she got situated, he turned and came toward the door.

Maggie came up out of the alley she'd ducked into just in time to see a rather large figure going up the hotel's interior stairs. A skirted figure.

There was no desk clerk on duty, and so she slipped through the front door, hand up to catch the bell and keep it from jangling, and crept up the stairs. But when she reached the top, the hall was deserted and all the doors were closed.

"Suds," she said under her breath, and trudged down the stairs again.

Eddie was on the desk when she reached the Famous West

Hotel. "How'd it go, Miz Maguire?" he whispered, conspiratorially.

"Fair to middling, Eddie," she said, her hand on the stair rail, her foot on the landing. "Did Grady—Mr. Maguire—get another room?"

Eddie opened his mouth to protest, but she quickly added, "For himself. Harriet and I are staying put."

Eddie looked relieved. "No, ma'am, he didn't. Is he your husband?"

People always made the same mistake. Well, she supposed she and Grady didn't look much alike. She had dark hair, his was sandy. He wore glasses, she didn't. She had brown eyes, his were lady-killer blue. She had her mother's face, heart-shaped, and Grady's was square-jawed, with a cleft in the chin. And naturally, he had the mustache in the family. No, they didn't look much alike at all—which came in handy every once in a while.

She said, "He's my cousin. Same last name, though, which I imagine he was in too much of a hurry to give you?"

Eddie shrugged and said, "Daddy was on the desk."

"Oh. Do you have anything close? Say, next door or across the hall?"

Eddie didn't have to look. "Fifteen?"

Fifteen was opposite her room, catercornered. Good. She said, "That'll be just dandy. Key?"

He tossed it to her, saying, "He'll have to come down and sign the—"

They both looked up as a crash, followed by a shriek, sounded from upstairs. Maggie took the steps two at a time. She ran down the hall, Eddie hard on her heels. It was coming from her room, all right: the sound of splintering furniture.

Grady cried, "Stop! Stop it!" as Maggie burst into the room only to find the rocking chair smashed, Grady greatly mussed and pinned to the bed, and Harriet on top of him, kissing him.

Grady wiggled his mouth free and yelled, "Stop it, I say!" in horror.

Maggie contained herself long enough to say, "Grady, really! Are you taking advantage of our little flower?"

"Me?" Grady managed to croak, his voice breaking, before

Harriet overwhelmed him again and planted another enthusiastic kiss on his mouth.

Still trying not to laugh, Maggie gestured toward the young desk clerk, who was standing in the doorway, blushing bright red. "Could you help Mr. Maguire, Eddie? He seems to have got himself"—a bubble of laughter escaped her—"entangled," she finished.

"Hattie like Grady," Harriet protested as Eddie pulled her off. "Hattie *love* Grady. Hattie give Grady ride for free."

"God," said Grady under his breath. His spectacles were askew, dangling from one ear, and his hair was sticking up at an interesting angle. "God."

"Good day, Mr. Applegate," Harriet parroted. "It is a pleasure to meet you. What fine weather we are have."

"Having," said Grady, combing fingers through his hair and straightening his tie.

"Having," repeated Harriet, and pulled against Eddie's restraining arms. "You take ride now, Grady-sweetie?"

"No," said Grady, fixing his spectacles with a slight shudder. "God, no."

"How 'bout you, cowboy?" she said, looking straight at Maggie, and it took her a moment to remember she was still in disguise.

She pulled off the hat and tossed it to the top of the dresser, then said, "I don't think so, Harriet. Why don't you get some sleep?"

"Mag-wire!" Harriet cried gleefully, having recognized her at last. "Pretty funny!"

As Eddie dragged Harriet back toward her own bed, Grady, now reasonably well put back together, whispered, "Are you sure there isn't some brain damage, too?"

"Don't be grumbly, Grady. She's been stupid for a long time. It's been to her *advantage* to be stupid since she was six years old. It'll take her a little while to figure out it's to her advantage to be smart. Well, not quite so stupid, anyhow." She watched as Eddie tried to get Harriet down on the bed. Harriet kept trying to pull him in with her. "Then again . . ."

Grady got up and went to help Eddie.

Maggie kicked the pieces of the rocking chair under the bed, and sat down on the spare mattress in a heap. As much trouble as Harriet was proving to be, and as much as she didn't want to take her to San Francisco yet, she had an itchy feeling, a bad feeling, that had been growing ever since she'd watched that slicker ride out of town.

They'd best leave Bent Elbow tomorrow, she decided suddenly. They could just lock Harriet up in the office until she was presentable, and leave Corinne's fate to the sheriff. A sobering thought, but sometimes you just had to cut and run. They'd have to pray that Quincy Applegate and Just-Call-Me-Ralphie wouldn't find out they were in town again until Harriet was ready for the unveiling. Quincy, because he could disinherit her. Ralphie because he could do the same—just much more permanently.

Harriet was still protesting loudly. Maggie got to her feet and opened her suitcase, rummaging through weapons and miscellanea until she found a small, slightly dented white box, from which she pulled a paper packet. Filling a glass with water and then emptying the packet into it, she gave it a stir, then moved between the men.

"Harriet?" she said, then "Harriet!"

Harriet looked away from Grady, who was on the other side of the bed, hands on her shoulders. "What, Mag-wire?"

"Drink this, Harriet. It'll help you sleep."

Harriet frowned. "Hattie no want sleep." She turned her face toward Maggie's cousin again, suddenly beaming. "Hattie want Grady. Grady cute!"

"Well, Harriet can't have Grady," she said firmly, much to Grady's apparent relief, and elbowing Eddie out of the way, took Harriet's jaw firmly in hand. "Now, drink!"

THIRTEEN

"**I** SWEAR TO GOD, MAGGIE, SHE BUSHWHACKED ME!"
Grady whispered later, after Hattie was asleep. Thank
God. It was a terrible thing for a man to have to fight off
a woman's advances, he thought. Absolutely nothing prepared
a fellow for it.

He was back in Maggie's room again after moving his
things across the hall, to his new room. It made this one look
like a palace.

Maggie had unleashed her bosom from its binding and
changed clothes to look like a girl again, and was leaning back
in her replacement rocker, which Eddie had just hauled up the
stairs, grumbling actively. The juggling balls rested in her lap.

She fingered one absently and said, "I'm sorry I dragged
you all the way out here, Grady. I think we ought to leave."

"What? And vacate this garden spot?" Grady said, feigning
umbrage. "I haven't even taken the scenic tour yet. If there
is one."

"Be serious."

"I am! Bent Elbow presents all sorts of possibilities! Why,
just the name itself conjures up myriad—"

"Grady."

Sighing, he leaned back against the headboard, stretching
his arms along its top. It wiggled and creaked and threatened
to give, so he sat forward again. "Yes, O Goddess of the
Dancing Balls. By the way, thank you for not throwing
knives."

She smiled. "I figured Eddie already had enough damage

to explain to his father. While you were getting moved, I had him let me into our old room. I heard shots on the street while I was down at the Purple Fox and—''

''I heard them, too,'' Grady cut in. ''Some of them sounded too close for comfort.''

Maggie nodded. ''I found two more holes in the wall. Didn't bother digging out the slugs. Somebody's got it in for us, though I'm a bit puzzled. It's as if they—or he, or whoever—are trying to scare me—or Harriet—more than anything else. They're sure not aiming to kill. Even to hit anything that's moving.''

Grady pointed to her ear, which was healing nicely, but nicked. ''And that?''

''I think it was a mistake, that's all,'' she said. She fingered it, then winced.

''Another half inch, and it would have been a rather large mistake.'' He placed his hand over his heart and raised his eyes heavenward. ''Here lies Maggie. The shooter didn't mean it. World without end, amen.''

Maggie ignored him, to his slight aggravation. She said, ''So someone's shooting at us, and Corinne turns up missing.''

Grady shrugged his shoulders. ''That's nothing unusual. Probably ran off with some cattle boxer.''

''Cowpuncher,'' she said absently.

''Whatever.'' He studied Harriet, who was sleeping fitfully. ''She probably glued herself to him, and he *had* to take her along.''

But Maggie was still ignoring him. ''And tonight, there was a suspicious character at the saloon.''

''All characters at saloons are suspicious.''

''This one didn't know how to ride a horse.''

Grady cocked a brow. ''Seems perfectly normal to me. Besides, you say that about anybody who can't do a handstand in the saddle at a full gallop while they're throwing a loop or tossing a rope or whatever you call it.''

''Hush,'' she said, looking slightly annoyed. ''All his clothes—boots and hat, too—were new, just off the shelf. I'm surprised they didn't still have the price tags on them.''

"A tidy man," said Grady approvingly. "Keeps the local haberdashers in business. Good for him."

"Oh, never mind," she grumped. "He had to be one of the slickers that made off with little Corinne Gish. How many men could there be in the same town with all new clothes and new boots? I mean a town like this. And I had a very bad feeling about him. I should have grabbed him while I had the chance."

Grady nodded gravely. "New boots. Let's hang him."

"Oh, hush. He rode into town, talked to the bartender, talked to someone in the office—I think it was Festing—"

"Festing?"

"Tom Festing. He owns the saloon, and he's Harriet's boss. And he's making a bid for the sheriff's job, come the next election."

Grady pursed his lips. "Can't blame the fellow. He's going to have to find another line of business if his girls keep wandering off."

"True," Maggie said. "Anyway, this slicker rode into town, talked for five minutes to the bartender and *maybe* Tom Festing, then rode straight out again. Didn't even stay long enough to finish his drink."

"And how do you know he hadn't been in town all day?"

"Because his horse was still sweated up, that's how. And the bartender took off a few minutes after he left. He went up the street to the Kid Concho Hotel and talked to a woman. A large woman."

"Good Lord," said Grady, pretending shock. "Another hanging offense! Is there no end? Which reminds me. I counted no fewer than four hotels, just looking up and down the street. Any particular reason you chose this flea-infested flophouse?"

Maggie paid him no mind. "You know, there's another thing bothering me. How come this whole town is named after a dead outlaw?"

Grady smiled. "Bent Elbow Smith, Bent Elbow Jones, or Bent Elbow Johnson?"

"Oh, you know what I mean. It's Kid Concho this and Kid

Concho that. The café, the livery, the dry goods store, another hotel . . ."

"Better than this one, I trust."

She tossed the first ball in the air, and the others followed. Grady knew he wouldn't get much else out of her.

He stood up. "You going to get the stage tickets, or you want me to?"

"No." She was concentrating on the balls. "I'll do it, first thing in the morning. I want to check in with the sheriff, worthless as that will undoubtedly prove. And you need your beauty sleep."

He made a face at her, but she didn't notice.

"By the way," she went on, "nice job on Princess Tosses Her Lunch. So far, anyway. Think I'll get her a dress while I'm out, now that she's done upchucking on her clothes."

She stopped juggling, catching all three balls in the fingers of one hand. He had yet to figure out how she did that.

She said, "I wish we could stay to help Corinne. But our first priority is to keep Harriet safe. Isn't that right?" Then, without waiting for an answer, she said, "By the way, what room are you in?"

"Fifteen," he replied, as if to an idiot. She'd seen him coming and going from it, and the number was right on the door.

"No, silly. I mean, is it named after anyone?"

He shrugged. "How should I know? Why? Does this one have a name?" He took in the shabby furnishings and the peeling wallpaper once again, then wished that he hadn't.

"It's the Doc Holliday suite," she said, tossing the balls into action once more. "Eddie says Kate Elder used to come, but she hasn't graced them with her presence for three years or so. And no, I don't know the last time Doc was here."

Grady took a last look at the mouse-chewed furnishings and let himself out, muttering, "And people wonder why Doc drinks."

WEDNESDAY, JUNE 6

>━┤━◆〉━○━〈◆━├━<

MAGGIE WAS UP AND DRESSED BY SEVEN, AND BY seven-thirty had purchased her tickets from the yawning Wells Fargo agent. She strolled down to Henderson's Mercantile, found it wasn't open for business yet, and walked up to the sheriff's office. The sign on the door said he wouldn't be in until nine, so she wandered back down the street, checking out the business signs as she went.

Randall Pharmacy, and above it, Alma's Place, whatever that was. The Kid Concho Mining Company. Bent Elbow Notions. Kid Concho Fine Dry Goods and Kid Concho Leather. All too much Kid Concho in the town.

The morning was overcast and dark, and getting darker instead of lighter. Gray clouds formed a solid mantle, the color of a dirty nickel, from horizon to horizon. Rain was coming, she could smell it. She hoped it would wait until nine-thirty, when the stage would come to carry them north to Sky Butte, and perhaps out of its path. To rattle and bang and bump them north, she thought unhappily. Her poor backside.

She was waiting when the proprietor of Henderson's Mercantile showed up.

"Looks like we got us a fierce'un comin'," he said, nodding toward the sky as he opened the door. The bell tinkled, and she stepped past him, inside. "Darker'n the inside of a black hog out there, yes, ma'am!"

"And that is decidedly dark," Maggie replied, while he brought out a lantern and lit it. "Where are your ready-made dresses?"

A half hour later she had picked two dresses, a pale pink and a soft blue, which she thought would suit Harriet's coloring, along with shoes, underclothes, a bonnet, and appropriate hair ribbons. She hoped to be able to braid Harriet's shaggy mop into submission. The girl was really much too old for ribbons, but they'd hide a multitude of sins.

Her stomach growled, and she hurried her step. Somebody from the Kid Concho Café would be over with their breakfast anytime now, and she had to wake Grady and Hattie so they could not only eat, but also be ready when the stage pulled in.

No time to see the sheriff now. She'd have to stop by on her way to the stage office. She wanted to tell him what she'd found out about Corinne, and her suspicions about the kidnapping, and to tell the sheriff which way the slicker had ridden out of town. And to tell him about the new bartender. Well, that was probably nothing, him running across to the hotel like that, but it never hurt to report everything. Everything you couldn't check out yourself, that was.

Not that it would do much good reporting any of it to old Seersucker-Sodbuster-Sapsucker, but her conscience was bothering her a great deal more than it should.

The front door of the hotel was standing open, and she stepped into the dark lobby. Too dark. Eddie's father had kept the night lantern burning, but now the lobby was deep in shadow.

"Hello?" she called.

No answer. She made her way to the desk, felt for the lamp, then felt through her purse until she came to the match tin. "Always carry sulfurtips, Magdalena, my dear," her father had said. "You never know when you'll want to light a stogie or torch a building."

She got one out and struck it, and lit the lamp. Oddly, the glass was still warm. The lobby eased into view. And so did the figure of Eddie's father, crumpled on the floor at the bottom of the stairs.

Maggie bent to him immediately. Blood trickled from a cut on his forehead, but he was breathing. She patted his cheek. "Mr.—"

Drat. She didn't know his last name, let alone his first.

She'd never thought to ask Eddie. "Wake up," she said gently, then shook him.

Whatever had possessed him to blow out the lamp, then try to navigate the stairs? He moaned a little.

"Hello? Sir? Can you sit up? Is anything broken?"

"Somebody . . ." he mumbled, shaking his head slowly from side to side, eyes closed. "Somebody . . ."

"Somebody what?" asked Maggie impatiently. *Somebody call a doctor? Somebody hit me? Somebody get this crazy room-swapping woman away from me?* "Can you hear me? Are you hurt? Beyond the obvious, I mean," she added.

"Somebody . . . get the sheriff," he said finally, then brought a hand up to his head.

Outside, lightning brightened the sky twice in rapid succession, followed almost immediately by a crash of thunder so loud that it rattled the windows. As the rain began to pelt down, a young girl bearing a covered tray burst through the doorway.

"Jesus, Mary, and Joseph!" she exclaimed, paying more attention to the storm she'd just escaped and the tray, which she slid onto the desk, than the scene in the lobby. "It's blowin' like the devil, Sam! You mind if I—"

Just then she saw Maggie, crouched beside Eddie's father. "Jesus, Mary, and—"

"Joseph," cut in Maggie impatiently. "Run and get the sheriff, then get the doctor."

"Sam?" the girl asked, staring dumbly.

"The sheriff and the doctor!" Maggie said again.

This time the girl turned to leave, but froze at the door. The rain was sheeting now, blowing sideways, pounding into the buildings, drumming on them. Lightning lit the lobby brighter than a thousand candles for the count of five, and thunder vibrated the floor. Maggie said, *"Now!"*

The girl ran, rain drenching her before she took two steps, the wind whipping her skirts.

Maggie eased Eddie's father—Sam, the girl had called him—to the floor. She wanted to ask him whether the man who'd hit him had been coming or going, but he'd passed out again.

Quickly, she grabbed her bag and searched through it again, this time locating her derringer. Only two shots, and an unpredictable sort of weapon unless you were up close, but she planned to be. As the storm howled between the buildings and hammered at the roofs, she started slowly up the steps, her mouth set, her eyes becoming accustomed to the darkness.

She paused at the top of the staircase. The hall stretched before her, black as the hard, dark center of night. The only window was at the far end. She waited, her breath coming in short, shallow bursts. Then the lightning flared, for one moment showing the passageway as stark and bright as a photographer's flash. Showing Grady's door, standing open, and hers, in the same condition. And a body, twisted and sprawled on the runner rug in the space between.

Grady?

She felt her way along, in darkness again, until her toe touched the body. She knelt, and immediately took a deep breath of relief. She hadn't realized she was holding it. He was breathing, too, but his pulse was weak. She started to roll him over in the darkness, muttering, "You've gained weight!" underneath the storm's roar, and almost had him turned when she felt the knife in his side.

Oh, God. Oh, Grady!

She eased him back onto his face. Jaw locked, back stiff, she rose slowly.

His door was wide open, and since it faced the street, was completely illuminated by the next flash. Empty.

She stepped over Grady, taking care that her skirts didn't catch on the knife grip, and flattened herself against the wall next to her door.

She waited for the next flash, and when it came, she leaped into the doorway, gun held before her.

Empty. No Harriet, no nothing.

"Blast!" she said, and her own voice sounded tremulous and small against the darkness, against the storm.

She felt her way across the room, which was lighted none too well even on bright days, and groped on the dresser top for matches. She found them, her fingers scattering the pile.

She lit the lamp, picking it up and turning to go to Grady, back out in the hall.

Except that when she turned, Grady was lying on the floor between the beds, in a small but slowly spreading pool of blood.

Who the devil had she found in the hall?

FOURTEEN

>─┼─◆─◯─◆─┼─<

"M R. MAGUIRE," SAID THE DOCTOR, SNAPPING HIS bag shut with a blessed finality. "I must say, I can't remember ever having had a worse patient."

"Thank you, I'm sure," said Grady, holding a compress to the new stitches at the back of his head. "My best to the wife."

Halfway to the door, the doctor turned. "I'm not married."

"Shame," said Grady, his voice dripping sarcasm. "You have such a gracious bedside manner."

The doctor slammed the door behind him.

Grady sat up, swinging his legs over the side of the bed, and grimacing when the change in pressure set his skull to throbbing. "So, who was he?"

"Who was who?" Maggie replied. "Why are you always so filthy to members of the medical profession?" She was looking out the window. The rain had stopped, and past her shoulder Grady saw single drops fall in an uneven rhythm as water slowly dripped off the roof, off the sill. The dark overcast of clouds had moved out, taking the storm to the east. It was light again.

"I can't help myself," he said. His head was starting to pound, now. "My mother was frightened by one while she was carrying me. And, of course, that charlatan bleeding her to death didn't help. Is there, by chance, any whiskey in the house?"

"They used to bleed everybody," Maggie said absently.

Maggie disagreed with his low opinion of the medical pro-

fession, but it didn't look like he was going to get a rise out
of her this time. She still hadn't turned around.

"And no," she added, "there isn't any whiskey."

"Wonderful," he said. "Who was the man in the hall?"
He took away the compress and to his horror felt the zigzag
of stitches. Weren't they supposed to be straight? The doctor
was a philistine!

"Biscuit Pete," Maggie replied.

"No, really," Grady said, still feeling his scalp. Sheer
butchery. "Who was he?"

Maggie turned at last. "Biscuit Pete. Really. He's down the
hall, temporarily. The doctor said he lost a lot of blood, but
he's going to be all right. Apparently the knife didn't do any
serious damage. That leather vest of his took most of the
knife's force, and the blade just skittered along his ribs. What
I'd like to know is what in the world he was doing here."

Grady put the compress back in place. *Scarred,* he thought
dismally. *Scarred for life.* Maggie, of course, didn't care. Maggie only cared about the case. He lay back down—that was
better—and said, "What I'd like to know is who the devil *is*
Biscuit Pete, and what was he doing being stabbed outside my
room? Didn't even ask my permission."

"Stop being cranky," she said, sitting on the opposite bed.
"Here, let me see."

He turned to the side and took the compress away. She
leaned over him for a second, her fingers gently combing his
hair aside, then sat back again. "You big baby!" she said.
"It's barely an inch long! You should be happy they used
brass knuckles—and not very well, I might add—instead of a
chair."

He arched a brow, but it hurt and he winced, ruining the
effect. "Brass knuckles? Good grief. And what makes you so
sure they didn't use a chair? It feels like they used a piano."

Maggie sighed. "Because of the bruises on either side."

"Bruises?" he said weakly, and felt the back of his head
again. There was probably concussive brain damage. A blood
clot!

Maggie clucked her tongue heartlessly. "Honestly, Grady.
Don't start with the I'm-going-to-die-any-second stuff."

"Well, in case I do—not that you'd care—make sure Otto gets my woodworking tools. And my set of Austrian wire nippers."

She patted his hand. "Yes, dear."

"You were saying? About the Biscuit person?"

She scooted back on the bed a little. "Biscuit Pete, Grady. Biscuit Pete. He carried Harriet over from the saloon for me."

He opened his mouth to ask a question, but she was already answering. "When I got here, she wasn't exactly able to navigate. Anyway, he carried her. Said all of maybe six words."

He snorted. What a ridiculous name for a grown man! "And unlikely to say anything else for some time, I take it."

Maggie nodded. "So what happened to you? What were you doing in my room, anyway, and in just your shirtsleeves?" Suddenly she grinned. "Harriet's allure finally get to you?"

He said, "Very funny. I was already up, if you must know. I'd just finished shaving when I heard noises from across the hall. In here. I came over, the door was unlocked, I walked in, and bang. No candles, no music, just *boom*."

He felt the back of his head again. "Are you sure this is stitched right? Are those little bumpy things supposed to be there?"

Maggie pulled his hand down. "It's just swelling against the stitches a little, that's all. Now, stop it. You'll only make it worse. Honestly, a grown man."

"Yes, Mother," he said dryly. "I'll be good."

"Anyway, Sam didn't see anything, either."

"Sam?"

"Eddie's father. Mr. Cross."

"You've been busy. A regular ferret." He raised his hand to his head again, but Maggie gave him a dirty look and he dropped it to the sheet. "What's the sheriff say?" Change the subject, that was the ticket.

Maggie got up and went to the window again. He didn't see why she bothered to stare out of it. All there was to look at was the weathered, unpainted, windowless side of the building next door.

"Hardly a thing," she said, her back to him, her arms

folded. "He'd barely got here when some kid came running in, whispered in his ear, and then he took off with the kid in a great big hurry. Somebody probably lost a cow or has a cat up a tree."

"Or has a cow up a tree."

Maggie turned long enough to glare at him.

"Well, it's more interesting," he said in self-defense. Then, "I'm guessing you don't have the highest opinion of the sheriff?"

She gave a small, frustrated kick to the wall. "He won't do us any good, anyway. All this mud. How am I supposed to track Harriet in all this damn mud?"

FIFTEEN

>━┥◆┝━━◉━━┥◆┝━<

MAGGIE HAD CHEWED TWO PENCILS TO THE NUB AND given up on juggling. She removed her throwing knives from their case. There were six lovely steel knives in the kit, all with sleek ivory handles and slim, sharp blades, all perfectly balanced. She hadn't brought the entire collection. She had, in fact, eighteen—well, eighteen that were her favorites now, and in current use. All lovingly purchased through the years in sets of six—odd that they should sell precision throwing blades in sets, like flatware, but there you were. She traveled with only the one set, however, and she currently had it open, throwing her knives at a particular rose in the wallpaper full of roses that graced the Doc Holliday suite.

It was five in the afternoon. Grady was across the hall, asleep. Sam Cross, Eddie's father, was downstairs in the same condition. Biscuit Pete had awakened, but when she went to question him, had turned his face to the wall with a terrified expression and wouldn't say a word. The doctor had asked her to leave.

"I thought cowboys were supposed to be tough," she muttered under her breath, and for the tenth or fifteenth time that afternoon, threw the last knife at the wall. As before, it burrowed in neatly with a low thrumming sound, exactly where she'd wanted it.

She'd had to change targets several times. The wallpaper was getting tattered.

She crossed the room, pulled the knives free, and walked

back to consider her new target. Yes. The rose just over the center of Harriet's headboard. The bed that had been Harriet's, and might be again if they could find her.

Maggie threw the first knife.

If she's still alive.

Maggie threw the second knife.

Where can she be?

The third knife, half a circle around the rose.

Just-Call-Me-Ralphie's out there somewhere, I just know it!

The fourth knife.

But Ralphie's a city boy if ever I saw one.

The fifth.

How does Tom Festing figure in?

Just at the moment the sixth knife flew from her hand, someone rapped at the door.

"Who is it?" she called as the knife found home. A perfect circle.

"Ma'am? It's Sheriff Sopsucher, ma'am."

Well, at least he'd left off the "little lady." For now. She let him in. "Good afternoon, Sheriff," she said caustically. "Nice of you to drop by."

If he noticed her tone, he gave no sign. He said, "I just talked to your cousin. And tried to talk to Soda."

"Soda?"

He tipped his head down the hall. "Pete Soda. Biscuit Pete? He ain't sayin' much, though. Mind if I come in?"

He stared at the knives in the wall for a second as if he were about to comment, then seemed to think better of it. He said, "I been out to the Lansing spread. That was Toby Lansing, Joe's youngest, that come for me. I thought you ought to know."

Maggie tipped her head to one side. "Know what, Sheriff?"

"I thought it might have somethin' to do with Hattie," he continued. "See, Toby found Tom Festing's other girl out there. Corinne Gish. Found her washed up beside the creek, dead as a stump. The thing is, her wrists was all swolled and chafed. I reckon she'd been tied up for a spell."

● ● ●

y lamplight, Maggie and Grady huddled over a table in
Grady's room, while Sheriff Sopsucher (who acted as though
e would rather have been anywhere else but with them) halt-
ngly drew the map.

"No, I reckon it takes a jog to the east there," he muttered
nder his breath as he kneaded the big eraser on the page
gain.

"Sheriff, it doesn't have to be *exact*," Maggie said. The
aper was already more holes than map. "All we need to
now is if there are any cabins along it. Miners' shacks or line
amps or—"

Sopsucher, brushing eraser leavings from the page, shot her
sidelong glance. "Wouldn't hardly be no line camps along
e creek this far down, Miz Maguire."

Grady merrily chipped in, "Well, of course there wouldn't.
Really, Maggie. Line camps."

Maggie gave him a dirty look over the top of the sheriff's
ead, which was bent to his task. Grady wouldn't know a line
amp from a bag of nickels, but she didn't say so. Instead,
he said to the sheriff, "Any sort of building? Any sort of
helter?"

"Yes, any sort," Grady said, and wiggled his eyebrows.
He'd found some whiskey, and apparently had administered
ome anesthetic. He was far from plastered, though. Just loose
nough to be cocky.

The sheriff placed X's here and there. He sat back. "Well,
reckon that's about the best I can do. This first one, here,"
e said, pointing to a gray, wavery X beside an eraser hole,
'is where Toby pulled the body out. Don't reckon she was
oating long at all, seein' as the body was still on the warmish
ide when he pulled her out. But that creek gets to movin'
wful damn fast when there's rain. Coulda traveled six, eight
niles."

He moved the pencil up the line of the creek. "Now,
his'uns a branch of Steadman's outfit. Used to be a trappers'
hack, now Steadman's got boys out there, watching his cattle
nd watching the creek."

Maggie lifted a brow, and Sopsucher added, "Water rights
re real important around here."

Grady piped up, "Water rights, Maggie. Of course." Sh
was about an inch away from smacking him. He pointed
the next mark rather grandly. "What's this one?"

"That's Chance Hoag's cabin. He's whatchacall, a re
loner. Ain't seen him but three times myself, and I been sheri
here for ten years. Nigh on blasted my head off the last time.

"A hermit." Grady pointed again. "And this one?"

"That's McCullough's place, but I don't think the bod
coulda come from there. Too far."

Maggie crossed her arms. "Maybe we're going at this th
wrong way."

"What other way *can* we go at it, Mags?" Grady aske
"They killed her and threw her in the creek," he said, wi
the solid gold voice of authority. "She was in the water for
term of perhaps no longer than fifteen minutes—if, as the la
who found her says, the body was still warm—and washed u
on a bank about here." He pointed, theatrically, to the ma
then crossed his arms and struck a pose.

The sheriff, his head bent, missed seeing Maggie take a
open-handed swipe at Grady's sleeve. He said, "Maybe n
even a quarter of an hour. More like ten minutes. That water
on the cold side. Could leech the warm right out of a body."

"Wait a minute," said Maggie, banging the side of her hea
with the heel of her hand. "How was she killed, anyway
Shot, stabbed, clubbed over the head? Poisoned, darted, stra
gled?"

Grady said, "You're reaching . . ."

Sopsucher shrugged. "Didn't see no marks on her, but sh
was pretty much a mess. Probably bashed over the skul
Clem'll tell me in the mornin', once he's gone over the body.

Maggie said, "Clem?"

"Clem Hastings. The undertaker."

"Where's your morgue?"

"My what?"

"Where's your mortician's office?"

Still wearing a napkin tucked into his collar, Clem Hasting
the undertaker, wielded the key and opened the front door
what Maggie was relieved to see was Hastings Fine Furnitu

and Funerals, not another Kid Concho namesake. Mr. Hastings was in a nasty mood, a fact that he took no pains whatsoever to hide from Maggie and the others.

"Sure sorry to take you away from your dinner, Clem," the sheriff said for the third time.

Hastings, a small, thin man with bug eyes and a narrow mustache, grunted. "Roast. The one night of the month when Nellie has roast that ain't burnt to a crisp, and you got to come knockin'. Ain't you got no sense of culinary decency, Sopsucher?"

As he lit a lamp and led them past finished furniture and the storefront, then into the back room past worked planks and half-turned table legs, then through a black-curtained doorway and into the viewing room, Maggie tried to soothe him. "I'm sorry, Mr. Hastings. Sheriff Sopsucher had you open the shop at our request."

"Peas," said Hastings bitterly, leading them between saw-horses waiting to display another occupied coffin. He lifted another curtain and ushered them into yet another room. This one was tiny, with rough, unfinished walls. A pine coffin, on end, leaned against one of them. Its lid was leaning beside it. "She had them new peas with it, and them little round potatoes with the skins on. And meat that wasn't brown right through to the center. Had pink to it. Yessir, a distinct cast of pink. Well? There she is."

He pointed to the sheet-covered corpse on the table.

Sopsucher said, "You can go on back to your supper, Clem. I'll lock up."

"I should say so," said the mortician as he took his leave. "I should certainly say so." He grumbled his way out of the room and to the front door, and kept grumbling until the clanging door closed between them.

"Guess she musta made him a real good roast," the sheriff said as the bell atop the front door jangled on Hastings's exit.

"So it would seem," said Grady, and Maggie could tell he was doing his best not to laugh, and only halfway succeeding.

She had more important things to do than get after Grady, though. Unpinning her hat, she said, "If you gentlemen wouldn't mind?"

Sopsucher looked at her curiously, and she made a *sho* motion with her hands. "Go on with you. Wait in the viewin room." When the sheriff started to protest, she said, "Co inne's been naked in front of a lot of men, I don't doubt tha But she's dead now and can't count any change. Don't yo think it was time she was treated with a little decorum?"

Sopsucher took off his hat belatedly and followed an alread hatless Grady through the curtain. Maggie watched as they l another lamp, its light turning the black curtain gray, showin their shadows.

She lifted the sheet from the dead girl's face. She was s pale in death. Blond, like Harriet. Light eyes, like Harriet' stared up at the ceiling, unblinking. Small, too. Like Harrie She couldn't have been more than five feet tall, and she wa all bones. Tom Festing was a harsh taskmaster.

Scratches on the face and throat, all minor. She carefull felt through the girl's hair, matted with mud, then felt throug it again, then rolled the body over and searched through i parting Corinne's hair and revealing the scalp a quarter inc at a time.

Now, that was interesting.

Grady checked his watch again—nine thirty-six, this time– and went back to staring at his shoes. His muddy shoes. Th streets outside were like quicksand, and although they'd bee able to stay on the sidewalks most of the way, they'd had t cross the openings of two alleys. He stared unhappily at h custom-made Newport ties, their jaunty tassels caked wit drying grime, their genuine French calfskin—hand-picke hand-measured, hand-cut, and hand-stitched by Mr. Garibal at Garibaldi & Sons—obscured by muck. All the scraping an buffing and soaping in the world wouldn't restore his shine.

The sheriff wasn't exactly glib. He sat there, not mindin his own muddy boots in the slightest, and he'd said exactl three words since they'd retired to the viewing room: "yup and "we'll see."

The "yup" had been in answer to Grady's saying he'd bet ter light a lamp, and the "we'll see" had been in reply t Grady's particularly eloquent paragraph—at least, he consi

ered it eloquent—regarding the possibility of another cloud-
burst. Currently, the sheriff was seated in a wooden chair
opposite him, legs stretched out straight in front of him, ankles
crossed, hat pulled down over his eyes.

Maggie was no help. She hadn't said another word. Every
once in a while he heard a rustle of fabric from the other room,
or a little grunt, or a footstep, but that was all. A person would
think she'd call out her findings. She had to be finding *something* after more than a half hour in there, didn't she? A person
would think that she'd want to be reminded there were living
people out here.

Ghoulish business, this.

He shivered, then checked his pocket watch again. Nine
thirty-eight. He closed the watch case with an echoing *snap*
this time but didn't get a rise out of the sheriff.

He was about to do something drastic—burst into a little
Gilbert and Sullivan, say, or belch loudly—when Maggie
pulled the curtain aside and stepped into the room, the lamp
held before her. The sheriff clambered to his feet immediately,
hat in hand, and Grady followed.

Maggie's face held no expression. She said, "I think we're
going to have to widen our search."

"Now, ma'am . . ." Sopsucher started.

Maggie held up a hand. "Coffee first. Is the Kid Concho
Café still open at this hour?" Grady, who knew better than to
argue, headed for the door.

SIXTEEN

>━┼━◆>━◯━<◆━┼━<

T HE KID CONCHO CAFÉ WAS A SMALL, OVERLY BLUE-
checkered establishment, where the table at which they
were seated was uneven and tottered toward him when
he rested his elbow on it. Grady turned his half-full coffee cup
in the saucer one-handed, casually observing the restaurant's
other customers—all four of them—while Maggie explained.
There hadn't been a mark on the body, she said.

"Did you check her scalp? Sometimes them head wounds
can be hard to find, especially when a gal has long hair,"
Sopsucher said condescendingly, and Grady was surprised that
Maggie didn't pour her coffee in his lap, or at least set his
nose on fire.

"I checked," she said, patiently.

It must be something in the coffee they served here, Grady
thought. Some sort of tranquilizer. He must remember to ask
them about it and stock up on whatever it was.

"I checked several times, as a matter of fact," she continued. "No bruising, no broken skin, no indentations of the
skull. Nothing. Tell me, Sheriff: When you found her, was she
wearing one shoe?"

Sopsucher lifted a brow. "How'd you know that?"

"Her feet. She'd run a great distance wearing only one
shoe. Her right foot was unmarked, but her left had quite a
few punctures and cuts. And scratches."

Grady sat back and lifted his coffee cup, smiling. There was
nothing in the coffee that had changed her, just the scent of
the prey, and the electricity of the chase getting under way.

Now she had something she could sink her fangs into, that was all.

Sopsucher, unfamiliar with the glint in Maggie's eye, said, "Well, I don't know how you figure she run a 'great distance.' Don't see how you can tell, one way or the other. Maybe she got them cuts on her foot earlier. Why, she coulda lost that shoe when they took her. Maybe she was in one'a them shacks and took off out the door when they weren't looking. It was awful dark. Maybe they held her under till she stopped kickin'. Or maybe she just stumbled into the creek and drowned."

It was a phenomenal speech for Sopsucher, and Grady was impressed with the length if not the content.

Maggie, though, seemed unimpressed. "You're partly right, Sheriff," she said magnanimously, as she signaled the waitress for more coffee. "I believe she did stumble into the stream by accident. But she'd been free a good amount of time. At least an hour."

Sopsucher gave a little sigh. "Now, little lady—I mean ma'am. How do you figure—"

"Her wrists. By the swelling there."

"Well, of course her wrists were swole up! She'd been hog-tied!"

"Yes," Maggie explained, and nodded her thanks to the waitress, who had just refilled her coffee. She waited for the girl to go away and then said, "That's my point, exactly. When you tie someone's hands, the flesh on either side of the rope swells, true?"

Grady watched as Sopsucher nodded. He was walking right into it.

"The flesh of Corinne's wrists—under the rope burns, too— was entirely swollen. If she'd been drowned while she was still tied—if they'd just held her under, as you suggested—I wouldn't have seen that. The heart stops pumping, the blood stops flowing. No blood flow, no swelling, to be simple about it. No, she was freed sometime earlier. Probably worked her way free. Too much abrasion for it to be otherwise. She was held for a time at—let's call it Camp X, shall we?"

Sopsucher nodded, and Grady thought, *Camp X? Couldn't you have done better than that?*

"Anyway, she was held there for a while, until they found
they had the wrong girl. Perhaps they were confused, perhaps
they were angry. What were they to do with the first girl?
Maybe they all left her to go and get Harriet, maybe one of
them took pity on her and set her free, maybe . . . well, there
are a great many maybes. But one way or another, she got
loose. And then she ran. It was morning, but it was dark,
remember? The storm was moving in. She loses her shoe, but
she's too frightened—or it's too dark—to look for it. She
keeps moving. She's moving toward town, toward safety."

Maggie was on a roll, speaking in breathless, hushed tones.
Sopsucher had leaned forward, mesmerized. And Grady found,
much to his dismay, that he was getting caught up in it, too.

"But it's getting darker and darker," Maggie went on.
"The rain starts to pelt down. She comes to the creek—she
can hear it rushing over the noise of the storm. She can follow
it to town. Except that it's risen higher than she figured, and
as she's running along the bank, she slips in. Maybe the bank
caved in, maybe the mud sucked her down, I don't know. But
the important thing is that she went under, and she drowned,
and she floated downstream no longer than ten minutes.
Which, taking the rapid current and the storm and the condition of the body into consideration, could have moved her
anywhere from a couple-three to, say, eight miles at the outside. And then she washed up, and that boy—what's his
name?"

Sopsucher was gazing at her steadily. "Toby Lansing," he
said.

"And Toby found her." She drummed fingertips on the
blue-gingham tablecloth, signaling, Grady knew, the end—almost—of the lecture. "Since we missed dinner, I'm in the
mood for a steak," she said, holding up one hand to call the
waitress again. "Anybody else hungry?"

"Make mine rare," said Grady, "with a side of eggs." He
smiled. There was no one better than Maggie when she was
on a roll. And he could tell that she wasn't done yet.

As the waitress ambled over, pad in hand, Maggie said casually, "There's just one thing."

Sopsucher sat back, waiting for the waitress. "Like, for instance, why didn't they just kill her and get it over with?''

Grady cocked his head. Something akin to surprise passed briefly over Maggie's face. "Exactly," she said.

"Maggie, it's late," Grady whispered, holding his watch to his face and squinting.

"The light's on under his door." She rapped on it. "I'm going to get this cleared up once and for all."

Next to her in the dim hotel corridor, Grady frowned. In a stage whisper, he said, "You'll wake the whole place!"

She ignored him. She knocked again, louder this time, and said, "Biscuit Pete, I know you're in there. I'm not going away. I can stand here all night, knocking and talking."

"Maggie!" Grady said with a hiss.

She knocked again, this time banging her fist against the wood.

Down the hall, a door creaked open and a balding head popped out. Groggily the man said, "Lady, please!"

"I'm sorry, sir," she announced in a loud voice, "but until the gentleman in this room has the courtesy to answer his door, I intend to—"

Another door opened. Maggie didn't see anyone, but a scratchy male voice called, "Let her in, dang blast it, and let the rest of us get some sleep!"

Maggie pounded on the door again. Grady, hand to his face, was trying to sink back into the shadows. She leaned over and grabbed his suit coat and pulled him back.

She was about to knock again when she heard the key in the lock. The door creaked open, just an inch. A voice stuttered, "Y-yes'm?"

"We want to talk to you, Biscuit Pete."

"Um, I don't—"

Maggie gave the door a shove and walked in, pulling Grady in her wake. A scattering of applause broke out in the hall as she left it.

Rolling his eyes, Grady closed the door behind them. Maggie allowed herself a fleeting grin. Then, hands on her hips, she looked at Biscuit Pete. "Well," she said.

Biscuit Pete's shirt was hanging open, and beneath it, his

midsection was wrapped tightly in bandages. He twisted his hands. "W-what you want?" he said, glancing from Maggie to Grady to Maggie again like a nervous hoot owl. "You already kidnapped my sweet Hattie and let her get took by thugs. What more you gonna do?"

Dryly, Grady said, "Maggie, you didn't tell me he could talk."

Maggie kept her eyes on Biscuit Pete. "What do you mean *your* sweet Hattie?"

"Well . . . well, I . . ."

"Sit down, old boy," said Grady, chipper as ever. "Ease the load on your brain."

Pete backed up and sat on the edge of the bed, swallowing hard. His Adam's apple bobbled up and down.

Maggie said again, "What do you mean, Pete?"

"Well . . . I mean . . ." He rubbed at his temples. "Well, I love her, that's what," he suddenly burst out, defensively. "There. I said it right out. I love her and we're gonna get married, and that's all there is to it. Except you took her, you took my Hattie. And now somebody else got her, and I don' know why. How come all of a sudden ever'body wants to steal my little Hattie away?" He stopped, exhausted from the effort.

Grady handed him a glass of water, saying, "There, there my man. These things happen."

Biscuit Pete drained the glass gratefully, then handed it back. "Reckon," he said, then stared at Maggie reproachfully.

"I see," she said thoughtfully. She dragged a wooden chair—the only piece of furniture besides the bed and the bureau—up to Biscuit Pete's mattress and sat on it, her knees almost touching his. Grady slouched against the wall, chewing a toothpick he'd plucked from his pocket.

"Pete," Maggie began, in a tone she generally reserved for her stray cats and dogs, "I didn't kidnap Hattie. I was trying to help her. Her father was a wealthy man. He searched for her for years—well, he hired people to look for her—after the Indians killed his wife and took Harriet captive. He loved her very much."

Biscuit Pete was following her raptly. She supposed she

could go a little farther into Harriet's father, and tell him how Horace used to flagellate himself and walk barefoot through the snow in search of some cosmic atonement, but she didn't want to scare him.

She said, "About six years ago, he had a stroke."

Biscuit Pete's forehead wrinkled.

She said, "An apoplexy."

"Oh," he said, nodding gravely.

She heard Grady give a little snort but didn't look his way. She said, "That's when he stopped looking, because he was too sick. And he died never knowing that his Harriet was alive, and that she'd been released from captivity." His brow wrinkled again and she said, "Rescued. From the Indians. He left Harriet a lot of money, Pete. And the insurance company hired me to find her, so they could give the money to her. Except that in order to claim the money, she's got to be sober."

For starters, she thought.

"I didn't know that," Pete mumbled. "I'm right sorry."

Sorry that Horace died and now Harriet would get his money, or sorry that Harriet had to sober up? She said, "Pete?"

He cleared his throat, then ducked his head down till she was staring at its shaggy crown. "I'm right ashamed I took them shots at you. I weren't tryin' to hit you or nothin', I swear. I was just tryin' to . . . to . . ."

She held back the satisfied smirk she felt pushing at her face. It had been Pete, after all. She said, "Scare me into leaving town, so you and Harriet could go back to the way it used to be?"

"Yup."

She patted his hand. "I thought so. No damage done, Pete. Not much anyway," she added, remembering her ear with a little grimace. And then the pattern of bullets on—or rather, in—the wall. "You're a pretty fair marksman."

"I guess."

"You came up to take Harriet, didn't you?" she said softly. "And they surprised you in the hallway?"

Pete lifted his head, and he looked at her with something akin to amazement. "I seen him goin' across the hall." He pointed to Grady. "I followed him. 'Cept when I got there, these other fellers come out. There was two of 'em, and one had my Hattie over his shoulder like a sack'a potatoes."

For the first time, Maggie saw Biscuit Pete's face twist into something akin to anger. Good. She could use that.

"And then . . . ?" she prompted.

Pete shrugged. "And then I guess somebody pulled a knife. The last thing I remember seein' was new boots."

"New boots?" Grady piped up from the corner.

"Yes, sir," replied Biscuit Pete, twisting toward him and wincing with the effort. He put a hand to his bandages and said, "The feller whose feet I landed next to had 'em on. I remember, 'cause they was the very same pair I been lookin' at for near three months down to Kid Concho leather goods, 'cept they sold 'em four or five days back." He turned toward Maggie again. "I remember thinkin' it weren't fair that the son of a bitch—beggin' your pardon, ma'am—had my Hattie and my new boots, too. Are you folks gonna find her? And see that she don't come to no harm?"

Maggie sat back. "Yes, Pete. We're going to find her and clean her up and make sure she gets her inheritance."

"Can I help?"

"You most certainly can. And once we get Hattie back and Grady works on her a little—"

Biscuit Pete's face darkened, and Maggie said quickly, "Works *with* her. Elocution."

Brow furrow, Pete leaned forward, as if to rise.

"I'll teach her to speak properly, coach her in syntax," Grady said, but Pete kept coming, and he hurriedly raised his hands and added, "Me teach Hattie talk good."

Under her breath, Maggie muttered, "Grady, really."

Pete, oblivious to her, sat back on the mattress.

Pete seemed to mull all this information over for a few seconds. Then he looked up, hope in his eyes. "That talkin' right—that's so Hattie can get the cash?"

Maggie nodded.

"How much money's Hattie gonna get? Maybe . . ." He swallowed, the Adam's apple bobbling again. "Maybe a hundred dollars?"

"No," Maggie said gently. "More like three hundred and fifty thousand."

Pete gulped. "T-three hundred and f-fifty—"

"Thousand," said Maggie.

Biscuit Pete swooned backward. It was a good thing he'd been sitting on the bed.

Grady studied him for a moment. Finally he said, "I think he took it pretty well, don't you?"

SEVENTEEN

CHAUNCEY GARRETT, HAVING BEEN DELAYED BY THE rain and the subsequent mud, hopped down off the five-o'clock stage, which arrived approximately six hours late. He stretched his legs on the way up the street, stopping to relieve his bladder in an alley along the way, and entered the Purple Fox. Stepping up to the bar, he called for a whiskey.

The bartender was a different man than the last time he'd been here, he noted. More customers, too, though by the looks of it, Tom Festing didn't pull much of a profit from the well. No girls to be seen. That was likely the big moneymaker.

He smiled. Well, Festing was one chippy short now. He hoped. He'd debated with himself, on the way out from Denver, whether to kill Festing now or later. To do it tonight would save him an extra trip down into this little shithole of a town, and that had pulled a lot of weight. But then, he supposed he should bide his time until he'd had a chance to dig around in the girl's mind. Later on, if he came up empty—if that shit, Ralphie, had sent him on a wild goose chase—Festing might come in handy.

For what reason, he wasn't sure. But it paid to keep an open mind.

He crooked a finger at the bartender, who sauntered down to his end of the bar, bottle in hand.

Garrett put his hand over his glass and said, "Festing in?"

The bartender set the bottle down behind the bar. He picked up a rag. "Who's askin'?"

"Old friend," said Garrett quite pleasantly. "My name's Jones. Bill Jones. Like to see him."

The bartender shrugged, then tipped his head toward the office. "In there. Knock first."

"Obliged," said Garrett, and made his way toward Tom Festing's door. And as he crossed the barroom, he pondered the various reasons why a bartender should be wearing a false mustache. Oh, it was a good one, no doubt about it. Probably fooled everyone else, but not him, not Chauncey Garrett, not a man who'd spent the greater share of his adult life on the stage and had seen some doozies.

Time enough to ponder it later.

He opened the door and found Festing seated at his desk, a scruffy terrier mix curled up on the floor beside it.

Festing looked up from his paperwork. "This is private," he said, with annoyance but no trace of recognition. "Get out."

"In a minute, Tom," said Garrett, smiling, fixing him with a blandly pleasant but wholly riveting stare. He closed the door behind him. "I'd like a word with you first."

EIGHTEEN

>─┤─◆─┼─○─┼─◆─├─<

JIM CAULDER PULLED OFF HIS FALSE MUSTACHE WITH
trembling hands and settled it in its case. Picking the last
traces of adhesive from his lip, he sat down and poured
himself a large whiskey from the bottle he'd sneaked out of
the Purple Fox.

A soft rap came at the door, and he pulled a pistol from the
bureautop and stepped beside it. "Who is it?" he asked.

"Cora, you idiot. Who else?"

He opened the door. She hurried in, making herself at home
in his chair. Primly, she folded chubby hands in her broad lap.
"Well?"

"Garrett's here," he said without preamble. "He was in
tonight. I think he spotted me." He picked up his glass again
and tossed back the remaining whiskey. "I know he spotted
me."

"Don't be silly," Cora said, her face holding no particular
expression. "He wouldn't be looking for you at all. What happened?"

"I think he spotted my mustache, I mean. Stupid idea,
Cora." He poured himself another drink. "He came in and
asked for Festing. Stayed in the office about twenty minutes,
and then he left." He raised the glass to his lips and took a
drink. He'd stopped shaking. "I told Festing I was sick, but
he wasn't going to let me go, so I stuck my fingers down my
throat and puked behind the bar."

He made a face, and then tossed back the rest of his whiskey. He set the glass down on the bureau. "Jesus. Do you

know how disgusting that is? Anyway, then he let me go. I followed Garrett up the street—the best I could, with Festing holding me up like that—and saw him just turning into the Crazy Horse Saloon. Stuck my head in the door long enough to make sure it was him, and see him settle in at a poker game. Then I came here.''

Cora pursed her lips. "Festing appear odd when you spoke to him?''

"A little fuzzy." He'd crossed the room, and was staring out the window at an angle, up toward the Crazy Horse. "Did you expect him to say, 'Help, help, I've been mesmerized by a crazy killer'? That guy gives me the willies, Cora.''

She didn't look at him. She said, "A coded telegram arrived while you were at the Purple Fox.''

He turned from the window. "And?''

"They've picked up most of the extras. Got Skerrit and Tibbs up in Squeaky Hat, Muldoon and Anderson in Reno. They found Norton in an empty warehouse in San Francisco. Bullet in his chest. No signs of a struggle.''

"Garrett?" Caulder asked, tugging at his collar.

She lifted a hand, palm up. "Probably.''

"What'd they get the others on?''

Cora shrugged. "Does it matter? The important thing is that they're out of the way. Temporarily.''

"So that leaves Garrett and Scaggs and his detective. And the three up in the hills.''

"Case and Kramer, for certain. And Monroe," she said. "We think. Why Scaggs would ever hire those lamebrains is beyond me.''

"Because he hired them before he hired Silas Corcoran," Caulder said, glancing once again toward the Crazy Horse. Garrett was still inside.

"No excuse. Although I suppose they did better than Corcoran's men did, with the exception of Garrett.''

"No, Ralph Scaggs hired him, too.''

She grimaced. "At Corcoran's behest. Happy?''

He nodded. "Just like to keep things straight, that's all. I don't understand this case. I mean, I don't understand certain things about it. Why Scaggs hired who he hired, for instance.''

"If you understood it, I'd be worried about you," Cora replied. "Ralph Scaggs is a dolt. But make no mistake, he's a dangerous dolt. I wish we'd picked up Corcoran." Cora tapped her index fingers together twice. "Slime. The scum of the earth."

"Why didn't you grab him when you had him, then?"

"Because Miss Maguire was riding the same stage, you fool," she suddenly barked, startling him. "And when we stopped—well, I couldn't very well have taken him in town, now, could I? Not without calling attention. The trouble is," she said, eyes narrowing, "nobody's seen hide nor hair of him since."

"Do you want me to follow him? Garrett, I mean," he said, hoping that she wouldn't. He was tired and hungry, and frankly, Chauncey Garrett scared him. He didn't flinch at the idea of bushwhackers or armed robbers or even assassins. But Chauncey Garrett, a man who came at his prey with a smile and soothing talk and who then proceeded to blow their brains out—or their hearts or their eyes or worse—was an entirely different matter.

"No," Cora said, and he exhaled loudly. He hadn't realized he was holding his breath. "We know where he's going."

He raised his eyebrows. "We do?"

Cora nodded. "Where Miss Maguire is going. Up into the hills."

"We're going, too, then?"

"No. We'll wait."

"But Cora! You can't turn that spellbinding snake loose on a little thing like that!"

Cora stood up. "Yes, I can," she said, straightening her skirts. "Obviously I have more faith in Miss Maguire than you do. We'll wait and see who comes back down the hill."

"But—"

"That's final, Jim."

THURSDAY, JUNE 7

>─┤─◆─○─◆─├─◄

"**W**ELL, YOU CAN TRY THE OLD DAWSON PLACE, here," said Sopsucher, pointing to the map. "And the old miners' shack, here. But dollars to doughnuts she ain't in either of those places." It was morning, and the sheriff sat back from his desk. Behind him, the wall was papered three times over with outdated wanted posters. He folded his hands in his lap. "She's long gone by now, probably to be with Jesus. No offense, Soda."

Grady caught Biscuit Pete's arm before he could do serious damage to Sheriff Sopsucher, and Maggie put herself between them. "I don't think so, Sheriff," she said as calmly as she could manage. "They didn't kill Corinne. On purpose, anyway. Why don't you come with us?"

The sheriff sighed and closed his eyes for a moment. He said, "Darlin', I'm gonna go over to the saloon and have a little talk with Tom Festing just as soon as he comes in, and—"

"When's that, Sheriff Sodbuster? Noon? Two o'clock? We've already wasted enough time waiting for you to show up! We can talk to Festing anytime."

"Sopsucher," he said, caught on the first sentence. She doubted he'd even heard the rest.

"*Miss* Maguire!" said Maggie, standing tall.

"All right. *Miss* Maguire. Dagnabit, lady, you are about to drive me loco!"

"I might say the same for you," Maggie said with a growl, snatching the map off the desk. Harriet wasn't dead, she was certain of it, but she might not have long. "Go ahead. Talk to Mr. Festing. Talk all afternoon. Knock back a few beers! Play cards! But *I'm* going to *do* something!"

''Gonna knock back something, all right,'' the sheriff grumbled under his breath, but Maggie heard it.

She spun on her heel and stalked from the office. Outside, she went directly to the rail and her horse. They hadn't wasted the early morning hours while waiting for Sopsucher to show up. Biscuit Pete had been to the livery and rented horses, and outfitted them for a trip out of town. Maggie had been to the Kid Concho Café and ordered a lunch packed.

Grady had complained, mostly.

She put her foot in the stirrup and mounted. She gathered her reins. Biscuit Pete was ready to go, but Grady stood on the walk, eyeing his mount.

''She's not going to lift you into the saddle,'' Maggie said. ''Hurry up.''

Grady just stood there.

''Come on!''

Grady looked up. ''Are you sure I wouldn't be of more use in town?''

''Grady . . .''

Tentatively, he untied the horse and threw the reins over her neck. His foot went in the stirrup. He began to bounce on the ball of his foot.

''Just get up there!''

After two tries he made it, and sat hunched over the horn, both hands locked to it. One hand uncramped long enough to find the reins and take them up unevenly. ''Ready,'' he said, his nose six inches above the horse's dandery mane.

Honestly. She'd offered to teach him to ride more times than she could count, but he was always too busy. Well, this little jaunt might just change his mind.

They turned away from the rail. As they started down the street at a jog, Grady hanging on for dear life, Biscuit Pete drawled, ''Sheriff Sopsucher ain't so useless as he puts on, Miz Maguire. He used to be a real fast hand with a gun. A real dangerous feller.''

''That's what they tell me,'' said Maggie, eyeing Grady. ''Good gravy! For God's sake, let go of her mane and sit up!''

NINETEEN

>━┼━◆❯━━◯━━❮◆━┼━<

GRADY REINED IN THE HORSE AND SLID FROM THE SAD-
dle. "Stop!" he shouted, panting. Maggie and Biscuit
Pete, riding ahead among the trees, halted and twisted
in their saddles. Maggie, for one, did not look at all pleased
with him. Actually, Biscuit Pete didn't look too happy, either.

"Grady, get back on your horse," Maggie said crossly.
"We haven't gone four miles yet!"

But he didn't mount up again. He slid down till he was
sitting in the pine needles. "No."

"Grady . . ."

"No. I refuse to move from this spot. I'm sore. I have
blisters. My *blisters* have blisters. My ankles are raw from the
damn stirrups. My knees hurt. If God had meant for mankind
to ride around on horses, He would have . . . Well, He would
have made something differently, that's all."

Maggie's mouth was set. Biscuit Pete appeared disgusted,
or at least Grady thought he did. Pete's expressions ran the
gamut from A to B and therefore could be a bit tricky to figure
out. If one cared to decipher them, that was, and Grady was
in no mood.

"Go on," he said, pulling a handkerchief from his pocket.
"Go on without me." He wiped at his face and neck. They
were in the mountains, for goodness sake—in the foothills at
least. The pine trees were thick. A body would think it'd be
cool and dry, not hot and so muggy you could slice the air.

With a snort, Maggie pulled a packet from her saddlebags,

then tossed it down. Grady caught it and looked up at her curiously.

"Your lunch," she said. Then she leaned down over the saddle and hissed, "Grady, you're embarrassing me! *Now* will you learn to ride?"

He rubbed his ankles. They were scraped raw. He looked up. He whispered back, "No."

A *boom* sounded distantly, but not so distantly that its vibration didn't send shivers through the trees. Grady's mare skittered, and for a moment every pine needle and leaf danced. Grady jumped. "What in heaven's name is that?"

"Oh, good gravy! It's only blasting." Maggie sat back up. "All right," she said in a normal voice, so that Biscuit Pete could hear. "We'll go on without you. You send those wires we talked about."

Grady watched them ride away, disappearing among the trees. There were no wires to send. Just Maggie, trying to save his face.

He stood up slowly, put his sandwich in his coat pocket, and gingerly began leading the horse back the way they'd come.

It was beyond him why she thought everyone should learn to ride. It was almost a religious thing with her. People should stay in the cities, he reasoned. People should take cabs, ride the trolley. People should be more civilized! Why, any minute now some smart lad or other was going to invent a machine that would make horses obsolete. Maybe something steam-powered.

Steam—that's the ticket! he thought, cutting around a large outcropping of granite. Why, the whole city could be lined with tracks, and then they could build more tracks from city to city! Not those chains and pulleys the cable cars used or those big wide things like trains used, but smaller, a narrower gauge. More personal-sized. A locomotive—miniature, of course—in every carriage house!

Something was biting him.

Forgetting the locomotives, he slapped at his neck, and his hand came away bloody. Bugs. Heat and bugs and blisters. He would have given anything to find a four-star hotel through the trees. "Run me a bath and stable my horse!" he would have said. Then, "Bring me a magnum of champagne and another of liniment!"

Lord. Had anyone ever been in this much pain? He was walking stiff and bowlegged, and how far did she say it was back to town? Four miles? Good God.

It was better than going up the trail with them. Better than going another five or six miles to the old Dawson place and finding nothing.

Why was everything in the West referred to as "the old Such-and-Such place," anyway? The whole West was practically new! How could anything made by white hands be old? Now, if he was in England, say, and somebody said, "It's over at the old Swingle-Hyde-Thorpe place," he would have, by God, believed them! Probably five hundred years old if it was a day.

But no. This "old Dawson place" was probably five years old if that, ten at the outside, and already falling apart. Didn't anybody build things to last anymore?

He mopped at his brow again—damn this humidity!—and led the mare in a wandering path around a sticker thicket. Odd. He didn't remember that, but then, things looked different on the ground than they did from the saddle.

He supposed Maggie and old taciturn Pete were making better time, now that he wasn't with them. They were probably most of the way to the Dawson place by now. All right, not most of the way there. But they were making better time. And they'd find it empty. And then over to that old miners' shack—another "old" building. Probably hadn't even reached its teenage years.

He snorted. They wouldn't find anything there, either. A wasted trip. It wasn't that he agreed with the sheriff, not totally. He didn't believe Hattie was dead. He believed the cabin and shack would be empty because the kidnappers had moved.

After all, Corinne had run off on them. They might not know she was dead—in fact, they probably didn't. If they thought she'd made it to town, they would have run, and they would have taken Harriet with them—the direction was anybody's guess, though. No, Maggie wasn't going to find a blessed thing up in the mountains.

The foothills, he reminded himself. The mountains were those giant snowcapped heaps of rock off in the distance. Snowcapped. He'd like a little of that snow right now.

Grady led the horse around a clump of trees, then skidded down an incline, the horse sliding after him and knocking him flat on his back.

"Fine," he said as he lay half on pine needles and half in the mud, the horse nosing him. "Bug-bit, sweltering, blistered, and now muddy. I hope you're happy." The horse snorted in reply, leaving a damp spray of stain on the front of his suit coat.

Batting at it disgustedly, he clambered to his feet. "Remind me to— Ouch! Get off! Get off my foot, you obstreperous beast!"

After some thought, the horse moved.

"You could at least apologize," said Grady through clenched teeth, hopping on one foot. And it was while he was hopping that he realized that nothing looked familiar. He couldn't see the trail that he and Maggie and Biscuit Pete had cut coming up here.

He took off his suit coat, folded it, and after some soul-searching, put it on the saddle. He was going to have to do it.

He said, "I apologize profoundly for every bad thing I've said about you. Now, hold still, old girl." He put his foot in the stirrup and tried to mount. The mare stepped to the side, and he went *splat* in the muddy pine needles again.

He got up, brushing himself off.

He went to the horse's head and took hold of the cheek-straps. "Now, see here! I've said I was sorry. We're lost, and I need to get up on your back to see better. I'm not any happier about this than you are. So be a good girl."

He went back to her side, gripped the saddle horn, put his foot in the stirrup, closed his eyes . . . and swung up into the saddle!

"Humph!" he sniffed, suddenly full of himself. "And Maggie says I'm not a horseman!" Carefully he gathered his reins, straightened the suit jacket beneath his sore backside—oh, blast! He was sitting on his sandwich!—then cast his gaze about for the trail.

It was nowhere in sight. Troublesome but not unfixable. He thought about retrieving his lunch, but decided it was already smashed flat, and he didn't want to have to get off the horse again to get it. After all, he might not be able to get back up.

He gave the horse's neck a few cautious pats. "All right, girl. We'll go back the way we came." One hand locked to the saddle horn, he reined the horse around and started her back up the hill. "We're bound to come across— Whoa!"

Another blast rumbled the ground just as a covey of quail broke cover under the mare's nose, and just as suddenly, she jumped to the side, taking Grady with her, and broke into a gallop.

"Whoa! Stop!" he yelled, too afraid of serious bodily injury to let loose of the saddle horn and rein her in.

He ducked down just in time to avoid a low-hanging branch. "Stop, horse!" he cried against the wind. "Stop, I say! *Maggie! Help!*"

TWENTY

>━┥━◆━◯━◆━┝━<

"**T**HERE IT IS," WHISPERED BISCUIT PETE. HE AND MAGgie had led their horses as close as safely possible, then crept through the undergrowth on foot. Carefully, Maggie parted the sugarbush branches and peered at the clearing.

The Dawson place consisted of a crudely built cabin, which was falling in on itself; an outhouse, which already had; and three pole corrals, with most of their poles missing. There were no signs of life, let alone of recent activity.

Maggie rose out of her crouch. "Nobody's here," she said, giving a snap to her riding skirt, shaking twigs and grass and dirt from the hems. "Nobody's been here for a long time."

"No, ma'am," replied Biscuit Pete. He followed her as she walked down the slope, to what was left of the house. "I reckon not. Not since I seen 'em hang Teddy Dawson, leastwise."

Maggie stopped, and he nearly ran into her. "You hanged him? What did he do?"

Biscuit Pete ducked his head and scratched the back of his neck. "Horse-thieving, ma'am. We come up here, my pa and me and the Joyner boys and Kid Concho and Hashknife Jack, and got the drop on him. I was just a young'un, but I remember it good."

Maggie was glad Grady wasn't there. He'd have some pithy remark about the cherished code of the West or starting youngsters out on the path of righteousness early or something. She said, "Kid Concho's all over town. He certainly gets a lot of publicity for a hired gun who's been dead ten years. Pretty fast, wasn't he?''

Pete looked at her oddly for a second, then stared off into the distance. "Yup, he was fast. So was Hashknife Jack, till they caught him cheatin' at cards over to Carson City a few years later. Shot through the lungs," he said matter-of-factly. "Took him four days to die."

Maggie said, "How colorful."

But Pete wasn't listening. "Teddy Dawson got hanged from that sycamore, yonder." He pointed toward a large tree at the edge of the little clearing, then suddenly his eye lit on something. "Well, I'll be dogged! They's still some'a the rope up there!" He pulled out a pocket knife. "You mind, ma'am?"

Maggie rolled her eyes. "Oh, don't stand on ceremony."

Pete's face wrinkled quizzically—as it had several times previously that day—and before he could ask her to explain, she said, "Go ahead."

As Biscuit Pete trotted toward his hanging tree to fetch down the scrap of rope—strange, the things people got sentimental about—Maggie walked down toward the cabin. The door had long since vanished, the chimney had crumbled, and the roof had caved in. The only tracks to be seen in the rubble of the interior were those of squirrels.

A wasted trip.

But there was still the miners' shack. Not that she was hopeful. She was beginning to think that Grady was right about going back to town. Not his reasoning, exactly—her motivation was much more convincing than a bruised backside. She was beginning to think that they wouldn't find Harriet out here, at least not where they were looking. With Corinne vanished from their grasp, the kidnappers would have to think she'd gone to town for help. They'd have to think a posse would be bearing down on them at any moment.

And they'd be gone.

She sighed. She wished she'd brought her knives. At least she could have taken out her frustration on that sycamore. She walked out around the side of the house, only to spy Pete, standing on his horse's saddle so he'd be tall enough to reach, sawing away at that scrap of rope.

She closed her eyes, breathing, "God save me from drunkards and fools," then walked to the tree, her skirts swishing high weeds.

"About done?" she said, taking hold of his horse's bridle. Just then the rope came free in his hand. Still standing on the dappled gray, he casually tucked the rope in his pocket and folded his penknife. "Yup," he said, and then he was down, sitting in the saddle. "No need to hold ol' Nickel's head, ma'am. He's real steady."

"Oh," she said, and let go. Pete wasn't much for brains, but you had to admire the way he handled himself on a horse.

He'd brought her chestnut, too, and before she mounted up, she dug out lunch. It was past noon, and she was hungry. Tossing a packet to Biscuit Pete, she said, "Roast beef sandwich," and mounted up. "We can eat while we're riding. I'd like to take a look at that miners' shack."

"Is Hattie gonna be there?" he said, fiddling with the rope. He held the sandwich, still in its paper, under one arm. "I gotta get my Hattie back."

"I don't know, Pete. If she's not, then hopefully we'll find out which way she went. At least." Maggie squeezed her horse with her knees, and they moved out at a walk. The horse was really quite decent, for a rental. It reined fair to middling, and had a reasonably smooth jog. "Why'd you climb up there and get that?" She nodded at the rope. It was gray and frayed and probably rotting.

"It reminds me of my pa," he said, and Maggie was surprised when his voice shook.

She cocked a brow but didn't speak. Thoughtfully, she unwrapped her sandwich as they rode out through the woods.

TWENTY-ONE

>──┼─◆◇◆─◇─◆◇◆─┼─<

"**F**INALLY!"

Grady slid gratefully to the ground. His jacket, which he'd been sitting on, had bounced out from underneath him a good two miles back. He was in his vest and shirtsleeves, which were sweated through, and if his backside had been sore before, it was on fire now.

The horse wasn't in such good shape either.

He snatched the reins down, and began—haltingly, between his aching ankles and sore thighs and blistered behind—to walk the horse. She followed, head down and blowing hard, sweat soaking her flanks and neck.

"That'll teach you, you bag of bones," he muttered as he walked. "That'll teach you to run off with somebody who can't get you stopped. Ran yourself into the ground, didn't you?" He wiped a hand down her neck, scraping lather away.

"Well, let this be a lesson to you. If you run away with me again, you're just going to have to keep running until you die or fall over, whichever comes first."

He switched the reins to his other hand, then rubbed carefully at his backside. Oh, for a bucket of liniment! He would have bet that when he eased himself down into it, steam would rise in billows.

This would teach him to complain. Just when you thought things couldn't possibly get any worse, you ended up walking bowlegged in the middle of absolutely nowhere—not a hotel in sight!—with your tailor-made suit coat lost forever and your lunch with it, your Newport ties encrusted in mud, and no one for company—no one to hear your tale of misery—except a sweaty, stupid horse.

He didn't even know which way town was.

His stomach growled.

"Oh, shut up," he said.

The horse snorted.

"You, too." He kept on walking. From Maggie, he'd learned, at least, that you couldn't let a sweaty horse stand. Or something like that. And you couldn't give it water. It seemed cruel to him, but if Maggie said it, it had to be true.

Most of what Maggie said turned out to be true, a fact he grumbled about but that secretly gave him no small amount of pride. Smart girl, his cousin. Smart lady. If he'd come across a woman half as sharp as Maggie Maguire on his nightly ramblings through the city, he would have snatched her up. If she would have had him, that was.

He pushed a low-hanging limb out of his way. He'd just keep heading downhill. A person couldn't go wrong if he just kept going downhill. Sooner or later, he was bound to hit civilization.

He walked on this way for roughly a half hour, limping and smarting and cursing softly under his breath, until he thought it was safe to give the horse a drink. He poured water from the canteen into his hand, letting her slurp with big, rubbery lips from his palm, until half the contents were emptied—as much on the ground as down her throat, he suspected—and then he took a drink and recapped the canteen.

"You're not only a disobedient, headstrong beast, you're greedy, too," he said in disgust, wiping his hand on his pants. The mare dipped her head down to nibble at a clump of grass. "And you don't pay attention to a word I say."

Actually, come to think of it, the horse was quite a bit like Maggie. He chuckled softly as he pulled the mare's head up and started walking again. And then he got to thinking that it was a good thing Miriam Cosgrove couldn't see him now. Ah, Miriam. So blond. So round. So flushed.

So tipsy.

He sighed just before another pine branch slapped him in the face.

"Feh," he said, sobering for a moment and picking pine needles out of his teeth.

And it was while he was divesting himself of pine needles that he noticed the mare had her head up and was staring to the right, through the trees. She whickered softly.

"What is it, girl?" he asked, and immediately gave himself a mental kick for even entertaining the notion that she'd tell him.

He cupped his hand over the mare's nose to keep her from calling—one of Maggie's tricks, that—and slowly started walking in that direction. It could be Maggie and Biscuit Pete coming back down the mountain, although he doubted it—it was too soon. But maybe they'd seen the error of their ways and started back early.

Too, it could be a miner or a trapper with a horse—he didn't imagine the mare would whicker at a human, no matter how friendly he might smell. A miner or a trapper would have food and, more importantly, directions. He could sit down for a while. No, on second thought, he couldn't. But perhaps, he thought hopefully, they'd have something he could lean against for a few minutes.

Then again, it might be someone he didn't want to meet.

Cautiously, he made his way through the trees.

TWENTY-TWO

"**A**IN'T NOBODY HERE, NEITHER," SAID PETE, WAVING off a bee. They had dismounted twenty yards from the miners' shack.

"But they *were* here." Maggie walked toward the corral, which had been recently shored up with poles. Not very well, but someone had made an attempt. And the corral was full of fresh hoofprints and manure, and there were plenty of bootprints outside and in.

She looped her horse's reins over the fence, then reached into her deep skirt pocket for the Colt. She eased it onto a full chamber—she always carried it with an empty chamber under the hammer for safety's sake—and started toward the shack.

"Ma'am?" said Biscuit Pete from behind her. "Miss? You reckon you should be carryin' a big ol' gun like that?"

"Quiet," she said. They'd made so much noise already, it was a little like closing the barn door after the horse had gone East, over Egypt. Her mouth crooked into a smile. Her father had always said that whenever one of the acts had skipped out during the night—or when they and the carnival had to disappear under the cover of darkness. "Gone East, over Egypt, Magdalena," he'd say, which meant that they'd parted the Red Sea. Which meant that they were permanently long gone.

"Ma'am?" Biscuit Pete was looking at her curiously. At least his expression was leaning toward it, as far as she could tell.

She made herself appear serious. "Nothing. You go around the back. I'll take the front."

Giving a shrug to his lanky shoulders, Pete wandered through mud and knee-high weeds toward the back of the building, then stopped and bent over, lifting something from the undergrowth.

"What is it?" she called.

Silently, he held it up. A woman's shoe, muddy. Corinne's.

Maggie stared at it for a moment, then stiffened her shoulders. She signaled for Pete to go on around back, and proceeded to the front of the cabin.

This structure, which bore no one's name, was in somewhat better shape that the old Dawson place. It still had its roof and chimney, at any rate, and when she peeked around the front, she saw the door was still on its hinges, and closed.

Maggie edged around the front of the shack, stooping before she came to the window. She listened. It was quiet. She peeked over the sill. The interior was deep in shadow, but she could pick out signs of recent habitation: a candle and dirty plates on the table, and an empty whiskey bottle.

No movement, though.

She went to the door, thought about kicking it in but then decided that was too dramatic, and lifted the latch instead. Slowly, on leather hinges, the door creaked open.

Rubble. Broken glass, more dirty plates, empty tin cans, more whiskey bottles. She picked up one of the cans. The label said Peaches, and it was full of ants swarming over the last drops of sticky juice. Tossing it into a corner and flicking ants from her hands with a little grimace and a large shiver, Maggie turned and went back outside.

"Pete?"

"Ma'am? Back here."

His shout had come from the backside of a shack. She followed the sound and found Pete. He was bending over a man lying on the ground.

Pete stood up. "I didn't do it," he said a little defensively. "He was already shot when I got here."

The man, eyes closed, moved his mouth.

Maggie said, "Get me some water. Now."

As Pete took off at a lope, she knelt to the man. He was of middling height, dark-haired and ordinary-looking, perhaps

thirty years old or thereabouts, and dressed in new clothes.
New shirt, new pants, new boots, and his shirt and Levi's still
bore the faint creases left from sitting folded on the mercantile
shelf. You could have put the shirt back up on the shelf, it
looked so brand-spanking-new—except for the bloodstain,
crawling with flies, that covered most of his belly.

That, and the bullet hole that centered the stain, and from
which blood was still thickly oozing.

He tried to speak again, and Maggie said soothingly, "It's
all right. We're here to help," even though she knew they
wouldn't be able to help him at all. She whisked the flies
away, but they landed again the moment she took her hand
away. He'd been here all night, she suspected. His face was
already gray under the sunburn, his fingers and hands bluish.
It was only a matter of time. Of minutes.

Pete was back. He handed her the canteen and she unstop-
pered it, propping the man's head and holding it to his lips.
He tried to drink, but most of the water coursed over his chin.

"Scaggs," he managed, choking.

Maggie handed the water back to Pete. "Yes," she said.
"Ralph Scaggs. You work for him, don't you?"

"Joke's on them," the man whispered, the flies buzzing,
his head lolling, his beard stubble scraping Maggie's wrist.
"Killed me for my—" A cough took him, and he shuddered,
and for a moment Maggie thought he was gone. But then he
seemed to brighten. His eyes opened and he looked up. They
were blue. He whispered, "Scaggs promised ten percent to
those boys. They figured to kill me and split my ten, too."

He laughed suddenly, just the ghost of a chuckle, really,
that brought up a huge bubble of blood. Maggie wiped his
chin on her sleeve.

"You're real kind, miss." A whisper.

Maggie leaned closer. "What did you mean, the joke's on
them?"

"I was—" Another cough, another bubble of blood. "I was
only gettin' five." Suddenly he clutched at her sleeve. "My
name's Monroe, Sully Monroe. See they get my marker—"

A seizure took him, stiffening his body beneath her hands
and his grip on the bloody fabric of her sleeve, and just as

quickly he went limp, his hand dropping to the ground. A trickle of thick, dark blood drooled lazily from one corner of his mouth.

"He a goner, ma'am?" said Biscuit Pete, behind her.

Maggie closed Sully Monroe's eyes. "I guess he is, Pete."

"You want I should start diggin', or you want to follow them boys? I seen a trail yonder, where they went."

TWENTY-THREE

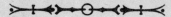

GRADY COULD HEAR SOUNDS NOW. MEN ARGUING. He tied the mare to a tree and deftly unbuckled his saddle-bags, pulling free a short-barreled Peacemaker. Checking to make sure the hammer rested on an empty chamber, he stuck it in the back of his waistband, then pulled his shirt free to hide it.

No sense in taking any chances.

Leaving the mare behind, he crept forward.

And then he could see them through the brush: two men, as far as he could tell, in a clearing. And beside them, in the damp weeds, a girl. Harriet. She was either sleeping or passed out. Or dead.

Not the happiest thought.

"I said, gimme that!" said the taller of the two. He was light-haired and stockily built, and wore his jeans—brand-new, by the look of them—rolled wide at the cuffs. Definitely not a fashion plate, this one.

"Bugger off, Kramer," replied the short, dark fellow. He appeared slightly younger, too, perhaps twenty or twenty-two. "You're gettin' half his percentage and you already got his pocket knife. I get to keep the watch."

"Jesus, Case! Why the hell do you care what time it is, anyway? We're lost in these goddamn woods. We're probably gonna die out here in these stupid clothes!"

"Somebody's gonna meet us, I tell you. That is, if they can find us. And if they don't find us, at least someday somebody'll find my skeleton with a gold-dipped watch on it!"

Case threw himself at Kramer, and the men began to scuffle on the ground.

They didn't sound like locals. In fact, they sounded like city boys, like Grady himself. Well, certainly not so cultured, he thought with a sniff. More like he had sounded in the old days, before he turned legit and ground off the rough edges. Ralph must have hired talent—if you could call it that—back home. And what percentage were they talking about? The one called Case said someone was meeting them. That was all he needed. More buffoons with which to be lost in the wilderness.

What to do, what to do . . .

Suddenly he had a stroke of absolute genius.

Congratulating himself on his cleverness, he reached for his pistol and eased it onto a full chamber. Trying not to limp, he went forward, out of the trees and brush; forward, across the clearing, until he was practically on them. They were so engaged in beating each other to a bloody pulp that they hadn't even noticed him.

He glanced over at Harriet—still out cold—then said, "Gentlemen!"

Case heard him. He started to open his mouth and point, but Kramer slugged him in the jaw.

Sighing, Grady pointed the gun overhead and fired one shot. Both men froze.

Remembering what the fight was over—a pocket watch that obviously belonged to neither of them—Grady said, "I thought there were supposed to be three of you."

Kramer got off Case, dusting at his shirt and pants. "Mr. Garrett, sir? I thought you'd be taller."

Grady nodded. If he could just pull this off, he wouldn't have to pull that "client confidentiality" ploy with Miriam. She'd fall into his arms and practically scream, "Take me!" But why stop at Miriam? He could milk this story for years, toppling blondes, brunettes, redheads. . . .

"Mr. Garrett, sir?" It was Case, now on his feet beside Kramer, his hat in his hands.

"What happened to the third man?" Grady said, standing up straight and taking care to keep his voice and manner clipped and short. The way he imagined a kidnapper would talk. Well, a real kidnapper, not these two idiots. Oh, Miriam was going to love this!

"Well, there was three of us, but we kind of had, um . . ."

"An accident," finished Kramer, stepping on Case's toe. "He sort of got killed."

"He was cleaning his gun," offered Case through clenched teeth.

"And it went off," said Kramer. He shook his head. "A terrible thing. 'Fore he died, he said, 'You boys split my cut of the take.' Didn't he, Case?"

Case, having got his toe free, hopped on one foot.

Kramer snarled, "I said, didn't he, Case?"

"Yeah. Yeah, that's what he said, all right, Mr. Garrett."

Morons, Grady thought. But they were armed morons. What was he supposed to do, pay them now? Out of his pocket? All he had was twelve dollars and a linty peppermint. Well, a pair of dice, too, but he doubted they'd accept those, even if they did roll a consistent eleven.

Stuck for something to say, he just nodded and said, "That's fine, boys."

And then, to his amazement, Kramer said, "Well, good. That's fine. Um, I guess we'll be goin' now." He tipped his head toward Harriet. "She's sozzled, but she's in one piece. Just like the man said." He turned toward Case. "Oh, quit hoppin' around like some baby. Let's go."

Case mumbled something Grady couldn't hear, and hobbled after Kramer, toward the horses.

Grady stood there, watching them saddle up—or attempting to. Even he was better at it than they were. Finally they were both mounted, and though Grady didn't put much faith in Kramer's girth strap (since he could see light between it and the horse's belly), he held steady while they rode over to him.

"Which way is out?" said Kramer, looking down from the heights of the saddle.

"Just go down the hill." Grady pointed across the clearing. "You can't go wrong."

Case said, "We been goin' downhill since last night, and we still ain't nowhere! We tried to take another route comin' down from the shack. Bet they got posses out, don't they? I mean, since *somebody*"—he eyed Kramer—"let that other gal light out on us."

Grady said, "They're searching." He tipped his head in the opposite direction he'd told them to go. "Over to the east."

Kramer said, "How'd you find us, anyway, Mr. Garrett?"

"Trailed you," Grady replied, trying to appear as if he knew what he was talking about, and fervently wishing they'd be on their way before they asked him something he couldn't bluff his way out of. He slapped Kramer's horse on the shoulder. "Get going."

Kramer reined away, but Case hesitated. He leaned toward Grady, his formless hat nearly toppling from his head. "Can I watch? I never saw nobody kill a woman before. You gonna cork her while she's tranced?"

Grady swallowed hard. Tranced? Kill her? What in the world was this Garrett being sent to do? Suddenly he didn't feel so brave anymore. The real Garrett might show up at any moment, and Grady didn't think Garrett was someone whose acquaintance he wished to make.

He fixed Case with a gaze he fervently hoped was steely. "I said, get going."

Case opened his mouth, then thought better of it. He reined his horse away and joined Kramer at the edge of the clearing. Kramer turned back long enough to call, "See you in Frisco!" Both of them disappeared into the trees.

"Thank you, God," Grady whispered, and tucked the Colt into his pants, then hurriedly pulled it out again and fixed it on an empty chamber. After what he'd just been through, the last thing he needed was to shoot his own backside off. Although it was already so sore, he doubted he'd feel it. He was sticking it back in his waistband again when he heard another *boom* of a blast, then a thump and a crash of brush. Then Kramer, his voice distant, swearing a blue streak.

He smiled. The girth.

He waited until the sounds of travel resumed, thinking that, all right, maybe he wasn't so handy on a horse. But he could still talk the birds from the highest branches and into the cookbag. Smiling to himself, he saddled Harriet's horse—quite a bit more handily than Case and Kramer had done, he thought, allowing himself a little cockiness. He'd even remembered to rock it back onto the blanket, and he didn't get kicked when he reached for the girth strap.

Satisfied, he hoisted Harriet up across the saddle. She was soused again. Maggie wasn't going to be amused. Well, there was nothing he could do about that part.

Once he was sure she was balanced, he led her horse from the clearing, going in the opposite direction as Case and Kramer, back toward where he'd left his mare. Best to get as far away as possible. Pity there weren't any street signs out here.

Well, Maggie would find him. Maggie always found him. Some Indian—what was his name? Floating Bear? Diving Ox? Waltzing Muskrat? Some animal doing something, anyway— had taught her how to track when she was a kid.

And he was thinking, as he reached his mare and began to lead both horses, that it was a handy thing to have had a father who owned a carnival. His father, her father's half brother, had run a floating crap game, and a fine one it was, too. When you wanted a square game—as square as they got, anyway— you saw Conner Maguire.

Not everyone's father was destined to be in show business like Maggie's dad, he mused as he limped his way down the endless hill, through the infinite trees. Some people's fathers had *real* professions.

He gave his glasses a cursory wipe on his shirtfront, replaced them on his nose, and kept walking.

TWENTY-FOUR

>━┼━◆━○━◆━┼━<

MAGGIE LEANED BACK IN THE SADDLE AND BRACED herself as her horse skidded down a muddy incline. Biscuit Pete rode about fifteen feet ahead of her, following a trail that three horses had cut the night before, and the newer, fresher tracks left earlier today by a fourth horse, following the first three. How much earlier, it was impossible to tell. Maybe several hours, maybe twenty minutes.

"Did you hear something, ma'am?" Pete had stopped, and was sitting up very straight, craning his head from one side to the other.

"Hear what?"

Pete shook his head and started forward again, his gray's tail swishing. "Nothin', I reckon. Them boys sure was ridin' all over hell and gone. Excuse me for cussin', ma'am."

"Yup," she said, imitating him. "They sure was. And you're excused."

The trail wandered and rambled and doubled back on itself, and she was beginning to think the men she was following were as lost as she was becoming. She said, "Any idea where they're headed?"

"Well, I woulda said Green Butte. That's a little town south of the ridge. 'Cept now we're goin' down toward Hobson's Ferry." The trail took a swing to the left, and as he ducked under a pine bough, he added, "Or Crowfoot."

Maggie sighed and ducked for the same limb. Coming up, she said, "In other words, you don't know either."

Pete thought about it for a moment. "Nope."

Biscuit Pete continued in the lead and she let him, for he'd proved to be a fair hand at it, and the men hadn't done anything to obscure their trail. They might as well have left a red stripe in their wake. As she rode, Maggie puzzled over this new set of tracks. She supposed Sheriff Sopsucher could have changed his mind about their errand and ridden up anyway, bypassing the old Dawson place. Maybe he thought he was following them, for he'd have no way of knowing that Grady had turned back and that they were no longer a party of three.

Highly unlikely, but still a possibility.

For the life of her, she couldn't figure out why Just-Call-Me-Ralphie had hired these men, and promised them a grand total of 25 percent of the proceeds. It was staggering amount to pay to common kidnappers. If she'd wanted it done, she could have had Harriet snatched for fifty dollars, including expenses. But then, perhaps Ralphie didn't know where to hire talent.

Which brought up another point, one of which the sheriff had reminded her: Why on earth had Ralphie bothered to kidnap Harriet in the first place? Why hadn't he just hired one man to kill her? That was what he wanted, wasn't it, a clear path to the inheritance?

She turned the picture over in her mind—a stranger enters the saloon, goes upstairs with Harriet, slits her throat, goes out a window, and hightails it. He'd be long gone before anyone discovered the crime. And Sopsucher, layabout that he was, wouldn't even go down the street to stop a bar fight. He certainly wouldn't be enthusiastic about mounting a posse to chase after any killer, let alone a killer of whores.

It would have been so easy. So why go to all this bother?

It didn't make sense.

There had to be something else to this, something Quincy Applegate hadn't told her. Or maybe something he didn't know either.

The thought of Quincy brought a smile to her lips. Really, he was quite nice, wasn't he? Such a nice, gentle voice that vibrated all the right places inside her. Such a nice man. Maybe, when they returned to San Francisco and had Harriet all stowed away, he'd ask her to dinner again, at one of those swank restaurants. Real high-tone, like her father used to say. She'd wear her blue satin, the one with the plunging neckline, and then she blushed, just thinking about wearing it to dinner, wearing it with Quincy.

But then she straightened in the saddle. Why *shouldn't* she wear it? Good gravy, she'd paid thirty-two dollars and seventy-five cents for it—at Grady's insistence, she hastened to add, though he'd never so much as seen her in it. She'd only worn it twice, and it was bound to go out of fashion soon. At that price, she should be wearing it every day!

The thought of dragging blue satin through the mud while running after felons and tackling burglars and riding after kidnappers—then dazzling them into submission with her décolletage—tickled her and she let out a little hiccup of laughter.

Ahead, Pete reined in and twisted in his saddle. "Ma'am?"

She shook her head, still smiling. "Nothing, Pete."

"No, ma'am, I mean, they stopped here."

She had been so lost in blue satin that she hadn't been paying attention. That would teach her to daydream. She said, "They certainly did, didn't they?," got down off her horse, and walked out into the light of the clearing. Pete followed.

"There was a fight," she said, as she bent to the crushed and uprooted weeds. A few drops of blood had dried on a patch of brown needles. She stood up and began to walk in circles, eyes flicking over the ground. "Three of them came in. That would be Harriet and the two kidnappers. And they rested here for a while. Harriet was there."

She pointed to a depressed place in the grass, and Biscuit Pete brightened, then frowned.

"It don't look like she moved much." He looked up, concern denting a small furrow in his brow. "She's all right, ain't she?"

After spending the entire day with Biscuit Pete—the last few hours alone—she was finding him incredibly annoying. She almost snapped back, "How the devil should I know?" but she tempered herself. He couldn't help being stupid. So she said, as to a child, "She was probably passed out, Pete. Drunk."

Strangely, this seemed to make him happy. He said, "Oh. Okay," and went back to quietly holding the horses.

Well, it took all kinds.

Maggie continued to walk the clearing. Their mysterious fourth rider had come through, too. Had halted his horse in the center of the clearing—probably looked around, just like she was doing. And then he'd mounted up and ridden off to the west, in the wake of two riders.

The third had . . . She bent closer, really looked at the boot-prints. She'd seen them before, but she'd just assumed they belonged to one of the outlaws. But they didn't. They weren't even bootprints.

Suddenly she slapped a hand against her temple. How could she have ever confused those low-heeled, flat-footed city shoes with boots! Grady. Tiny shivers began shooting up her spine.

Grady had been here, too. How or why, she couldn't imagine. Well, yes, she could. He'd gone and got himself good and lost, and he'd lost his horse, too. But what on earth had he been doing mixed up with these boys?

His trail exited the clearing, moving east, and he was walking. The tracks of a single horse—a mounted man?—followed his footprints.

Suddenly the shivers turned to ice.

Quickly, she went to Biscuit Pete and snatched her reins from his hand. "C'mon," she said tersely, swinging up into the saddle. Without waiting for Pete, she reined toward the trees, patting her pocket unconsciously to check that the Colt was still there.

Pete caught up with her about twenty yards back into the woods. The scuffled tracks and stripped brush told her a horse had been tied to a sapling for a time. Grady and the second horse had walked right to it, and then the two horses moved out together, Grady still afoot. The tracks wove ahead of them, through the woods.

"I think it's all right," she said, although for the life of her, she could not imagine how he'd done it. "I think Hattie's with—"

Distantly, a gun barked twice, its thin report echoing off the tree trunks, the bare, upthrusting rocks.

Pete was already turning his horse toward the sound.

"No," said Maggie, and her voice was deadly serious. "Whoever was trailing those boys found them. And I've got a feeling he'll be coming for Harriet next."

Maggie leading this time, they set off through the trees, following Grady's trail.

It didn't take them long.

After ten or twelve minutes of skittering down slopes and circumventing fallen trees and boulders, they spotted Grady through the trees. He was trying to lift Harriet off the ground and back on her horse.

Holding the unconscious girl under her arms like a giant rag doll, he glanced up as they rode in, a perturbed expression on his sweaty face. His glasses were fogged, and he seemed to have lost his jacket. "Well, it's about time," he said, puffing.

"Nice to see you, too," Maggie replied with a straight face, then crooked her finger at Pete. "Help him, would you?"

With a muttered "yes'm," Pete stepped down off his horse and went to Grady, taking the limp Harriet from him with almost no effort and lifting her up, across the saddle. If she hadn't known he was wounded, his actions certainly wouldn't have given him away.

"We're not going to make it to town," Maggie said.

"Thank you, oh, thank you," Grady said with a growl, ignoring her. "Yes, I managed to rescue her myself, at great peril to life and limb. But it was no trouble at all, I assure you."

"You can tell me all about it later, Grady." Maggie was watching Biscuit Pete tie Harriet to the saddle. He was the strangest man, really. He'd professed his love and said he wanted to marry her, yet he was hitching her to that saddle like she was a deer he'd just shot.

She turned her attention back to Grady. "I think we heard somebody shoot those two fellows. There were two, weren't there? That you met in the clearing?"

Grady was polishing his glasses. "It's not fair, Maggie. I never get to tell you anything." He held them up to the fading light, then gave them another rub and settled them back on his face. "I didn't hear any shots."

Biscuit Pete had finished securing Harriet, and he swung back up on his horse. "Sounds are tricky up here," he muttered.

"We'd better find a good place. A cave or something." She studied the sky, where it peeked through the treetops. It would be dark within an hour. "Something easy to defend. And we'd better find it soon. Pete?"

He studied on it for a moment. "Ain't no caves," he said, shaking his head. Then, "How 'bout a mine shaft?"

"Lovely," said Maggie. "Grady, you'd better mount up."

"Not on your life," he said, picking up his horse's reins and Harriet's. "Well? Lead on!"

"You know the way, Pete," Maggie said. He set off at an angle, and they followed.

Grady walked beside Maggie's horse. "Do you know a gentleman named Garrett?"

"Know some, know of more," she said, trying to keep her eyes on the surrounding woods as well as to the path Pete was cutting. "Bob Garrett over at Acme Indemnity. Then there's Booger Nose Bart Garrett. Used to run a badger game with Eva Muller. There was Evil Eye Garrett, who used to mesmerize his victims. And Little Jimmy Garrett, down at the docks, and his father, Big Jimmy, of course, and—"

"Stop," said Grady. He really was limping, and she felt sorry for him, but there was nothing she could do until they got to a safe place. He said, "I mean a Garrett who kills people. They were waiting for him. They thought I was him."

Quickly he told her the details of what had happened, and if she could have stopped the horse long enough to get down and hug him, she would have. And then she would have smacked him for taking such a big chance. Even she wouldn't have been foolhardy enough to just walk into their camp.

Well, maybe not.

"You'll be the death of me yet," she said when he finished. "You know that, don't you?"

He snorted, but she noticed he was smiling. He said, "And what have you and God's gift to sheep been up to?"

She laughed out loud, then slapped a hand over her mouth. "Grady!" she scolded, when she thought she could talk again. And then she told him.

And when she finished, he said, "How did you know that I wasn't in the fight and lying somewhere, beat to a bloody pulp?"

"Because your tracks walked straight over the battle scene, that's how. I take it Case and Kramer had a small disagreement?"

"Correct. And how did you know I had Harriet?"

Maggie shrugged. "Didn't at first. Watch out for that—"

A sapling smacked Grady in the face.

"Branch," Maggie said, too late.

Straightening his glasses, Grady plucked free a leaf that was caught on his watch chain and grumbled, "Aspen. A change of pace from pine needles, at any rate. And what do you mean, you didn't know at first?"

"Not until we found where you'd tied your mare." She nodded at the riderless horse plodding behind him.

"And you came after me instead of Hattie?"

"Hattie could have been either—"

"Maggie, you know perfectly well I can take care of myself!" he said angrily. "Given a year or two, I would have found my way down off this mountain—"

"Hill."

"All right, *hill*. I would have found my way down just fine." He walked on a few steps. "Maggie?"

"Yes, Grady?"

"I don't suppose you'd have an extra sandwich on you?"

From up ahead, Biscuit Pete chose that moment to call, "She's just up ahead."

Grady craned his head up toward Maggie. "She?"

"He means the mine."

"Oh."

They came out of the trees into a tiny clearing, perhaps twenty feet across, that brush and saplings were already reclaiming. Before them the hill rose up dramatically, and into its face was cut a squarish, yawning mouth that was haphazardly boarded over, though most of the boards had fallen to the ground. Someone had painted the words "Keep Out" on one of them, and sketched a crude skull and crossbones on another.

"Ah," said Grady. "Nevada's answer to the Palace Hotel, I presume?"

Rolling her eyes, Maggie followed Pete's lead and stepped down off her horse. A stream was close by, for she could hear the sound of rushing water coming through the trees. She hooked her stirrup up over the saddle horn and began to loosen the girth. She said, "Let's get the tack off these horses, then you boys can get Harriet inside. I'll water the horses and fill the canteens."

She was just sliding the saddle down when a creamy voice that belonged to no one in the party said, "That's a good idea, my dear. All except the part where you go to the creek, of course."

Standing half shadowed in the mouth of the mine was a tall, blond man in his late forties, with a pistol in each hand. He was pointing one of them at Pete, the other at Grady, and he was smiling at her.

TWENTY-FIVE

"YOUR GUNS, GENTLEMEN?" HE WAS LEAN BUT POW-erful, and dressed much like Grady, except for the boots and the fact that he still had his suit coat and derby hat. "Kick them over, if you'd be so kind?" he said to Pete, who had obediently dropped his pistols to the ground.

"And you," he said to Grady, in a voice that was low and smooth and strangely lulling. Like warm pudding, Maggie thought.

Grady held out his hands to show they were empty, but the man, who could be no one else but Garrett, clucked his tongue and said, "Back of the pants, Mr. Maguire. That's it, nice and easy. If you'd kick it over, please?"

He hadn't asked for Maggie's gun. But then, how would he know she had one? Come to think of it, how would he know Grady was armed? Until Garrett had mentioned it, she'd still assumed Grady's short-barrel was in his saddlebags.

"Over there, now, gentlemen," Garrett said, motioning with the barrel of one gun. "Together, if you'd be so kind?" He holstered one of his pistols, and keeping an eye on Grady and Biscuit Pete, kicked their guns back into the darkness of the mine shaft.

He said, "And you, miss." Again, the little gesture with the gun's barrel. She moved over with the others, but he mo-tioned her back. "Just so I can see you. About five feet to the side, if you please." His voice was like caramel and custard, flowing thickly over her mind.

"How'd you get in front of us?" she asked with some effort, playing for time. He'd killed those two men. He was going to kill them, too.

He smiled, exposing white, even teeth. "It was easy. I could have ridden around you on a tortoise. If you gentlemen will be so kind as to sit down?"

Biscuit Pete and Grady sat. Pete's eyes were locked to the man's. Grady sat, blinking.

"You're very tired," said Garrett, his voice like water in the desert. "You gentlemen could use some sleep. Some nice, deep sleep. And Maggie needs to relax." Maggie felt herself wavering, then suddenly she dug nails into her palms. No! She knew who he was, or at the very least she knew what he did. Another few seconds and Grady and Pete would be no good to her.

"Relax," said Garrett. "You've had a hard day. A very hard day indeed."

Pete's head sagged on his shoulders. Grady began to nod. Still standing, Maggie said, "But you knew where we were going."

"Voices carry in the woods," he said, and his voice sounded melodic, strangely rich and inviting. To the men, he said, "You're very sleepy. Your eyelids are so heavy. They're weighted, heavy, so sleepy. You can't hold them up any longer. There, that's right. That's good. So comfortable. So pleasant. You hear only my voice, only my voice, only my soothing, calming voice."

Grady was fighting it, she could tell, but Garrett consoled, "Why, you're all worn out, Grady. So tired. You deserve some peace. Some rest. Some sleep. Some deep, deep, sleep. Deep, deep, deeper, deeper."

Beneath her skirts, Maggie stepped on one foot with the other, digging her heel down, and began to silently recite the catechism. Even though she knew, she asked, "What . . . what are you doing?" Her face felt numb, as if she were talking through a mask. She switched from the catechism to the multiplication tables. Two times two is four. Two times three is six. Two times four is . . . is . . .

"Why, I'm easing your friends into a trance, Maggie." Grady's head dropped to his chest, his glasses sliding down his nose. "Now I'm going to let them sleep forever, and then we'll have some fun while I wait for Miss Hogg to wake up. And sober up. Your legs are so stiff now, Maggie. Why, they feel as if they've turned to stone. You can't move them at all, now, can you?"

"No," she answered, her voice small. And with what part of her brain was still functioning, she thought, *Concentrate on what he's doing, damnit! Analyze it. Think about the process. Grade him against your own performance.*

"You can put your hands down, now, Maggie. It's awfully warm. Terribly warm. It's so hot you're sweating through your dress. Be a shame to ruin it, now, wouldn't it? Why don't you unbutton your dress?"

Slowly, she let her hands drop. She fumbled with the buttons at her waist, numbly thinking how good he was. The power of suggestion. Don't demand, suggest. Don't order, ask. The subject would always comply. *Oh, yes, he's superb,* she thought groggily. She'd give him an "A." She was going under. Analysis wasn't working, at least not well enough. She turned her thoughts to a song, a popular song, one she found hideously irritating.

"That's good," he crooned. His voice was at the perfect pitch. Melted butter, flowing over her. An "A+."

The song. Think about the song. *Hinka-chinka Chinee-man, Ugga-wugga Injun Sam, Inky-stinky macaroni . . .* Feh! Despicable! Now the tune was all she could hear. *How'd you get your hair so squirrely, In a braid just like a girly. . . .*

He said, "Very good. Keep going. It's so terribly hot. And now, I'll just take care of your friends."

Her head was clear of everything but the song now. It was past annoying, and she was almost wishing he'd shoot her so she could get rid of it.

Carefully, he took aim at Grady, bracing the pistol with both hands.

Swiftly, Maggie reached into her pocket (*Hinka-chinka, Chinee-man*), knowing the gun was on an empty chamber and hoping she could fire in time. Before he saw her, she brought it out and pulled the trigger once, on the swing up, to an empty click. And by the time he wheeled toward her, a mixture of rage and disbelief on his face, she'd leveled the gun and fanned it twice more. (*Ugga-wugga Injun Sam . . .*)

This time the chamber wasn't empty.

He dropped to his knees in the mud, staring at her.

"I hate that song," she said under her breath.

The gun fell from his fingers, his lips forming a silent, "How?" And then he toppled face forward, to the ground.

She went to him and kicked his gun away. She poked him with her shoe, though with that messy exit wound he couldn't be alive.

"It takes a carnie to beat a carnie, that's how," she muttered, bending to roll him over. (*Hinka-chinka Chinee-man, Ugga-wugga Injun Sam . . .* Drat it!) She finally managed it, and he flopped onto his back. The slug had gone through his heart.

Could this be Evil Eye Garrett? She'd never heard tell of anyone else mesmerizing their victims. She dug through his pockets, finding several expensive trinkets, and finally his wallet. *Chauncey Garrett,* his card read. *Stage Work and Private Matters.*

She stood up and wiped her hands on her skirts. These days, she was used to the sight of dead bodies. Well, as used to them as she ever expected to be. But this one—not to mention the song, which kept repeating in her brain—filled her with repugnance. She supposed there was something to be said for anesthetizing one's victims before the final strike, but fair play demanded they have at least a chance to fight back.

Especially when their killer was such a lousy shot that he had to immobilize his victims first.

She got up and began to drag Grady, then Pete, into what looked like more comfortable positions. And she thought, as she loosened Grady's tie and vest and stuck his glasses in his vest pocket, that it all harked back to her days with Pinkerton, and the day he'd blown up the James house. That had been unfair, too, especially to the little boy he'd killed.

She stood up, staring at Pete and Grady, blissfully snoring in the weeds, and not likely to be awake for some time unless she could manage to imitate Garrett's voice, which she could not. She wondered: If she had been there that night, the night that the Pinkertons bombed the James gang's home, would she have shot Allan Pinkerton to keep him from ordering the bomb hurled?

On the horse behind her, Harriet moaned. Maggie went to her and began the unstrapping process, tugging at the bonds that cut into Harriet's arms and legs, and silently cursing Pete for having been so enthusiastic. *(Inky-stinky macaroni . . .)*

"Whiskey," Harriet breathed as Maggie slid her from the horse's back and dragged her to the mouth of the mine shaft, to the beat of that stupid, degrading, ridiculous song.

Harriet was alive and well and oblivious to the four deaths that had taken place this day: four deaths today and poor little Corinne yesterday, all for the sake of a drunken, illiterate ragamuffin. Maggie leaned over her. "What is it, Harriet? What's your story?"

The presence of the late Chauncey "Evil Eye" Garrett presented Maggie with a whole new slew of questions. Why in heaven's name would Ralphie hire a mesmerist?

This was the question she asked herself as she led the horses down to water. Why, out of the hundreds of hired guns available for a drink and thirty dollars, had Ralphie hired this man? She knew he didn't come cheap. And judging from Ralphie's payroll habits with his men—25 percent to those incompetents!—he'd probably promised Garrett the moon.

Why a mesmerist, why someone so specialized? Harriet had been an Indian captive since she was a child of six. She barely remembered the English language, let alone the rudiments of hygiene. What could be locked up inside her that was so important?

Garrett had very kindly tied his horse—and the two belonging to the hapless slickers—down by the stream, and she led them, along with the others, back up through the trees to the mine shaft's opening, all the while trying to beat the song—that horrible, hideous song!—from her mind. By the time she finished stripping them of their tack and scrounging through the saddlebags for feed, it was dark, and she was still stuck on *how'd you get your hair so squirrely.*

She chewed on a piece of jerky she found in Garrett's saddlebags while she scraped together some deadwood and kindling. And then, just inside the mouth of the shaft, she nursed them into flame. Harriet, stretched out on the other side of the burgeoning fire, mumbled softly in Apache and twitched.

Grady and Pete snoring in the background, she stepped over Garrett's body and began to search the ground. As she searched, wandering back into the trees, she tried singing a new song under her breath to counteract the hinka-chinka one—"The Six-Penny Waltz" was good—and she turned the questions over and over in her head.

What could Harriet know that was so important? Maybe she didn't know anything at all. Maybe Ralphie was just incomprehensively inept at hiring his people. But maybe Ralphie hadn't hired him at all, maybe someone else was involved.

No. It was Ralphie. Had to be. No one else could possibly profit from Harriet's death. But then, they weren't killing her, were they? They'd gone to great pains to keep her alive.

Having found what she was looking for—and having switched to "Mighty Max O'Banyon" since "The Six-Penny Waltz" kept turning into the hinka-chinka song—she went back toward the fire to find Harriet flat on her belly and cozied up to Garrett's stiffening body.

"You buy Hattie Backwash, cowboy?" she slurred to his staring profile, her eyes swollen and slitted.

"I don't think you're going to have much luck there," Maggie said, stepping over Garrett's corpse, then bending to close his eyes. Unnerving, him staring like that. Like he was still trying to mesmerize her from the Great Beyond.

"Hattie give ride?"

Maggie stepped to the side and sat down, cross-legged, and reached into her pockets. "Go back to sleep, Harriet. You've got a big day ahead of you."

Harriet put her head down, more out of drunkenness than obedience, Maggie suspected, and began to breathe heavily, her mouth open.

Taking up the tune again, Maggie pulled the pine cones from her pockets, sorted them for size, and picked the best four. Then, snugging her back against the hillside, she began to juggle as she sang, "Mighty Max O'Banyon went in twilight to the glade, Downward in the gloaming to meet his fairy maid. . . ."

FRIDAY, JUNE 8

W E MUST MAKE SOME KIND OF PICTURE, MAGGIE thought as they rode into Bent Elbow late the next morning. She was leading Harriet's horse—Harriet herself being tied into the saddle and too sick and delirious to navigate—with the kidnappers' horses, tied nose to tail, following. Grady was behind her, probably still standing in the stirrups, and tied behind his horse was Garrett's bay—Garrett's body strapped across it—and a glassy-eyed Biscuit Pete, riding Nickel. Just barely.

By the time they reached the sheriff's office, they'd gathered a little crowd.

Maggie swung down off her horse and put a hand to the small of her back. She'd give anything to crawl into a nice goose feather bed and sleep for a week. Her own goose feather bed, if at all possible.

Well, it wouldn't be long now. A goose feather bed. Nice, clean hardwood floors. Soft rugs, Ozzie purring in her ear, a good book, indoor plumbing. Lord, she'd kill for indoor plumbing.

She hitched her horse to the rail, said "Shoo!" to a kid who'd wandered too close, and proceeded to untie Harriet, who was, at least, too sick to complain.

Grady had dismounted, too, and walked toward her stiffly, scratching an insect bite on his neck. Blood stained his pants at the ankles and made damp, rusty spots at the insides of his knees.

"Oh, Grady," Maggie said. "You're a mess. I'm so sorry."

"I don't know how you stand it," he said, then to the gawkers, "Go home, please. Go on. Scat!"

Just then Harriet toppled into Maggie's arms, and she said, "Help!" Grady leapt to aid her with the girl, although it seemed a miracle he could move at all after what she'd put him through. As they dragged Harriet to the sidewalk, she thought it might be a good idea, once they got back to San Francisco, to treat him to a night on the town or something. And maybe a bucket of liniment here. No, not liniment, she thought with a cringe, imagining the fire when it hit those open sores.

She propped Harriet's head against the hitching post and said, "How I stand what?"

Grady grimaced. "The great outdoors. Mud. Bugs. Sleeping on the ground. I won't mention armed killers."

She shrugged. As bad as she felt for Grady, never in a million years would she admit she'd been yearning for a soft bed and a flush toilet. Ignoring the question, she nodded toward Biscuit Pete, who was struggling to get off his horse but couldn't seem to remember how. "Help him, would you? That trance is sure taking a long time to wear off. And keep an eye on Harriet."

Slowly, Grady moved toward Pete, muttering something lengthy—and very probably profane—under his breath.

Maggie went into the sheriff's office.

Sopsucher was sitting at his desk, eating peppermints. "Who's the dead one?" He offered her the bag, and she noticed that his knuckles were bruised. Probably from a door banging him as he exited, she thought with a sniff.

She waved the bag away. "Why don't you come out and see?"

"No need. I reckon you can tell me. He's more Clem Hastings's business now." He bit down on the candy in his mouth. Maggie could hear him crunching from across the desk.

"Aren't you going to send for him, then?"

He reached into the bag for another mint. "Oh, he will've heard. Be up here anytime now. Who's the deceased?"

"One Chauncey Garrett," she said, digging the contents of his pockets out of hers and placing them on the desk. "Better known as Evil Eye Garrett. I shot him, purely out of self-preservation, you understand. And there are three more bodies

up in the hills. Two of them, he shot. Grady says they were
called Case and Kramer. The other one—that was Sully Monroe—was killed by the aforementioned Case and Kramer.
You'll have to go up after them.''

Nodding, Sopsucher sucked the peppermint into his mouth.
''Reckon we can do 'er this afternoon. Case and Kramer and
Monroe, you say?''

Maggie nodded.

The sheriff stared out the window for a second. ''Never
heard tell of any of 'em.'' He turned back toward Maggie and
waved a hand toward the spare chair. ''Why don't you take a
load off and tell me why the hell all these fellas are murderin'
each other.''

Sopsucher continued to crunch peppermints while Maggie
told him what had happened up in the hills, although she didn't
know why she bothered. He didn't seem to be listening to a
word of it.

When she finished, he held out the sack of candy again and
said, ''You sure?'' When she shook her head, he rolled the
top up neatly and stuck the bag away in a drawer. ''Bad habit.
Gonna rot my choppers for sure. You say these fellas were
gettin' a percentage. Ten and ten and five and you ain't sure
how much for Garrett. That right?''

He had been listening after all. She said, ''That's correct.''

''So that's twenty-five plus something. Let's figure another
ten for that Garrett fella. Likely more, him bein' so specialized
and all, but let's say ten for the sake of argument. So that's
thirty-five percent you're up to so far. With Festing's fifteen,
that makes—''

Maggie stood up. ''What?''

He motioned her down. ''I know you don't figure I do much
besides sit on my backside, missy.''

The ''missy'' grated, but she decided to let it pass. She said,
''Tom Festing got fifteen percent? For what? You said that
neither of those shacks we looked at belonged to him. He
wasn't even in town when Harriet was kidnapped. . . .'' She
stared blankly out the window for a moment, considering the
possibilities, then turned back to the sheriff. ''Who hired him,
and when? Was it Ralph Scaggs?''

Sopsucher held up his hands. "Just slow down there, gal. One thing at a time. See, I had me a little talk with Festing yesterday afternoon. Didn't want to say much at first, but he kind of got convinced."

Maggie glanced at his knuckles again, and he covered the bruises with his other hand and shrugged. "Well, I never much liked him, anyway. Skinny little two-faced back-East weasel's butt, tryin' to take over my town. . . ." He glared past Maggie's shoulder.

"And?"

"What? Oh. Well, the short version is that somebody offered Festing a bunch of money if—"

"Who hired him?" Maggie broke in.

"Not your Ralph Scaggs. Festing looked real vacant when I described him. Way he told it—finally—it was a real average man, brown and brown."

"Height?"

"Between five-foot-eight and five-foot-ten."

Maggie slumped back in her chair. "Average."

"Yes'm. Though he was still pretty vague. I'm beginnin' to wonder if maybe he wasn't hired by your fella out there." He nodded toward Garrett's body. "Anyway, he was offered fifteen percent of three hundred and fifty thousand. By my reckoning, that's—"

"Fifty-two thousand, five hundred!" Maggie interrupted with a snort. Imagine handing out that kind of money!

"Fifty-two thousand, five hundred dollars," Sopsucher repeated testily. "If he'd sort of look the other way, and maybe take care of the moppin' up afterward. Well, he couldn't pass up that kind of money. Who could? Seein' as how he was thinkin' about runnin' for sheriff—that *was* thinkin' about it—he figured the best thing to do was just leave town. Thought maybe he'd come back and run for governor, though why anybody'd want to be governor with all that loot's beyond me. Hell, I just woulda said screw the whole damn place and bought me Texas or something. Anyway, he did what he did, the dumb son of a bitch—'scuse me—and when he come back to town and found out those other boys had loused it up—"

"Did he know them?" Maggie cut in.

"Only seen but the one who come to his office that night. Listen, do you mind if I finish?"

Maggie sucked in her lips and crossed her arms.

"Anyways, when he found out, he directed 'em to the hotel. And you folks. But he swore it wasn't one of his boys shootin' at your windows. Still got to puzzle that out." He turned to stare out the window again. "What's Biscuit Pete doin' out there?"

Maggie looked, too. "Sitting," she replied. "Garrett's whammy hit him hard. He's still a little dazed."

Sopsucher shook his head. "No, I mean, what's he doin' ridin' with you?"

"Why, he's—"

The office door banged open and Clem Hastings, dressed formally in undertaker's black, stuck his top-hatted head in. "Okay to take him?"

Sopsucher nodded. "Name's Garrett. Chauncey Garrett."

Hastings took a little black book from his pocket and scribbled with the nub of a pencil. "Spelling?"

Maggie picked the card up off the desk and handed it to him.

He said, "Don't suppose you'd have a date of birth? For the stone."

Sopsucher looked at her and she shrugged. He said, "You're on your own, Clem."

Clem Hastings slammed the door behind him and the sheriff winced in advance of it, as if Clem were in the habit of slamming things. He turned back toward Maggie. "Where was I?"

"You were asking about Biscuit Pete. He shot through my window, Sheriff. He admitted it. It seems he's sweet on Harriet, and he was trying to scare me away. He didn't understand what was going on."

Sopsucher sat back in his chair, folding his arms across his stomach. "Now, that's right odd," he said, pursing his lips.

"Why so? It seems perfectly normal to me. Well, not shooting at an open window, perhaps. But normal that he'd want to ride along to rescue her."

"Maybe so. I suppose you're right. 'Cept I never heard that Biscuit Pete was sweet on her. Not no more than any other whore in town, anyway. But I guess I can't keep my finger on everythin' that goes on around here. I expect he was a good'un to take along, though. Mighty slick with that six-gun.'' He straightened a little, then said, ''So. You folks goin' to leave our fair city?''

Maggie smiled. ''Don't look so hopeful, Sheriff. I don't know that it's safe to travel with her.''

''Why? Seems to me the boys who was out after her have all killed themselves off. With a little help from you.''

She stood up and propped her hands on the back of the chair. ''Crooks are like roaches, Sheriff. Where you see one, there are a lot more.''

''Gosh,'' he said, in such a manner that she couldn't tell whether he was putting her on or really serious. ''Wish I'd thought of that.''

She chose to ignore the comment. ''I believe that Evil Eye Garrett was trying to get information from Hattie. Exactly what, I don't know. But we're going to sober her up again, and then I'll have a crack at her.''

He cocked a brow. ''You know how to spellbind a person?''

She smiled, on surer ground. ''My father ran a carnival, Sheriff. One of our acts, for about a summer, was Mesmo the Magnificent. I'm a little rusty, but I'm willing to give it a whirl.''

She glanced outside. Garrett's body was gone, and so were Grady and Harriet, probably back to the hotel. Biscuit Pete was weaving away, leaving the string of horses, half of them still tied nose to tail and trailing out across the street to block what traffic there was. She said, ''Oh. I forgot to tell you about the bartender.'' Quickly, she gave him the highlights. ''Maybe you should check it out. Find out who that woman is. It's probably nothing, but . . .''

He puffed out his cheeks, then let the air out with a *whoosh*. ''Maybe later.''

Well, she'd told him. She said, ''Should I take the horses down to the livery?''

Sopsucher put his feet up on the desk, in obvious preparation for a nap. ''Nope. Leave 'em. Somebody'll tell Hiram, down to the livery.'' He closed his eyes.

''Are we finished?''

''For now, I reckon.''

TWENTY-SIX

A T THE KID CONCHO HOTEL, JIM CAULDER WALKED
into Cora Trimble's room without knocking. "They're
back," he announced, and Cora could hear the relief
in his voice. "Pete Soda rode back in with them. I still can't
figure that out. And they brought Garrett in, slung over a
horse."

She was sitting beside the window, taking the air and peeling an apple. She didn't get up, seeing no need to discomfit
herself. She said, "Dead, I assume?"

"Yes."

She smiled. "I knew we could count on Miss Maguire. Pity
they didn't get Soda, too, but then, I suppose we can't have
everything. 'If wishes were horses,' and so on."

"Now what?"

She paused, the peel in a long curl trailing almost to the
floor, and looked up at him. "You're so antsy, Jim. Just calm
down."

"But this is big, Cora. This is the biggest case I've ever
been on!"

A big case? How many cases had he been on, anyway?
Five? Seven? Calmly, she said, "It's been that way from the
start."

"Yes, but now with Garrett on ice, that is, I mean—"

"Now that you believe we might actually come through
with the goods?"

Caulder nodded. "Well, yes, actually."

"And everybody's going to be proud of you?" she said,

attending to her apple—the peel was growing longer now. "And you'll get a raise and everybody will call you a hero and the president will pin a big shiny medal on your chest?"

"Sort of. Yes."

Sighing, she set the paring knife in her lap, the apple alongside it. "There won't be any medals, Jimmy boy. No presidents, no marching bands. If we should happen to bring it in, it'll be kept quiet. You'll be asked to sign a paper saying you never heard of it."

Caulder's brow furrowed. "What?"

"That's the spirit," she said, keeping her face straight. He was so young, so filled with enthusiasm. She hated to be the one to kick the slats out from under him, but it had to be done.

"If anyone is thanked at all," she continued, "it will be our fearless leader, and that in a closed room at night in the rear of the White House. Because, if the truth be told, we haven't solved this case. We've had it for almost twenty years, and haven't solved it yet. Still might not. It's an embarrassment. And if we should solve it, it'll be on account of Miss Maguire and that insurance agency."

"But—"

"No buts." She picked up the apple again. It was almost done. "All we've done is follow her. And we'll continue to do so for however long it takes. You want to do something, you can go to the stage office and get me a schedule. I imagine we'll be pulling out of here tomorrow."

"You think she's leaving?"

"I would. Whether Garrett had time to rattle anything loose in Harriet's skull or not, Miss Maguire is bound to have figured out something's not quite on the square. My guess is that she'll try to mesmerize Harriet herself. Either way, she'll get out of town, probably tomorrow. North, to Sky Butte."

She was concentrating on the apple, but she knew Caulder was making a face. "It's not fair," he said at last. "Not fair at all. And how could she possibly—"

"Next time, read the dossier," Cora said, cutting him off. "Miss Maguire has many unique talents, mesmerism among them. And we have ours. The main one of which, currently, is to sit on our backsides and let her do the work for us. Now, go get me that stage schedule.''

Cora finished the apple at the same moment the door closed behind Agent Caulder. She held the peel up, a red spring, and smiled.

TWENTY-SEVEN

>━┼◆━◯━◆┼━<

THAT EVENING, GRADY STOOD IN THE LAMPLIT HALL-way, waiting for Maggie to tell him it was all right to come in. He stood because he couldn't do anything else. Never in his entire life had he been so cruelly bruised and abraded, so physically insulted. With each step, he felt as if his skin were being sandpapered by a three-hundred-pound carpenter in a hurry, and he ached down deep in his bones.

He wanted nothing more than to hobble back across the hall and lock himself in that dingy hotel room and lie prone for a week and a half. He had decided it would take at least that amount of time before he could move without screaming. And then he wanted to go home to San Francisco and never, never, ever leave it again.

He'd thought it was bad yesterday, but a night spent sleeping on mud and rocks followed by another morning in the saddle had just about done him in. As it was, when Maggie had called him, saying she thought Harriet was sober enough—and suggestible enough—it had taken him a full three minutes to slowly squirm his way, like a sprained snake, to the edge of the bed.

Standing up had taken another three minutes.

And so now he was propped in the hallway, waiting for Maggie the Mesmerizing to cast her spell over Harriet the Hopeless, and find out exactly nothing.

When Maggie was finished—which he trusted she'd be very soon, because he was certain Hattie wouldn't remember a thing, no matter how much faith Maggie placed in this hocus-

pocus—he'd fall on his bed once more and have Eddie run
and get him a bottle of good whiskey.

Good thing his arms still worked well enough to hoist a
glass. Worked just fine, thank you very much. He wondered:
Could one drink on one's belly? Well, he was going to find
out. He was going to drink until he was too drunk to drink
anymore, and then he'd pass out of consciousness—and out
of the pain. And if he threw up, he'd just have to drown in it.

Maggie's door creaked open. She poked her head out and
said softly, "Come in, Grady."

Slowly, he began to move. Maggie crossed the room and
lit another candle. She'd only had one lit before, he saw. Probably used the light from the flame to heebie-jeebie Harriet,
who was lying on the bed. She looked to be sleeping. No bug-
eyes, no blank stare: Her eyes were closed and she was
breathing normally. He wasn't exactly sure what a body
looked for, but Harriet didn't look very spellbound to him.
Perhaps Maggie had failed after all.

The candle in her hand, Maggie turned around and said,
"It's all right, Grady. You can come in."

He said with a grunt, "I am. It just takes time."

Maggie gave him a sincerely kind look, the sort that almost
made him forgive her until he remembered it was the same
look she gave to three-legged dogs and lame cart horses. Quietly, she said, "I'll fix that up for you after we finish here.
And we'll send Eddie for some medicinal Scotch, if this burg
has such a thing."

Scotch? He brightened somewhat. She must really be feeling guilty. He put on his best hurt-puppy face.

Maggie whispered, "She went under just fine. Guess I'm
not so rusty, after all. I've suggested that she can only hear
my voice when she's addressed directly. Why don't you sit—
well, you can lean against the bureau."

He did, putting his weight on his elbows. It helped a little.
"Ready when you are."

"I think you're going to be surprised, Grady."

"Amaze me."

Maggie perched on the bed opposite Harriet's. "Harriet, can
you hear me?"

"Yes."

The tone of voice was so different from normal that for a moment he thought someone else was in the room.

"Harriet, I want you to go back, go back in time, far back, before the Indians came, when you lived with your real mama and daddy. I'm going to count to three, and when I snap my fingers, you'll be there. One, two, three." Maggie snapped her fingers.

Harriet's face changed from relaxed to soft to crabby. "Can't find Annie," she said suddenly, in a singsong sort of baby talk.

"Is Annie your doll, Harriet?" Maggie's voice was low and even.

"My kitty. Can't find her anyplace."

"How old are you, Harriet?"

"Four. Will you find her? She goes behind the coal bin sometimes."

Grady was amazed, quite frankly. He watched and listened, almost forgetting his bruises, as Maggie promised to look for the cat, then gently brought Harriet forward through time, little by little. She was having little success discovering what, if anything, was hidden in Harriet's brain that had caused the deaths of four men and a woman, but the process was fascinating.

She'd gotten Harriet up to her sixth birthday, now, and Harriet was describing the party and the cake and the presents. Dear Daddy Horace, it seemed, was not present, having departed for the Northeast better than a year back, but he'd sent her an Indian doll.

And Harriet's tone was much changed. She sounded like a very sophisticated young lady, extremely well spoken for six years old. Her speech was certainly nothing like her normal pidgin-English patois.

"Harriet," Maggie was saying, "did your daddy ever tell you a secret?"

He was about to tell Maggie that she was really reaching now, when Harriet smiled, and across the room, he leaned forward.

"Was it a good secret?"

"Yes." The smile opened into a grin.

"Can you tell me?"

Harriet's lips tightened. "It's a *secret,*" she said, as if talking to a dolt.

Maggie tipped her head back, staring at the ceiling, and Grady wondered how she was going to work her way around this one. Had Horace, all those years ago, told Harriet something worth the lives of five people?

Suddenly Maggie's head came down. She said, "Harriet, your daddy's here. He wants to talk to you."

Grady started to look behind him until he realized she meant him. He shot her a pleading look, but she only smiled back and said, "You can hear your daddy now, Harriet. He's right here."

For the life of him, Grady couldn't think what to say. Maggie made a little hurry-up motion with her hand and Harriet said, "Daddy?"

Silently, Maggie mouthed, "Grady!"

"Um, hello, Harriet," he began.

"Daddy!" The delight on the young woman's face struck him almost painfully.

"Yes, Harriet. Daddy's here."

Maggie was nodding encouragement.

"Do you remember that secret I told you?"

Harriet nodded. "Yes, sir."

"You haven't told anybody, have you?"

"Not even Annie."

They'd found her cat, then. That made him feel better somehow. He said, "Tell Daddy the secret, Harriet," and felt like a cad. "Just so I know you didn't forget."

Suddenly serious for the test, Harriet recited, "Daddy will save Harriet from the Lake of Fire if she's good, because he knows Jesus. Daddy has coffee with him and they talk."

That stopped him. Apparently it stopped Maggie, too. She sat on the bed, scratching her chin.

Finally he said, "That's good, Harriet."

Maggie said, "Yes, that's good, Harriet, that's very good. Now, I want you to sleep, sleep until I snap my fingers again.

And when you wake up, you won't remember that your daddy was here. Do you understand?''

"Yes," said Harriet.

"You will remember what you and I talked about, and you'll remember how to speak correctly. Do you understand?''

"Yes."

Grady waved his hand till he caught Maggie's eyes. "No booze," he mouthed, and Maggie nodded.

"You will have no desire for liquor. The idea of whiskey will make you sick to your stomach. Do you understand?''

"Yes."

"All right. You're quite sleepy, Harriet. In fact, when I wake you from this trance, you'll be so tired that you'll nod off again and sleep until morning, when you'll awake fresh and full of vigor, and remembering what I've told you. Understand?''

"Yes," said Harriet.

"All right. On the count of three I'm going to snap my fingers. One, two, three."

Harriet's eyelids didn't spring wide at the snap, as Grady had thought they would, but slowly fluttered open. She looked around the room, blinking sleepily, then at Maggie, who had picked up her hand.

Maggie's fingertips soothed Harriet's brow, and she whispered, "Go to sleep, now."

Harriet yawned, and said, "Yes, ma'am." She rolled onto her side, and in no time was breathing deeply and evenly.

A moment later, Maggie and Grady were out in the hall. "This is not good," Maggie said, his arm over her shoulders, her arm around his waist. "Nothing! I didn't get anything out of her!"

"Oh, I don't know about that," said Grady. "I think she's a charming little girl. Or she was. Don't you think it's refreshing that Horace chattered with our Savior over crumpets and a cup of ground roast? I wonder if Christ prefers Colombian or Brazilian beans."

She opened his door.

"And really, Mags, you've got this hypnosis thing down pat. Should've gone on the stage. The Magnificent Magdalena or something. Did you say something about Scotch?''

Maggie helped him inside. "Shut up or I'll let you fall.''

There was a knock at the door, and Maggie threw the cover over Grady's bruised and raw and purple legs, and answered it. It was Eddie, with the Scotch. He handed it in, then gave over another, smaller bottle.

"What's this?'' she asked.

"Horse liniment. It'll burn like all heck, but it'll toughen him real good up for the next time.''

Behind her, Grady groaned, "Oh, God . . .''

Eddie sniffed the air. "Oh. You already used witch hazel,'' he added with a degree of disappointment before he added, "Sheriff Sopsucher just come in with the bodies.''

"That's good, Eddie.'' She handed the liniment back.

He didn't take it. "No, I mean, he come in *with* the bodies. He was one of 'em.''

From the bed, Grady said, "I beg your pardon?''

Maggie just stared.

"Yup,'' said Eddie with an air of sorrowed importance. "Whole town's real upset about it. The population was right fond of him. Ain't never gonna be another one like him.''

Maggie finally managed to ask, "What happened? He just went up there to collect the bodies, didn't he?''

Eddie nodded. "Yes'm. Went up the hill with Biscuit Pete and Wiley Shoop.''

"Pete wasn't in any condition to—''

"The sheriff and Wiley dunked him in a horse trough, ma'am. He was fine, then, right as rain. Well, kinda soggy, but they needed him to take 'em to where the bodies was layin'. The sheriff knows—I mean knew—them hills like the back of his hand, but there's a lot of territory to—''

"What happened?'' Maggie broke in. She set the whiskey down.

Behind her, Grady gave out a little frustrated grunt, and Eddie peeked around her.

"He's pretty bad, ain't he? Saddle get your knees, Mr. Maguire?''

Maggie stood her ground. "Eddie?''

"Oh. Well, Wiley tells it that the sheriff sent Pete to find them two. Chase and Kruger?"

As one, Grady and Maggie said, "Case and Kramer."

"Yeah, that's it. And he sent Wiley up to the shack to get, um . . ."

"Monroe," said Maggie.

"Yeah. And then he sat down and rolled himself a cigarette, and nobody saw him alive after that. Wiley said he never saw nothin'. Just went up to the shack and packed up Monroe— by the way, Clem Hastings asked me to ask you if that's got an 'e' on the end."

"I don't know, Eddie," said Maggie testily. "He didn't spell it for me. What about the sheriff?"

"Oh. Well, when he got back down—Wiley, that is—Biscuit Pete was just comin' in with them other two, and the sheriff was lyin' beside the very same tree they left him under, deader'n a hammer."

"Heart attack?" Maggie said, hoping fervently for natural causes.

But Eddie replied, "Shot clean through the head. Well, I guess it wasn't so clean. There's a lot of mess when a fella gets shot in the head," he said philosophically, " 'specially if it's a big caliber and comes out the other side like—"

Maggie stopped him. "Eddie."

"Oh. Sorry, ma'am. The mayor figures it was probably somebody from back in the olden times, holdin' a grudge. Tom Festing sure ain't sorry, though. He's having a party down to his place. Well, as good as he can, being so stove up and all."

Maggie asked, "What happened to Festing?" before she remembered he'd had a visit from Sopsucher.

"Somebody beat him up. Got a cast on his leg and a couple of black eyes and everything. I hear tell it was the sheriff that done it, but I don't know that I hold with that. He hasn't beat anybody up for two, three years, now." He shook his head slowly, then looked up. "Bent Elbow's never gonna see his like again, no, ma'am. The funeral's tomorrow, if you want to pay your respects."

"Thanks, Eddie. Good night." Maggie shoved the liniment

into his hands, then closed the door before he could tell her more about exit wounds.

"The plot thickens," said Grady, face-down in the pillows.

Maggie picked up the Scotch and sat down next to him. She poured him a drink, and then, after a slight hesitation, poured out one for herself and downed it in one gulp. It wouldn't help any—she wouldn't even feel it—but it seemed the thing to do.

Grady held out his glass again, and she handed him the bottle. She said, "Tell me it's a coincidence."

"It's a coincidence," he said obediently. He was propped on his elbows, balancing his glass on the pillow, and trying to pour. He looked up from his bottle. "All right, it's not a coincidence. What do you want to hear?"

Maggie sighed. "The truth, for a change. This case was so simple in the beginning! Find the heiress, clean her up, bring her back, collect the fee. The end. Period. Now I've got bodies falling every which way. Harriet knows something she doesn't *know* she knows, and I'll be damned if I can pry it out of her when I don't have a clue where to start. And the sheriff is dead, not to mention Case and Kramer and Monroe and Corinne. And Garrett. Grady, I'm beginning to think we ought to cut our losses and run."

Grady grunted. He'd managed to down his second drink and was pouring a third.

She said, "Hadn't you better slow down?"

He shook his head. "This is purely medicinal. I intend to become unconscious as quickly as humanly possible. Besides, it's wretched stuff." He sneered at the label. "The finest Scotch, bottled in Illinois. Ought to call it Old Argyle. Or New Argyle. Probably aged a grand total of the week it took it to get here. Best not to taste it."

He fumbled with the stopper and she helped him hold the bottle steady. "Thank you," he muttered, and downed the third glassful. "That should do it. Now I've just got to wait for it to kick in."

Maggie took the glass and placed it on the bed table, alongside the bottle and his spectacles. "You're not being any help. Tell me what to do."

He shrugged, or at least it looked like it. "You're the sixty percent, I'm only forty. You have the decision-making twenty percent."

"Grady!" Every time she asked for a teensy piece of advice, it was always the same thing.

"All right," he said. "Let's go."

"We can't," she said, standing up. "We still haven't found Ralphie. He's out there somewhere, hiring people left and right."

Grady crooked his arm under the pillow. "You don't know that."

"Well, I feel it. And I don't want to be trapped on a moving train."

"All right, then," he offered, yawning. "We'll stay."

"With the sheriff dead and somebody getting shot every five minutes?" Maggie clutched her elbows, working at them.

"See?" Grady said, his eyes slitted. "I didn't do you any good . . . at all. Thank you for tending my wounds, seeing as how"—another yawn—"seeing as how I couldn't lick them myself." His head sagged into the pillow.

"I don't know. I just don't know." Maggie was pacing, staring at the floor. "Maybe if I put Harriet under again. Maybe if I took her right up to the Indian attack. No, that might be too traumatic. I feel awful about the sheriff. He was a nice old bird, even if he was— Grady?"

He was asleep. Maggie blew out the lamp, picked up her bottle of witch hazel, then closed the door behind her and walked slowly across the hall, still wondering what to do.

SATURDAY, JUNE 9

>━┤━◆❯━◆━Ⓞ━◆━❮◆━┤━<

IN SKY BUTTE, THE DAWN WAS BREAKING, AND RALPH
Scaggs was already awake. He paced his hotel room, back
and forth, back and forth. He should have heard something
by now, should have heard from somebody.

He went to the wall and pressed his ear to it. Snores. That
so-called detective, Corcoran, was still snoring in there. He
never should have hired him. He should have . . .

Well, he'd done it, hadn't he? Promised him 20 percent of
the proceeds—no, make that the inheritance—for his trouble.
The proceeds were something entirely different. Still, you'd
think he'd work harder. You'd think the sonofabitch would
work, period. After all, he didn't know his final payment was
going to be a bullet through the head.

It was going to be everybody's final payment. Except his,
naturally. Just like it had been that detective's, the one who
kept following them around all the time. After Ralphie had
snuck up behind him in an alley and drowned him in a rain
barrel, he'd rolled him. Habit, really. And he'd found a Pinkerton card.

Ralphie didn't know much, but he knew a person couldn't
go around knocking off Pinkerton detectives and expect to
remain a free man for long. He'd hidden the body in the
alley—it was coming on night, anyway—and after dark he'd
wrestled it into a buggy, driven it out onto the desert and
buried it, and burned all its identification.

Still, it had him on edge. Where there was one Pinkerton,
there were likely more. He just couldn't figure out why one
of them would be on his tail.

He perched on the edge of the bed, nervously drumming

his fingertips. Why hadn't he heard from the men who were supposed to have kidnapped Harriet? Why hadn't he heard from Garrett?

"Ralphie, you ain't got no patience!" That was what Lulu was always screeching at him. "For such a lazy bastard, you ain't got no patience at all!" Well, he'd had patience, all right. He'd lived with the old whore for four whole years before he'd finally had enough one night and throttled her and thrown her body into the bay, weighted with enough bricks to keep her at the bottom till doomsday. So long, Lulu.

"No patience, eh?" he grumbled aloud, then laughed. The sound startled him, rising as it did from the silence, and he stopped abruptly. Could the Pinkertons be after him because of Lulu?

No. Nobody'd missed her. And besides, that had been six or eight years back. No, not Lulu.

He stood up again and went to the window. An early-rising Chinaman, long braid bobbing, slowly trotted up the deserted sidewalk. The Chinese were even here, in Nevada. Ralph watched him, thinking that very soon he'd never see another Chinaman again. He'd never have to bilk another greenhorn or crack another crib, never have to roll another drunk or jay-hawk another Webfoot or clip another opium-smoking uptown boy. And why? Because he'd be as rich as any uptown boy ever hoped to be, that's why. Because crazy cousin Horace Hogg—bless his ever-loving, hatter-mad, larcenous heart—had done it for him almost twenty years ago.

It was buried out there somewhere, buried in the desert. At least he hoped it was. It had to be! Hadn't Horace spent all those years trying to find Hattie, because she was the only one who knew? Hadn't he spent half his fortune looking for her? A fortune that was paltry compared with what was locked up in the girl's head, granted; but crazy as Horace was, he wouldn't throw good money after bad, now, would he?

Would he?

A wave of doubt sickened him momentarily, but he pushed it aside. Horace was crazy, but not that crazy. It was out there somewhere. It had to be. Horace had babbled about it at the end.

It was a lucky thing he'd gone up to Washington. Lucky that he'd stopped in at Cousin Horace's, hoping to float a loan. Which, of course, he had never planned to pay back, not one red cent. He didn't get the loan, but he got something much better, because Horace talked; talked to him when the nurse was out of the room, just him and good old Cousin Horace, all alone.

Of course, Horace didn't know that. Horace had thought he was Jesus. Confessed the whole thing to him, although why on earth Horace would think Jesus would come to his house with gaiters on his feet and a worn beaver hat on his head was beyond Ralphie. He didn't do anything to dissuade him, though. He just drank it all in, and then he said something— "That's okay, my son. Everything's square," he thought it was—and then he left.

Cousin Horace had died a few days later.

Of course, Ralph, like everybody else, had thought that Harriet was long dead. He'd figured that what was buried in the desert would just have to stay that way, and he was more than content that he'd inherit Horace's fortune. But when that dandy from the insurance company had called him in and he'd found out that Harriet was alive and they were sending a woman—a woman!—to find her, well, everything changed.

He clasped his hands, wringing them in sheer frustration. Why was it moving so slowly? Surely he should have heard something from Garrett by now! Surely Kramer would have wired!

Jesus, he hoped he'd buried that Pinkerton deep enough.

Suddenly he turned and left the room, went four steps down the hall, and began to bang on Corcoran's door. A moment later, the little man answered it, blinking and looking not the least bit happy.

"What?" he said, groggily. "What on earth is it this time?"

"I want you to go down there and check on things," Ralphie said. "I want you to get up and get on a stage and hustle your lazy butt down there right now."

"Bent Elbow?"

"Yes, Bent Elbow! Get your ass into some clothes and git."

Corcoran closed his eyes and leaned against the doorframe.

"It's not even six o'clock in the morning, Ralph. Now, you've had these little nervous times before. Why don't you—"

Ralphie grabbed Corcoran by the front of his nightshirt and yanked him forward. "I ain't having a 'little nervous time.' I'm havin' a *big* nervous time, and I want you to go. Now," he growled, an inch away from Corcoran's face.

Corcoran's eyes were open now. He sighed. "All right, all right. Want to let go so I can get dressed?"

TWENTY-EIGHT

>⊱—¦—⊰⊹⊱—◯—⊰⊹⊱—¦—⊰<

MAGGIE WOKE EARLY, AND SHE WOKE UP JUST AS she'd fallen asleep: fully dressed, with the juggling balls in her lap, and sitting in the rocking chair at the foot of Harriet's bed.

Frowning, she worked her fingers against the knot at the back of her neck, then gave up and checked her watch pin. Six thirty-five.

Harriet was sound asleep. Grady wouldn't rise for hours if left to his own devices. Maggie stared at the spare bed longingly.

No. No time to go back to bed now. She stood up, slowly stretching backward and side to side, her hands in the small of her back. There was a time when she could have spent a three-hour night in a chair and jumped up, ready to wrestle a bear, or at least rope and hogtie one. Not anymore. She shuddered to think what it would be like when she was thirty. Thirty-five. Forty.

She stopped at forty—no sense in completely horrifying herself so early in the morning—and set to the business of changing her clothes.

She'd come to the conclusion, late last night, that they'd have to take a chance on getting Harriet out of town, and as quickly as possible. The train wasn't safe, but neither was Bent Elbow. It was better to be a moving target. The trouble was that they'd have to catch the train in Sky Butte, twenty miles to the north, which meant twenty miles in an unprotected stagecoach. As she stepped into a clean petticoat, she decided that after she finished dressing she'd go down and send Eddie over to the Kid Concho Café to pick them up an early breakfast. Then back upstairs to wake Grady and have him hobble to Wells Fargo for the tickets. That was, if he could walk today. They'd be in trouble if he couldn't. And Grady wasn't going to be a bit happy about the stage, either.

Then she'd wake Harriet, who she hoped would be a little easier to communicate with this morning. Maggie wasn't holding her breath, though. Trance suggestions that were to make a powerful change in the subject's expression were seldom heeded at first.

If at all.

And then, if there was time, she'd try to put Harriet under again. Last night had been easy—the girl was so worn out that she'd been very susceptible to a soothing voice. Today she'd be fresher, and one night farther away from the whiskey. But Maggie hoped the girl would be amenable—she wanted to follow up on that Indian doll Horace had sent her. Maybe that was something.

Maggie shimmied into a fresh dress—at least a fresher model than the one she had on—and washed her face and brushed her hair. After the last pin was in place, she caught herself leaning toward the mirror and giving her cheeks a pinch. Now really, who was there to impress at seven in the morning in Bent Elbow, Nevada?

She crossed her eyes and stuck out her tongue at her reflection, then quietly let herself out the door.

The dirty breakfast dishes were stacked haphazardly on the bureau, which Grady was leaning against, absently toying with a few leftover shreds of hash browns. Hattie was still in her nightgown, sitting up in bed.

Maggie dragged the rocking chair over to her and said, "You're sure you don't mind, Harriet?"

The blond girl, somehow prettier today, sat up a little straighter than before. "Hattie no mind. Make Hattie feel . . ." She seemed to be searching for a word, a word she once knew and used, but couldn't find it. She settled for, "Feel good.

And some sad. Mostly good. Like to remember. Do again please, Mag-wire ma'am.''

Well, that was new! A ''please, ma'am'' out of Harriet! Maggie shot Grady a smug look. Grady rolled his eyes. She noticed he had on a suit coat again. Clever of him to have brought a spare.

Bringing up the candle, she said, ''All right, Harriet. Now watch the flame . . .''

Five minutes later, Harriet was in a deep trance. Unfortunately, so was Grady, and Maggie had to escort him into the hall and bring him out of it.

''Honestly, Grady,'' she said, her hand on the latch. ''You're hopeless.''

''The least you could have done was ease my pain,'' he whispered.

''Why? You're walking today, aren't you?''

''But every move's torture, Mags, sheer torture.''

''Hush,'' she said, and led him back inside. Grady, too, had the family idiosyncrasy with alcohol, although in a completely different way. While Maggie could never get all the way drunk, he could. And while Maggie suffered the agonies of the damned on the mornings after, Grady never felt a blessed thing, not one beastly twinge.

It wasn't fair.

Grady settled inside the door, and she went back to Harriet's side. They covered the birthday party again and came a few weeks forward in time, to when Harriet and her mother were packing for the long trek West. Maggie asked what had become of the doll Horace had sent.

''Lost it.'' Harriet pouted. ''Mama says I lost it, but I didn't, I left it on the shelf.''

''It's all right, Harriet. Now, let's doze for a moment . . .''

She brought the girl forward in small increments, getting closer to the massacre but no nearer to the solution to the problem. Grady was holding his pocket watch and pointing at it.

''One more,'' she silently mouthed at him, then turned back to Harriet before he could shake his head.

''We're coming forward in time, Harriet, forward in time

just a little. When I snap my fingers, tell me what you see." Maggie snapped her fingers.

Suddenly, Harriet let out a high-pitched, keening sound, then screamed, "Indians! Indians are coming! Get in the wagon! Get the box! Indians!"

Maggie panicked and seized Harriet by the shoulders. "It's all right, it's all right!"

But Harriet didn't hear her. "Wild Indians going to scalp us all! Mama? Mama! Hide the box, hide the box! Mama, please don't make me! Lake of Fire!"

Harriet began a frantic digging motion, scrambling the bed-clothes with her hands, her terror-stricken face turning quickly from side to side, tears of panic squeezing through closed eye-lids to stream down her face as she feverishly dug and dug and dug.

"Harriet!"

The girl pulled at the sheets, the mattress. "Hide the box, baby Jesus help me hide the box! Oh, the wind! Please don't let the Indians scalp me! Daddy's gonna feed me to the devil!"

A damp stain began to spread from beneath the girl, and Maggie knew Harriet had wet herself out of sheer fright. "Harriet! Grady!" she called, although she realized, as she said it, that Grady was already on the other side of the bed, his hands on Harriet's shoulders. She'd lost control of the sit-uation, and she didn't know how to get it back. "Harriet!" she called again. "Harriet, be still!"

Grady, trying to press the frantic girl back against the pil-lows, shouted, "Do the father thing again!"

"What?"

"Just do it!"

Maggie was willing to try anything. Above the frantic girl's wails, she shouted, "Harriet, your father is here! Harriet, listen to me. Your daddy is here. You can hear him. You can hear your daddy now." She snapped her fingers, praying the girl remembered the cue and that she could hear it over the noise she was making.

Wild-eyed, Harriet suddenly raised her head, almost as if scenting the air, and Grady immediately took her in his arms

and stroked her hair and said, "There, there, Harriet. It's all
right."

"I hid it, I hid it, don't be mad, don't make Jesus and all
His holy witnesses throw me in the Lake of Fire! Oh, the
devil's come for me, the devil's come for me!"

Grady hugged her tighter, a look of something akin to horror on his face. "It's not the devil, Harriet. No devils. And
Daddy isn't mad. Nobody's going to throw you in the Lake
of Fire. Hush now, hush."

He held her while her sobs gradually abated. Maggie sagged
back into her chair, stunned. That dirty old lunatic self-
righteous stinker! He'd managed to scare a little girl enough
that she was more afraid of him and his God than the Indians
who had borne down upon them and killed forty-three settlers
that day, her mother among them.

She waved a hand until she had Grady's attention, and then
she mouthed, "Ask her about the box."

"Harriet, dear, did you bury Daddy's box for him?"

The agitation began again, and again he calmed her, and
Maggie tried another tack. "Harriet, from now on, I want you
to be like a little bird, high above the scene, all right? You
can see your body, and you can see what's going on and hear
everything, but you're not in your body. You're floating in
the clouds, watching." She snapped her fingers, and Harriet
instantly relaxed.

Maggie nodded at Grady, and he tried again.

This time Harriet said, "Yes, sir. By the big rock. Mama
said if I didn't she'd tell you, so you could tell Jesus I was
bad and then he'd throw me in the fiery lake."

What little respect Maggie had for Harriet's mother was
fading rapidly. And even though the greatest part of her didn't
want to know the answer, she asked, "Your mama sent you
out from the wagons?"

"Yes."

"While the Indians were attacking?"

"When we first saw them coming." The answer was mat-
ter-of-fact. "While the men tried to circle the wagons. Mama
said to go out and bury it now or she'd tell, and don't ask any
questions, scat."

Maggie covered her mouth with a hand to hold in the sob.

Grady asked, his voice breaking, "What was in the box, Harriet?"

"Don't you know?"

Maggie said weakly, "Daddy's . . . . Daddy's just asking to see if you do."

Harriet shook her head slowly. "Mama kept it secret. A secret metal box. I didn't tell anybody she had it, Daddy."

Maggie had herself under control again. She said, "Harriet, did the Indians dig up the box?"

A proud smile broke over Harriet's face. "No, I hid it good. I hid it good for when I could come back and get it for Mama and Papa and Jesus." Then the smile collapsed. "The Indians found me, though."

Maggie began to talk Harriet down into a deeper, more forgetful sleep, ushering Grady from the room when his eyelids began to sag. She instructed Harriet to forget that her daddy was there but to remember the attack—without emotion and from afar, as if she were that small bird on the wind. She reinforced the suggestions that the thought of alcohol would make her sick and that she remember to speak more clearly. And then she woke her up.

Harriet's eyes fluttered slowly open. "Did you do it?" she asked. Then her brow creased as she answered her own question. "Yes." And then furrowed as she felt the dampness beneath her. "I'm sorry."

Maggie patted her hand. "It's perfectly fine. Are you all right?" She had no words for the overwhelming sadness she felt for this girl. A tyrannical father—half mad, it seemed, even in those days; a mother who had sent her out into terrible peril to hide a secret; and years spent suffering lord knew what at the hands of savages.

Harriet looked up at her. "We go now?"

Maggie stood up. "Yes, Harriet. We get you cleaned up, then we go."

TWENTY-NINE

>─┤─◆─○─◆─├─◄

MAGGIE WOULD HAVE FALLEN HEADLONG OVER THE luggage if Grady hadn't caught her. "Get your nose out of that map," he said, grumbling. "And hurry! We've only got five minutes to catch the stage." He stuffed Harriet's frayed carpetbag under one arm, then lifted a valise in each hand. "The sooner we bid *adieu* to Bent Elbow, the happier I'll be. Come, Harriet."

He did an about-face and limped up the street. Harriet, scanty braids peeking from beneath her bonnet and wearing the pink dress Maggie had bought her, trailed meekly in his wake.

Maggie stood in the hotel doorway, folding the map and staring at the black bunting and banners lining the street, and which seemed to have sprung up overnight. All along the sidewalks, men were wearing black armbands. What few women there were had dressed in black, and the storefronts were swathed in it. That poor goat, the one with the bandaged tail, was back, except he now sported a black sash tied around his neck. He was trying to eat it. Directly overhead, going from one side of the street to the other, was a long swath of paper or cloth—which, she couldn't tell—that read *So Long, Kid Concho*.

Eddie, a black band around his arm, tapped her on the shoulder and presented the receipt.

"There you go, ma'am."

She glanced at it, saw that it included, under miscellaneous, "wall repair—two rooms." She tucked it into her bag, mumbling, "Yes, that's fine," and coloring hotly. Maybe she should save the knives for home. Just carry balls. Batons, maybe. Flaming batons, like LoLo Carré, the Fabulous Flame Dancer. No, that wouldn't do. Fire damage was so much harder to control. . . .

"Ma'am?" Eddie was staring at her.

"What? Oh, nothing." She stuck the map under her arm. "Aren't you supposed to be asleep?"

"Yup. But Daddy spelled me for a while last night. Whole town's turnin' out for the funeral."

She pointed to his armband. "For Sheriff Sopsucher?"

He nodded.

"And the banner?"

Eddie cast a reverent eye upward. "Sheriff Sopsucher, ma'am."

"No, I mean . . . I thought Kid Concho was dead."

"Yes'm, he sure is that."

"Eddie, I'm confused."

"Confused or not, you'd better be leaving town, lady," said a new voice. Maggie turned. A man, who would have been rather handsome if it weren't for his blackened eyes and bruised face, angrily clomped toward her on crutches, his lower right leg in a cast. A small terrier followed him, grabbing at the cast and growling.

"Mr. Festing, I presume?" Maggie pulled herself erect. The sheriff had most certainly beat the stuffing out of him, and she tried as hard as she could to feel some sympathy.

He stopped before her, shook the dog off his leg, and swung out a crutch, gesturing up the street. "The stage is here. Get on it and get out of Bent Elbow, and take that stupid, troublemaking, skinny-assed whore with you. Take Biscuit Pete, too! This is my town now, and—"

"Was there an election last night, Mr. Festing?" Whatever sympathy she'd mustered withered away.

"There'll be one next week, damn it, after they get this nonsense over with." The crutch swung up, nearly clipping her nose, to wave at the banner. The terrier jumped for it and missed. "I cannot believe the way this town's been run! Outlaws and killers in charge! Well, it stops now." The crutch hit the boardwalk with a *thump,* narrowly avoiding the dog, who immediately attacked it. "It stops here." Then, to the dog, "Sit, Chico! Sit, goddamn it!"

The man was certainly annoying. Sheriff Sopsucher had shown restraint, if you asked her. She said, "I see. You're going to inflict your own moral code on the populace. Put the whoremongers and gamblers in control. Conspiracy to kidnap—not to mention murder—is an ugly charge, Mr. Festing. All in a day's work for you, isn't it?"

He colored. "That's slander. Libel!"

"Just slander. I haven't given it to the papers yet." She had a sudden urge to kick his crutches out from under him, but resisted. "Who paid you off, Mr. Festing? You've caused the death of one girl, at least indirectly."

"That's nonsense! Nobody paid me!"

"You're right, Mr. Festing. I apologize. You did it for free, through no fault of your own. Who promised you a fortune to look the other way?"

Festing was livid. He sputtered, then he shouted, "Just get out of my town!" He wheeled—the best he could on crutches, at any rate—and clomped away, down the street, the terrier nipping at his cast.

Eddie, cowed in the doorway, said, "He's a mite touchy."

At the corner, Festing gave a last angry poke to the air with his crutch before he turned and disappeared.

"I have a notion to stay, just to irritate him," Maggie muttered in annoyance, gazing at the place he'd been. "And what did he mean, outlaws and killers in charge?"

Eddie shrugged. "Aw, he's just sore because of the olden days, before he came. About folks bein' so attached to the sheriff and all. The Kid Concho thing. Mr. Festing's a city boy, like your cousin."

"Sorry, Eddie. Kid Concho? I don't get the connection."

He pointed to the banner, fluttering lazily in the breeze. "I thought you knew, ma'am, you being a detective and all. Sheriff Sopsucher used to be Kid Concho."

Maggie couldn't think of a blessed thing to say.

Eddie, with an air of exasperation, added, "Well, they

couldn't call him the Sopsucher Kid, could they? Or Kid Alvin?''

Maggie stared at him. "Alvin?"

"That was his first name," he explained. "Don't sound real western-like."

"Alvin Sopsucher," Maggie repeated, incredulously.

"He went over to his real name about ten years back, and took over sheriffin'. Said he was tired and wanted to settle down. 'Course, the town was a whole lot smaller then. One hotel and three saloons and Bertram's mercantile, like that. Hadn't hit the silver yet."

"But nobody called him Kid Concho! I mean—"

"Oh, he didn't like it, not one bit. After he shot five or six folks for callin' him the wrong thing, they sorta laid off it."

"Good gravy."

"Maggie!"

She glanced up the street and saw that, miraculously, the stage had come in nearly on time. Grady and Harriet were boarding, and Grady, boosting Harriet inside, waved frantically. Maggie said, "I've got to go. Thanks for everything, Eddie."

She heard him say, "Welcome, ma'am. It was real interestin' meetin' you."

She hurried along the walk and had no more swung the coach door closed behind her than it lurched forward. She flew backward, banging her head, and her hat tipped forward over her eyes. "Blast and damnation!" she growled, fixing it. At least they were alone in the coach. She could grouch with impunity.

She slid the pin back into place. "Grady, you've heard of Kid Concho, haven't you?"

"Well, of course I've heard of him, Mags," he replied. "The whole town's plastered with his name."

"No, I mean, had you heard of him before?"

Grady pursed his lips and stared at the ceiling for a moment, then closed his eyes. He wasn't much for the reality of the frontier, but he'd memorized more outlaw lore than she'd had time to read, and could recite it on demand.

"Gunslinger," he said, "birth name unknown. Shootist and

hired assassin. Participant in the Nola Valley War and the Hollow Creek shoot-out, among others. Hero of Greasy Gorge and the Albino Flats range war. Has the notoriety of being one of the few men missed by John Wesley Hardin. That he was shooting at, I mean. Principal in seven dime novels—four Ned Buntlines and three others. Disappeared ten, maybe eleven, years ago in northern Wyoming, never heard from again, presumed dead.''

He opened his eyes again and looked at Maggie. ''Why?''

''He was good to Hattie,'' Harriet said softly, and began sniffling. ''Dead now.''

Maggie ignored her. ''Alvin Sopsucher—our own Sheriff Sopsucher—was Kid Concho.''

Grady stared at her. ''You're joking.''

''Swear to God.''

Grady took off his hat and stared out the window. ''I'll be damned. I'll be goddamned.''

In an attempt to take her mind off Sopsucher, she shook out the map again. And nearly ripped it when the coach hit an unusually large pothole that lifted her out of her seat and sat her down again with a *crack*. ''Crimeny! You'd think they'd do something about these roads!'' Suddenly she remembered Grady's backside and said, ''Oh, Grady! I could unpack my suitcase. Let you sit on my dirty laundry. Folded up or something.''

He turned from the window, his hat in his hands. ''No need.'' He shifted to one side, exposing the edge of a hotel pillow.

''Eddie?'' she asked.

''To the rescue. Had to carry it out under my coat in case his father came out.'' He settled his hat back in place thoughtfully. ''Say . . . what about Biscuit Pete?''

Maggie smoothed the map out over her lap and chewed her lip. ''Oops. Forgot about him. I suppose we could wire. Harriet? Do you want me to wire Biscuit Pete for you?''

After a brief mourning period for Kid Concho, Harriet had dried her eyes, and she was leaning out the window, like a dog. She pulled in her head. Blond hair hanging in her eyes, she said, ''Huh?''

All that braiding, shot to pieces. With a sigh, Maggie said, "Do you want me to wire Biscuit Pete to meet us?"

"Who, Mag-wire ma'am?"

"Never mind." It didn't matter whether the girl had temporarily forgotten him due to the mesmerism or the fact that she was completely sober for the first time in three years. What mattered was that without Biscuit Pete she'd have one less chick to look after. One less big, lumbering, dull-brained chick, at that. She could always wire him later, from San Francisco.

She patted Harriet's knee. "When we stop, I'll fix your hair again."

Harriet shrugged, without expression, and stuck her head back out the window. What went through her mind? Did she think about what she'd done, where she'd been, what had been done to her in her miserable little life? Maybe she didn't think at all. That would be a soothing gift, not to think, and at the same time horrible. With a sigh, Maggie bent over her map again.

Mercifully, they'd hit a smooth stretch of road—well, relatively smooth—and after a few minutes of tracing lines with her fingers and twisting her face and sticking her tongue out the side of her mouth in concentration, she said, "How long before we get to Sky Butte, Grady?"

He tore himself away from the scenery, which wasn't much on his side of the couch, and looked at his watch. "We'll be at the first rest station in about fifteen minutes. After that, perhaps a half hour to Sky Butte, give or take. I'll be overjoyed to get back on a nice, mechanical train," he said, smiling dreamily. "Steam locomotion. First class, one way. It's the only way to travel."

Maggie sat back. "Don't set your heart on it yet."

Grady sighed and closed his eyes, consternation overtaking his face. "Now, Mags—"

"Well, don't you want to see what all these idiots are killing each other for? What somebody killed Sheriff Sopsucher for?" His death was eating at her more than she cared to admit. "Well, I do. We can get a guide in Sky Butte. It's not more than twelve miles."

"What is?"

"The site of the . . ." She glanced at Harriet, who was gazing blankly out the window at the mountains. She lowered her voice and leaned toward Grady. "The site of the massacre. Harriet's been working her way toward it for three years. I very much doubt whether even she's realized it."

"Well, that's just fine, Maggie," he said sarcastically. "Just fine. By all means, let's go off on a wild goose chase when there are probably killers all around us. They've murdered five people so far—"

"Six," she cut in. "Six, counting Kid Concho."

"Six. Pardon me. Well, why not add us to the total? What are three more? Oh, I'm all for it. Let's go, by all means." He folded his arms and turned to stare out the window, his mouth set. Maggie waited on him, and at last he said, "If you think I'm getting on another horse—"

"Carriage," she said, quickly. "I promise. You just aren't built for saddles, Grady."

"Oh, there's news! If I've told you once I've told you a thousand—" His eye lit on something, out the window. He reached toward his pocket, toward his gun. "Company's coming."

THIRTY

>───┼─◆─┼─◆─○─◆─┼─◆─┼─<

"**Y**OU HAVE THE COLT?" GRADY ASKED, EVEN AS HIS hand slapped his pocket. "Damnit! I packed mine!"

Maggie had already brought out her pistol—thank heavens for deep pockets—and had shifted to look out Grady's side of the coach. "Take this," she said, shoving the Colt into his hands. "I've got the derringer in my— Oh, suds." She snatched back the Colt and shoved it into her pocket again.

"Mags, what on earth are you—"

She tipped her head toward the rider cutting toward them, across the plain. "That's Nickel."

"What?"

"Biscuit Pete."

They watched as his figure grew large and larger against the desert landscape. He waved at them, then galloped up next to the coach. Trotting beside it, he stuck his head down to look in the window. "Hattie!" he cried, a wraparound grin splitting his face. For Pete, it was an emotional moment, Maggie thought. He was positively animated.

Hattie turned from her window. "Hello," she said, without expression, then turned back to watch the mountains roll by.

Pete frowned and called, "What'd you do to her?" over the rumble of the coach.

This was going to take a good bit of explaining. Maggie, unwilling to shout at length out the window, pointed to her ear and shook her head. She shouted, "Come inside!"

After he convinced the driver to stop the coach and tied

Nickel on behind, Pete joined them inside, and the stage
lurched ahead once again. Pete settled next to Maggie, across
from Harriet. "Honey?" he said, taking her hands. "Honey-
bunch?"

Harriet just looked at him flatly, then said to Maggie, "Who
this, Mag-wire?"

"It's Pete, dear," she answered. "Biscuit Pete."

"That's right, Hattie honey." He looked stricken. Well, as
stricken as it was possible for him to look. "I'm your ol'
Pete."

Harriet was still looking at Maggie. "He go with us,
ma'am? To the place?"

Maggie leaned forward. "To the place?"

"The place where . . . the place where blood runs?"

She'd been listening to their conversation after all. Maggie
kept forgetting the full ramifications of more than a decade
with the Indian tribes, one of which was that stony-faced sto-
icism. Harriet wasn't stupid. Beaten down, yes. But not stupid,
not by a long shot.

Grady had turned to look at her, too. He said, rather formally, "Harriet, do you wish to go to this place? We would
like to take you, but only if it's your wish."

Maggie gave his foot a little kick, but there was no need.
Harriet replied, "If Mag-wire say to go, it must be a good
thing. Hattie goes, Grady."

"Fine," said Grady, rubbing his ankle and looking daggers
at Maggie.

Pete asked, sniveling, "Well, what about me? How come
she don't remember me? Hattie? Sugar pie?"

"She's been through a lot, Pete," Maggie soothed. "She's
sober for the first time in ages. And we've, um, we've done
some deep . . ." Maggie tried to think of a word that wouldn't
frighten a rube like him, but couldn't come up with one. "I
hypnotized her, Pete. Mesmerism."

"Now?" he asked, outraged. He forgot where he was for
the moment and stood up, only to bang his head on the coach's
ceiling before he got halfway up. He sat down hard, rubbing
his head. "Has she got the spell on her now?"

"No, no, no. Last night and this morning."

"That's the devil's work! You folks stay away from Hattie from now on, you hear me?" He'd reached for Harriet's hands and pulled the poor girl so far toward him that she was practically lying on his knees. "Don't you go trancin' my gal again. Hattie, it's gonna be all right. You an' me are gonna take the next stage back to town."

"No pull Hattie!" the girl said, and tried to jerk herself free.

Grady said, "Pete, let go of her. It has nothing to do with the devil and everything to do with science."

Maggie decided she'd better butt in. Let Grady get started on science, and pretty soon he'd move from hypnotism to personal locomotives to pictures and voices flying through the air and into your house, and the next thing they knew, Pete would have them tied to the stake, a Bible in his right hand and a match in the left.

"*Medical* science," she said quickly, taking Pete's hand off the girl and pushing Harriet back into her own seat. "And Harriet is doing much better."

Pete frowned. "Don't you go witchin' my Hattie again, ma'am, or I'll have to get firm. I'd hate to do it, but that's a warning."

Maggie had just opened her mouth to ask what in the world he meant by "get firm," when the stage slowed and the driver called out, "Rest stop! Rest stop, folks. Singleton Station!"

While a crew changed the horses, Grady wandered off to talk with the men working on another stagecoach (which was, apparently, in need of a new wheel), Biscuit Pete busied himself with Nickel, and Maggie sat outside on a bench, in the purply shade of a thorny mesquite tree, rebraiding Harriet's hair.

"Harriet, you don't mind going to . . ." What was it she'd called it? Oh, yes. "You don't mind going to the place where the blood runs, do you? The blood doesn't run anymore. That was a long time ago."

The girl remained stone-faced. "Hattie knows. Hattie will go."

Maggie stopped braiding for the moment. "You don't have to, you know."

"Hattie goes, Mag-wire."

The statement had the ring of finality to it. Maggie changed the subject. "Biscuit Pete loves you very much. He really does, Harriet." She wanted to know that Harriet had someplace to go, someone to take care of her after the business at Western Mutual Specialties was finished. She didn't like to think of Harriet alone in the world, especially with all that money. She'd be a prime target for every two-bit hustler and con man who came along. She said, "Pete loves you so. Are you certain you don't remember him, just a little?"

Without expression, Harriet said, "Hattie love . . ." She said a word, a multisyllabic phrase that Maggie didn't understand. When she didn't respond, Harriet furrowed her brow, as if thinking how to translate, and then she said, "Tall Cougar."

"Oh," said Maggie. Had Harriet had a crush on an Indian brave? "That's his name, is it?"

Harriet nodded. "Hattie love Tall Cougar. Be his wife. Have his babies. One dies, but one is strong. Big strong boy." Her face softened, and a brightness showed in her eyes. "I call him Little Kitten. His father says is no name for a boy, but I call him that anyway. And he lets me."

Maggie slumped back, her hands in her lap. All this time she'd been thinking that Harriet was, well, not stupid, not stupid at all, but slowed down, somehow, by her ordeal. That all the trauma she'd been through had dulled her wits, made her unfeeling. She'd assumed that Harriet had been nothing but a slave within the tribe. The reality of it, that Harriet had been a wife and a mother, left her wondering if any of this—the army's rescue, and her own meddling—had been right. If perhaps Harriet wouldn't have been better off just left alone.

"What happened to Tall Cougar and Little Kitten, Harriet? Are they still at San Carlos? We could . . ." She let the sentence trail off. What could she do? Send for Tall Cougar and turn him loose with Harriet's money? He'd have no use for it, probably wouldn't even know what it was. Send Harriet back to the reservation with the money in a sack? The tribe would likely use it to line their moccasins if the Indian agent didn't steal it first.

But Harriet, still facing away, still patiently waiting for her hair to be braided, said, "Soldiers come. Kill many men. Kill many children. They take Hattie. Take me. I see Tall Cougar dead on the ground." Suddenly, Harriet whirled round. "He is brave. He kills five bluecoats to save Hattie and Little Kitten." She held up her hand, spread wide, to show five, and there was a proud, almost haughty expression on her face.

Maggie whispered, "And the baby. What happened to your baby?"

"After fighting is over, bluecoat tries to take him. Hattie fights, but two more bluecoats come. First bluecoat holds Little Kitten by his legs, says, 'You no need Apache baby where you go, white folks no want Apache baby,' and then he takes out his knife and then Little Kitten is dead. Cut up like an animal."

Harriet's expression was blank, but the tears suddenly streaming down her face told the true story. Faltering, she said, "Hattie cry inside all the time, many moons. Not show whites tears. Then Hattie find Backwash whiskey, and Hattie forget. No more whiskey now. Just sad." She put a hand over her heart. "Empty."

Maggie opened her mouth, but no words came out. She put her arms around the girl and hung on tight, and after a moment, Harriet embraced her, too, hesitantly at first, then tightly; sobbing, sobbing as if her heart would break.

"Get it out," Maggie whispered. "Cry it out." And then Maggie was crying, too.

THIRTY-ONE

>—I—<>—O—<>—I—<

ABOUT TWENTY MINUTES LATER, WHEN GRADY JOINED
Maggie and Hattie in the stagecoach, he took one look
at their red eyes and puffy faces and said, "Good grief!
What happened?"

"Nothing, Grady." Maggie said, wiping at her nose with a
handkerchief and giving him a look that said he wouldn't understand. But she said, "I'll tell you later."

"But Mags," he protested out of habit, "you look like—"
The stage door opened, and Biscuit Pete climbed over him to
sit across from Harriet.

"Why, plum puddin'!" he said, taking Harriet's hands.
"What's wrong?" He turned a troubled face to Maggie.
"What you doin' to her? You been witchin' her again?"

Grady put a hand on his arm. "Easy, there, son. Nothing
like that. The ladies have, I believe, bonded."

"Huh?"

"Sisterhood, and all that," he said, ignoring Maggie's evil
look. "The mutual travail of the species." Pete looked blank.
Grady sighed. "Pete, my friend, some things are impossible
to explain."

"Hold up there, Curly!" It was the stationmaster who
yanked open the door. " 'Bout forgot, you got another pas-
senger."

A small man, bearing a tidy satchel that Grady took to be
a sample case of some sort, clambered over his knees and sat
down between himself and Biscuit Pete. "Next time, mister,
make up your mind," the stationmaster said and slammed the

door, with a "Take her on out, Curly!" to the driver.

The coach started forward with a jolt that jostled Maggie badly—she was ethereal aboard a horse's back, but had absolutely no sense of balance in a coach or wagon. Well, it was jarring—almost knocked Grady off his pillow, as well. Thoughtful of Eddie, giving it to him. Nice boy. He turned to the little man next to him and said, "Make up your mind?"

"Oh, dear," said the man. "I was headed for Bent Elbow and prospects south, but I suddenly remembered a meeting in Sky Butte. This afternoon," he said. "Lucky for me that the coach needed repair, or I might have remembered in Bent Elbow, and then where would I have been?"

"Where indeed, sir!" Grady replied jovially. "Grady Maguire, at your service."

He held out his hand, but before the man could shake it and offer his name, Maggie said, "Silas Corcoran, I believe."

The little man cringed, and Maggie—wearing a predatory expression that Grady found delightfully amusing as long as it wasn't directed at him—added, "Ogled any new bosoms lately?"

In Sky Butte, which they came to none too soon for Grady's taste, he helped the ladies down from the stage, leaving Biscuit Pete to fend for himself. Silas Corcoran, the unfortunate salesman, scuttled off the moment the stage stopped.

Grady didn't know what got into Maggie sometimes. She could be a perfect lady when it suited her, but sometimes she had this fixation with men. Well, not a fixation, exactly. That made it sound like she liked them.

Well, she *did* like them, most of them. But she had a targeted dislike for men who, as she put it, took a less than polite advantage of the female sex: men who—quite naturally, Grady thought—looked a lady up and down in admiration of her figure, or used terms of endearment. It seemed that at some point in the past, Silas Corcoran had been guilty of the first offense, and Maggie wasn't going to let him off easy.

Frankly, Maggie didn't have that much to look at. Oh, she was all right, he supposed. She had a neat enough figure, but he was so used to her—and she kept herself so well buttoned

up—that he hardly took notice anymore. She was nothing like
the fair Miriam. Ah, Miriam. Now, there was a bosom worth
ogling! It spilled out over the tops of her gowns like—

"Grady! Stop daydreaming and help me with the bags."

His master's voice. Or should that be mistress's? "Yes,
Maggie," he said with a certain degree of overstated ennui,
and grudgingly made himself useful.

"If you don't mind my askin'," said Pete, shouldering his
saddle, "where the Sam Hill are we goin'?"

"Let me explain," said Grady.

Sky Butte was a fair-sized town, if you took into consideration that it was smack-dab in the exact middle of nowhere.
They had to walk three blocks to the livery, and then Maggie
sent him to buy a hat—to replace the one he'd lost in the
hills—while she arranged for the horses and a carriage. There
was no sense in him sunstroking himself, she said. He was
happy to comply.

When he returned to the stable, proudly sporting a new
dove-gray bowler he'd gotten at half price (the shopkeeper
having had no takers for it in three years), he found Maggie
had rented a buckboard—all the carriages being rented out—
for Harriet and him, and a horse for herself. Pete, who insisted
on coming along to "protect" Harriet and who had left his
gray back at the stage stop, had rented a horse as well. He
slung his saddle over the back of his rented mount.

"Let's go," said Maggie, her foot in the stirrup.

"What do you mean, let's go?" Grady demanded, craning
his head to and fro. "Where's the guide?"

She swung up and daintily slid into the saddle, though how
she managed in all those skirts was a wonder. It amazed him
every time. She said, "The livery man says we can't miss it.
Some sort of local tourist attraction. I like your hat, by the
way."

"Thank you. But what about lunch?"

"Grady, it's barely eleven."

"And we had breakfast practically before dawn!"

She sighed. "Oh, all right. We'll eat first, then the Devil's
Shute."

With a happy sigh, he climbed up on the buckboard, pillow in hand.

The Devil's Shute, as the locals called it, was easy to find. The wind rising, they went up the road ten miles through the tumbleweeded desert, then cut off on a rutted path for two more. They came upon it, just as the livery man had promised, over the crest of a hill: a valley—you could hardly call it a canyon—that sank down into the desert floor for as far as the eye could see.

It was full of craggy, yellow upthrusts of rock, some just a few feet high, some as tall as three men and as wide as ten, that rose from the desert floor like an old dog's teeth. And most of all, it was full of air currents, for the valley formed a kind of wind tunnel. The wind whistled through the yellow upthrusts, turning corners, throwing off sounds, tricking a listener, raising a knee-high mist of dust and grit above the ground.

It was the perfect place for an ambush if ever he'd seen one. Whoever had been leading Harriet's wagon train had been mad to go through here.

They traveled slowly down the canyon, twisting past one unearthly rock form after another, waiting for Harriet to give some sign. She seemed to grow more and more distraught, and at last, when they had gone about a mile, she stood up and said, "Grady, stop."

And then he saw it, through the mist of dust that shrouded the land. The wagons, what remained after the Indians had set their fires, had been left, as if as a warning to others. A scorched wheel here. An axle and wagon tree there. At least someone had buried the bodies, he thought gratefully.

In the seat beside him, Harriet was shaking.

"Maggie?" he called.

She was already off her horse. "It's all right, Harriet," she soothed, and helped the girl down. "Grady," she said, "did you get your pistol out of your bag?"

He patted his pocket.

"Good. Keep it close." She turned to Harriet. "You remember this place, don't you?"

The wind howled, and he had to lean close to hear. Biscuit

Pete had dismounted, too, and was coming closer.

"Yes, Mag-wire," said Harriet, trembling.

"No witchin', now," said Pete, stopping near them. He looked around. "This place gives me the spooks."

Grady concurred, but he didn't say so. Lord, but they'd named this place well. The Devil's Shute. He expected Old Nick himself to swoop down on them at any second, borne by the howling wind. He reluctantly climbed off the buckboard, cringing at his sore limbs as he took the long step down and joined the group.

"What now?" he asked.

"I don't know," Maggie replied. "That's for Harriet to say. Harriet?"

The girl was slowly wandering away, but with some sort of purpose. She walked out across the scene, scrubbed clean of carnage by time and desert winds. Left, then right, then left again she went, her feet lost in the blowing dust, searching for something, her skirts blowing.

"The wagon," breathed Maggie. "She's looking for the place their wagon was." Biscuit Pete started forward, but she put a hand on his arm, staying him. "Wait."

For twenty minutes Harriet roamed the site, sometimes pausing, sometimes squatting for a moment, then turning to face the west, as if looking for a marker. At last she seemed to find the place she was looking for. She sat down, almost lost in the blowing dust, her back turned to them.

"That's it?" Grady said over the wind's howl as they started toward her. "We came all the way out here so she could sit in the dirt?"

Maggie said, "Oh, hush," and walked out ahead of them, the wind snapping her skirts.

Grady said to Pete, "What do you . . ." and then remembered who he was talking to. "Never mind." He might as well try to make conversation with a tree. He clamped a hand over his new hat and kept walking.

When they reached the women, Maggie was down on her knees in front of Harriet, talking softly, stroking Harriet's hair. "It's all right, Harriet," he heard her say, over the whistling wind. "There's plenty of time."

"No," said Harriet, and struggled to her feet. "They come, they come."

She began to run, stumbling, toward the west, toward a thick upthrust of rock as tall as three men. She ran all the way to its base before she went down on her knees and madly began to paw the dirt, the wind hammering her now, lashing her skirts, her hair, as Maggie followed her, and he followed Maggie.

Maggie got there first and crouched five feet from Harriet, watching her dig. Grady stood behind her. "You don't suppose she's after—"

"Yes," said Maggie breathlessly.

"It can't still be there after all these years!"

"Why not?"

Just then Harriet uncovered something, less than an inch down: the gray metal corner of a box. She began to claw at the hard soil, and Maggie said, "Help her."

Grady bent and put out a hand, but Harriet slapped it away. Maggie said, "Maybe you shouldn't?"

"Whatever," he said with a sigh. He sat on his heels, the wind pushing at his back as he watched Hattie slowly unearth the box, then yank it free with a grunt.

It was not large, being the sort of metal strongbox a man might keep important papers in, and its time in the ground had scarcely damaged it at all. Harriet cradled it to her, rocking it like a child.

"Safe," she said. "Safe."

Maggie said, just loud enough to be heard over the wind's whine, "Harriet? Let's open it up, all right?"

The girl stared at her for a moment, then slowly relaxed her grip on the box. Maggie took it and tried the latch. "It's locked. Grady?"

"I knew you'd need me, sooner or later," he said brightly, and reached into his vest pocket for a small leather kit. Unsnapping it, he chose a pick, then lifted the box. He inserted the pick into the lock, and holding it close to his ear, fiddled a moment. There was a small, satisfying *click*.

"*Voilà!*" he said, and opened the box. He looked inside.

He looked at Maggie. "This is what we came for? This is what all those people died for?"

Harriet's eyes popped. With a squeal of delight, she reached inside and grabbed the contents, clutching it to her bosom.

"A doll? A damn *doll*?" He turned the box upside down and shook it, even though it was obviously empty.

"Sarah," said Harriet, her head tucked, rocking. "Sarah."

"It's not just a doll, Grady. At least, I don't think so. Harriet? Harriet, may I see Sarah for just a moment?" The girl gripped the doll harder. "Harriet, please? I'll give her back to you, I promise."

"Mag-wire sure?"

"Maguire promises." Maggie crossed her heart.

It did the trick. Harriet solemnly handed her the doll. It was an Indian doll, obviously the one Horace had sent her so many years ago. It was dirty and smudged and much loved, and made of leather with crude features painted on its face. It wore no clothes. Maggie turned it over, inspecting it, then rolled a leg between her fingers. She smiled. She held it out to him. "Grady?"

He took an arm and rolled it. "That's odd. It's stuffed with pebbles."

"I don't think so. Give me your penknife."

He handed it over, and she turned the doll over on its face and made a tiny incision along the seam. She parted it.

Grady swallowed.

Harriet cocked her head. "Stars inside."

Maggie breathed, "Diamonds."

"Golly," said Biscuit Pete, leaning close. Grady had forgotten about him. "If'n you folks—"

A new voice interrupted him. "Excuse me, but I believe I'll take that."

Two men had stepped out from behind the rocks. Both held their hats down with one hand, and their pants legs snapped in the wind. Shy and blushing no more, Silas Corcoran, the bosom-gazing drummer, pointed a rather large gun in their direction. Grady didn't recognize the other man, but Maggie did.

"Well," she said, standing up, the wind billowing her skirts. "If it isn't Ralph Scaggs."

"Just call me Ralphie," he said with a smarmy grin.

THIRTY-TWO

❧—┤◆❭—◯—❬◆┤—❧

"PUT DOWN THE DOLL AND MOVE AWAY," SAID COR-
coran, wiggling his pistol.

Maggie complied, laying the doll back in the box
and taking Harriet by the shoulders, and calculating how
quickly she could push Harriet out of the way and reach for
her pistol. That weasel, Corcoran, had the only gun, as far as
she could see. Of course, Ralphie might be carrying, too, but
it wasn't drawn. If she could just take him by surprise . . .

"Farther," he said. They all moved to the right, scuttling
like crabs.

"How did you know?" she asked Ralphie. The wind
whipped tendrils of hair over her face. She kept Harriet in
front of her, one hand on her shoulder, so that Harriet's body
hid her hip. She reached down into her skirt pocket.

"I got my ways, sweetcakes," Ralphie said. "Old Horace
was rambling at the end. Didn't know who the hell he was
talkin' to or where he was. Made some real interesting con-
fessions."

Corcoran said, "You. The big blond." He nodded toward
Pete.

Maggie's fingers closed around the grip of the gun.

"Who, me?" said Pete.

"Unbuckle that gun belt and throw it over."

Pete did what he was told, and Silas Corcoran swung his
gun toward her. She froze, her fingers on the grip. To Ralphie,
who had retrieved the box, he said, "I think I might like to

have a little talk with Miss Maguire, here. All about Chinese strangulation. C'mon over here, honey.''

It was too risky. Maggie dropped the gun and took her hand from her pocket. She moved in front of Harriet, whispering, ''Get back.''

Ralphie turned his back to the wind and peered inside the box. ''Oh, sweet Jesus,'' he muttered. She couldn't hear him, but she could see his lips moving.

Corcoran beckoned with his free hand. ''Don't be shy. C'mon over and tell me all about it. I'm just dyin' to hear about it, you buttoned-up little prude.''

Maggie shook her head.

Corcoran said, ''I've got the gun, remember?''

She stood her ground. ''You may have the gun, Mr. Corcoran, but I've got my standards.''

''What?''

''You heard me.''

''You little bitch!''

Maggie folded her arms. ''Bastard,'' she said, smiling.

Corcoran had the nerve to appear shocked. He said, ''Why, you dirty-mouthed tart!''

''Can't have it both ways, Mr. Corcoran. I'm either a buttoned-up prude or a—''

''Jesus!'' Ralphie broke in, closing the box with a snap. ''Will you two quit it?''

''Move,'' Corcoran snarled, ''or I'll shoot the squaw.''

Maggie gave an exaggerated sigh and unfolded her arms, holding out her hands. ''Don't get your underpants in a knot, Mr. Corcoran. I'm coming.''

She heard Grady say her name, but she moved toward Corcoran, through a wall of wind, until she was standing three feet away.

''Well, well,'' Corcoran said. ''Not so high and mighty now.''

''Be a pity to do that Chinese choking thing on her without we have some fun first,'' Ralphie offered, the box now trapped tight under his arm. ''I got a handful of her skirt in Frisco. I'd like to have me a look-see at what's underneath before you cap her.''

Corcoran said, "C'mere, baby," and reached for her arm, which was just what she wanted him to do. In a blink, she grabbed him by the forearm, ducked down, and flipped him over her shoulder.

An easy toss, she thought, as he landed with a surprised *oof*. She wheeled around and clipped the wrist of his gun hand. His Smith & Wesson went flying.

Pete scurried to reclaim his holster, but Ralphie had beat him to it. She felt the cold steel barrel of a gun press against the back of her neck.

He said, "Slow down, cowboy," and Pete froze. "Back off," he said. Pete did.

And then she heard Grady—foolish, gallant Grady—say, "Drop it right now, Ralph Scaggs."

The second she felt an absence of pressure from Ralphie's gun, she reached into her pocket and rolled and fired even as she heard two other shots—Grady's and Ralphie's. Her bullet took Ralphie in the throat, but he was already falling, shot in the upper right chest, clutching the box. Grady was down.

She leapt to her feet, kicked the pistol away from Ralphie, and ran to Grady.

He was still breathing.

"You idiot," she scolded, weeping, and checking his clothing. "You silly fool!"

His eyelids fluttered. "At least my skirt isn't on fire."

Smoke streamed from her pocket, caught by the wind, and she beat it out, cursing softly. She hadn't had time to clear the material before she'd fired.

"That's better," he said. "Am I going to die, Mags? I'd rather not die in a place called the Devil's Shute."

"You won't. Not unless you get blood poisoning, you dear old goof." She was tugging at his coat, pulling it off. When he cringed, she said, "Don't be a baby," and worked it off his arm. "There. You see? Passed right through the meat. You'll be fine."

"That's easy for you to say. You haven't been shot."

"Not today, anyway," she said, ripping his sleeve.

"Fine. Try and one-up me. Here I am, lying helpless as a puppy, and you—"

They both jumped as the report of single shot ripped the air. Maggie spun around to find Biscuit Pete with his arm around Harriet's throat. The box was in Harriet's hands now. A thin trail of smoke blew sideways from the barrel of his pistol. It was pointed at Corcoran, who was now the late Mr. Corcoran.

"Pete?" she said.

"You folks are really pretty good," he said over the wind, swinging the muzzle toward her, and he didn't sound like himself at all. Gone was the lazy drawl, the slow, stupid air. Gone, too, was the slightly glazed expression. Suddenly he had a sharp, piercing look, like a bird of prey. "Real good, in fact. Seems a shame to kill you, but I can't leave any witnesses, now, can I?"

From the ground, Grady said, "What the hell is going on? I mean, if you're going to shoot me, I think I have a right to know. Who the devil are you?"

Pete snorted. "I'm the man with the diamonds, that's who. That's all you need to know." He turned to Maggie. "You still got that Colt in your pocket?"

"No," she lied.

He cocked his pistol and brought it up to Harriet's temple. "Bullshit. Reach in there real easy and bring it out. Two fingers."

Harriet's face was expressionless, and Maggie had no idea whose side she was on, or whether she'd gone into shock. Slowly, Maggie reached into her scorched pocket, found the gun, and plucked it out with her fingertips.

"Good," said Pete. Just then the wind gusted and took his hat, but he didn't flinch, didn't even look to see where it had gone. He said, "Now toss it over by the bodies."

She did. She still had her derringer, and he was only fifteen feet away, maybe fourteen. She thought she could hit him at this range. But what if she couldn't? The gun was famous for bad shots, and you had to be within ten feet, fewer really, to be sure. What if she missed and he shot Harriet, or worse, *she* shot Harriet? Grady's pistol had flown wide when he went down. There was no possible way she could reach it.

Playing for time, she said, "I think you owe me an explanation."

He snorted. "I don't owe you a damn thing, lady."

"Then humor me, Pete. Did Ralphie hire you?"

"Never seen him before in my life."

"What?" That took her by surprise.

"You heard me. Stand up."

Maggie got to her feet, glancing quickly at Grady.

"Him, too."

"He's wounded!"

Pete let out an exaggerated sigh that the wind whisked away. "He's only shot in the arm. He can stand up. I don't like to shoot people when they're lyin' down."

Maggie tipped her head toward Corcoran. "Didn't stop you there, I see."

"I made an exception."

"Oh." With Maggie's aid, Grady took his feet, and as he did, he passed something behind his back, into Maggie's hand. His pocket knife. She thought, *God bless you, Grady,* and took it without giving a sign.

Pete said, "All right." He still pressed his gun to Harriet's temple. "I reckon you could know some of it. Hate to see you die with a mystery still burnin' on your brains. Nobody hired me. I followed Hattie up from Moldy River. Didn't know her from squat and paid my fifty cents like everybody else, but Hattie, here? She talks sometimes when she's drunk and not quite asleep. Started talking about hidin' the box. Got to hide the box, she says, her mama's tellin' her to hide the box. Had me kind of curious, but not much to remark on until I was talkin' to some feller in the bar who'd known her right after she first started out, after she came out of Rusty Hinge. He told me her real name."

Maggie opened the knife behind her skirts. It had, perhaps, only a four-inch blade and a disastrous balance, but it would have to do. She said, "What would her name mean to you?"

"Wouldn't have meant nothin', except I'd just been up to Seattle, tracking down the last of the Joyner boys."

"The Joyner boys?" Maggie searched her memory, and the name clicked coldly into place. "The cabin. The old Dawson place. The Joyner boys were with you when you hanged Dawson.''

He gave a curt nod. "They were. 'Cept I didn't help 'em. Fred Joyner held me down while they did it.''

Beside her, Grady whispered, "What in the world is he talking about?''

Maggie ignored him. She'd just had a revelation. "You didn't ride up there with them, did you, Pete? And that rope wasn't a souvenir. You just couldn't stand to see it up there, because Dawson was *your* father. You killed that other man, too, didn't you? What was his name? Hashknife something.''

"Hashknife Jack. He was easy.''

"And the Joyner boys.''

"All three,'' he said proudly. "Took me a few years, but I tracked 'em down.''

"And then there was just Sopsucher—Kid Concho. Except he never left town. You couldn't do it, there wasn't any chance.'' Her stomach sank. "Not until we sent him up into the hills to collect those bodies.''

"Bingo. It took me eleven years to get my revenge, but by God, I done it. My name's Teddy Dawson, by the way, like my pa. Took on the Pete Soda handle a few years back from a feller that sort of died. Somebody else gave me the Biscuit.'' He smiled. "You're good, lady. Too bad I'm gonna have to kill you. Witnesses, and all that horseshit.''

"Excuse me,'' said Grady, over the wind, "but if you don't mind, how did you know about the diamonds? Even Harriet didn't know.''

Pete shrugged. "Didn't. Just put two and two together—Hattie mumbling about a box and her mama making her bury it, and Horace being so rich and all, and beating the bushes for Hattie for so long. I checked into it. Figured it was good odds there was something valuable in there. Cash or gold or something. Didn't figure on anything near so fancy. I figure, now that I'm done and Pa can rest easy, I could use a nest egg. I want to thank you folks for bein' so helpful.''

Dryly, Grady said, "Delighted, I'm sure.''

Pete said, "Well, I guess it's time I got movin'. Good-bye, folks.'' He grabbed the box from Harriet, shoving her away.

And as he did, Maggie hurled the knife.

She was right about the balance being off, and instead of his throat, where she'd aimed, it took him high in his shoulder. He stared at it for a second, then pointed his gun directly at her and said, "Why, you—"

Even as Maggie jacked the derringer down into her hand, Harriet let out an ear-spitting Apache cry that nearly startled Maggie out of her shoes, and leapt upon Pete. The gun went off, high, hitting nothing, as she tore the knife from his flesh, stabbing him over and over again. He fell, fending her off the best he could, but the knife kept rising and falling, and soon he lay still.

By the time Maggie could pull Hattie off of him, her bodice and arms were red with blood. She retrieved the box and took the doll out, clutching it to her bosom with bloody hands, and dropped to the ground, cross-legged. Diamonds slowly dribbling into her lap, she said, "They come no more. Not hurt anybody anymore." And then she sat, silently, in the shimmering, blowing fog of dust.

"Good Lord," said Grady, his own blood soaking his arm, his hat long since blown away. "Good Lord."

THIRTY-THREE

>——I—◆——O——◆—I——<

A T LAST THE BODIES WERE LOADED INTO THE WAGON, and Grady was fussing with his arm again. Maggie's rented horse had bolted at the gunfire, but Pete's remained. Both Grady and Maggie wore scarves over their noses and mouths—Grady, a bandanna taken off the late Silas Corcoran; Maggie, a wide strip torn off her petticoat.

Harriet was up on the buckboard seat, hunched over and holding her doll.

"Don't pick at that, Grady," said Maggie, sitting on the tailgate between the boots of corpses, her legs wide beneath her skirts, mopping her brow. She was exhausted. "You'll get grit in it, and then you'll really be sorry. Good gravy, but they weighed a ton! Even that little Corcoran. I'd sure like to know what his story was."

Grady took a last peek under his bandage, which Maggie had hastily torn from his shirt, then went back on all fours, searching through the blowing dust. "Not as heavy as Pete. Or Teddy, or Billy Bob, or whatever the devil his name turned out to be. This thing hurts like sin, Mags. You sure I'm not dying?"

"The only thing killing you is this wind. I swear, I've swallowed a pound of dust." Maggie turned her head so that the wind pelted her in the back of the skull instead of her face. It was a small relief. "I've never seen the like, not when it didn't turn into a thunderstorm. Or a full-blown dust storm."

"And this isn't?"

"No, this is just enough to be annoying." She slid down

off the tailgate and checked the saddle horses' tie ropes to see they were secure. Altogether, there were three horses, with Corcoran's and Ralphie's. She stared at Grady for a moment. "You sure you've got them all?"

Grady stood up stiffly and beat his hands against his britches. Billows of dust bloomed, were caught in the wind, and disappeared. "Just the three," he said, walking toward the wagon and digging in his pocket. He held his cupped hand out to Maggie. Three cut diamonds—the smallest two were at least one carat, perhaps a carat and a half. The largest—about two carats—winked up at her along with the others.

"Stick them in your pocket for now," she said. "Let's get out of this blasted wind." She climbed up onto the wagon seat. Harriet hadn't said another thing, not even when they moved her, dribbling diamonds, to the wagon. Maggie had a pocketful of them. "Harriet?" she said softly, leaning close. "Harriet?"

Slowly, Harriet turned her grimy face. She said, "We go now, Mag-wire?"

"Yes, Harriet," she said, as Grady climbed up on the other side. "We go."

"You drive," said Grady, dryly. "I may pass out from my injury at any moment."

Shaking her head, Maggie took up the reins and they started the dusty drive back to Sky Butte.

Once they climbed the hill, up to the road, the wind calmed abruptly. In fact, the breeze was light and pleasant. "How very odd," observed Grady, pulling away his bandanna. "It seemed more gradual on the way down. And I'll be damned if I can see those rocks from here. Strange."

"Must be some trick of the topography," said Maggie, more to herself than to him, then giggled.

"What? What's so funny?"

"Nothing," she said, and drove on, pulling her own scarf off, scrubbing it quickly over the upper portion of her face. It came away black.

Grady had taken off his glasses and was rubbing them with the inside of his shirt. She broke out laughing.

"What?" demanded Grady. "What?"

She elbowed Harriet and pointed, and a grin burst over Harriet's face. She said, "Raccoon man!"

"Oh, for the love of Mike!" Grady rubbed at his forehead. "Why didn't you tell me? Isn't it bad enough that I'm practically shot to death, without having to suffer indignities as—" He stopped, staring ahead. "Maggie, look."

Another wagon was approaching them, from the direction of Sky Butte.

"Probably just sightseers," Maggie said, but she reached into her pocket anyway, feeling for the Colt.

Grady stuck his glasses, half cleaned, back on his face and groped beneath the bench for his pistol.

"You really ought to invest in a shoulder holster," Maggie said, and wondered how in the world they'd explain three bodies. The wagon was nearing. She could make out a man and a woman. The man wasn't dressed like a local. He wore a light brown suit and a bowler hat. And the woman looked faintly familiar.

"What do you think?" said Grady.

Maggie kept her eyes on the approaching wagon. She'd seen that woman before. The woman raised an arm in greeting. "Hello, Miss Maguire!" she called, and Maggie knew. It was the woman from the stage. Cora. Cora Trimble.

To Grady, she said, "She was on the stage with Corcoran."

"I've been meaning to ask you—"

"Later," Maggie said, cutting him off. The wagon was pulling even with them. "Just keep that gun ready."

"Whoa!" The driver of the other wagon reined in his horses. Maggie did likewise.

"Afternoon," she said. She nodded at the woman. "Mrs. Trimble. What an unexpected pleasure to see you again."

"Likewise, I'm sure, Miss Maguire," she said with a cheery smile. She fluttered a hand toward their cargo. "You've been busy, I see. Three?"

Maggie opened her mouth, but Cora kept talking. "Let's see . . . there's Ralph Scaggs and Silas Corcoran." She stood up in the seat, peering over Grady's shoulder. "The third one's Pete Soda, isn't it? Or should I say, Teddy Dawson. Messy." She sat back down and smiled brightly. "Excellent, Miss Maguire, excellent! You've made our job so much easier.''

Shaking her head, Maggie said, ''Wait a minute. What job? Who are you people, anyway?''

''Oh, dear,'' said Cora, plump hands working the fastening of her handbag. ''How remiss of me.'' She pulled free a small alligator card case and passed it to her driver, who in turn passed it to Grady, who peeked inside and handed it past Harriet, to Maggie.

''You're going to love this,'' he muttered.

Maggie opened the case one-handed. She stared at the card inside. She closed it again. She took her hand off the gun in her pocket, and sat erect, staring at Cora Trimble.

''Pinkertons,'' she said with disgust.

''I'd like to thank you, Miss Maguire, for doing our legwork for us.''

''Legwork?!'' she spat, suddenly so angry she could have eaten a lizard and spat alligators. ''I solved the whole blasted case for you and brought in Biscuit Pete Soda to boot! And who hired you, anyway? If Quincy Applegate doesn't trust me to—''

Cora held up her hands. ''Calm down, Miss Maguire. We never so much as spoke to Mr. Applegate. Our orders came from a higher source. The government, to be precise.''

Grady leaned forward. ''You expect us to believe that the government is even slightly interested in—''

''A little Indian captive? No, not very much. Not any more than is appropriate, anyway. But diamonds? Yes, indeed, Mr. Maguire. Another matter entirely.''

Just then, another stone fell from Harriet's doll and into her lap. ''Star,'' she said, without expression.

''Miss Maguire,'' said Cora, redirecting her attention to Maggie, who sat stiffly, seething and thinking nasty thoughts about Pinkerton agents, ''your cousin needs medical attention. I suggest you trade places with my driver, and we all go into town. We'll chat.''

''Yes,'' said Maggie, ice in her voice. ''Let's.''

''Now, Mags . . .'' Grady warned.

She paid him no attention, and hopped down off the buckboard. She marched around the horses to Cora's buggy, passing her companion. She stopped. She grabbed his arm. She said, "You look awfully familiar."

He crooked a finger beneath his nose in imitation of a mustache and said, " 'Nother beer, sonny?" And then he had the gall to wink.

"Blast!" she said. She heard him chuckling as she went around the side of the wagon and climbed aboard, next to Cora.

She heard him give a curt hello to Grady, and then, "Hello, Harriet. Don't be afraid. I'm Agent Caulder."

Grady's wagon moved out at a walk, and Cora reined her team around to follow them. Staring at the dead men, their bodies jostling in the back of Grady's wagon, Maggie said, "I'm waiting for an explanation. And it had better be good."

"Certainly, Miss Maguire. I'm glad to give it." Cora took the reins in one meaty hand and gave Maggie her purse. "There's a mirror and brush in there. Perhaps you'd care to fix your hair while we talk? You look blown to pieces."

THIRTY-FOUR

B ACK IN SKY BUTTE, WHILE GRADY WAS ACROSS THE
street at the doctor's office, and Cora's companion, that
sneaky now-he-has-a-mustache, now-he-doesn't Agent
Caulder, unloaded the bodies with the help of a deputy, Maggie sat down in the sheriff's office and took Harriet's arm.

"These people want to look at your doll for just a few
minutes, Harriet. They'll give it back to you. All right?"

Harriet, who had been silent all the long trip back, said,
"These people nice?"

"Yes," said Maggie, although if she could have smacked
Cora Trimble, she would have. "They're friends."

"Not want to hurt Mag-wire?"

"No," she said. They certainly didn't want to hurt her physically. They'd just taken a few good shots at her pride, that
was all. She'd almost rather they'd come at her with a knife.

Harriet suddenly stuck her arm out, handing the doll to Cora
and saying, "Then lady can take."

"You might as well take these, too," said Maggie, delving
into her left skirt pocket. She came up with a handful of cut
stones, which she spread on the sheriff's desk.

Cora Trimble busily cut seams in the doll's arms and legs
and poured more diamonds on the desk. Hattie watched stoically. Maggie took in the process with something akin to stomach cramps.

Satisfied the doll was empty, Cora handed it back, a shapeless rag of leather, and said, "Pardon me for asking, Miss
Maguire, but are you certain your pockets are empty?"

Anger surged through her, but she said, "Absolutely, Mrs. Trimble. However, you can search me if you like." She held her arms out from her sides, staring Cora in the eye.

Cora wisely demurred. "I, uh . . . I don't believe that's necessary. Sheriff?"

The sheriff of Sky Butte, who had been standing back, wide-eyed at having real Pinkertons in his office and dumbstruck at the diamonds, said, "Ma'am?"

"Could you arrange for the reward on Theodore Dawson, alias Pete Soda, to be sent to—"

"Me," Maggie cut in, handing the sheriff her card. "If you don't mind, Mrs. Trimble?"

Harriet tugged at her sleeve. She turned, and Harriet held up what was left of the doll. "Flat," she said unhappily.

"We'll fix it," Maggie said, then turned back to Cora. "And now, if you don't need any more dirty work done, I believe I'll take my leave."

The Pinkerton agent folded her arms across her ample belly. "I believe that will about do it." As Maggie squired Harriet out the door, she heard Cora Trimble behind her, talking to the sheriff. "One more thing," she was saying, her voice growing faint as Maggie gained distance. "One of our agents has gone missing . . ."

"Well, it just makes me mad, that's all!" Maggie said, stabbing at her chicken. "I mean, here I get shot and you get shot—"

"An ear hardly compares with what I've suffered, Mags. I can't even *see* yours anymore." He hugged his sling, trying to look pitiful.

"All right, I get nicked and you get shot. Better?"

"Don't forget the stitches in the back of my head. I'm disfigured for life, I tell you!"

"Your hair covers it."

"And my saddle sores. Don't forget about my saddle sores!" Then he thought of Miriam Cosgrove, and how unromantic saddle sores sounded. "On second thought," he added, "maybe we'd best forget about those."

They were taking supper in Maggie and Harriet's room. The

hotel was much finer than the one in Bent Elbow. It served from its own kitchen till ten, and the menu, if not exciting, was at least filling. He lifted the lid off another dish. Noodles in some kind of sauce.

He offered the plate. "Harriet? Noodles?"

She picked up her fork in her fist and stabbed at it, and he said, "No, no. Remember what I told you?"

Harriet stuck out her lip and furrowed her brow in concentration, then took back her fork. She lifted the serving spoon and ladled noodles over the top of her string beans.

He said, "Well, that's better, anyway. We'll work more on it later." Then to Maggie, who sat across the little table chewing angrily, he said, "Well? So far, all I've heard is a great deal of complaining, and I have yet to hear the story. How long are you going to make me wait?"

She swallowed. "The short version or long one? I warn you, the long one makes me angrier."

"By all means, short."

She took a drink of water. "All right. It seems that Horace was more than a crackpot Bible-thumper with a knack for cutting lumber and marketing it."

"Funny," said Grady. "I should think that would be enough for any man."

"Do you want to hear it or not?"

"Sorry. Go on. Harriet, use your napkin."

Maggie waited for Harriet to wipe the gravy off her chin. "Back during the Civil War," she said, "two shipments of gold went missing."

Grady opened his mouth, but before he could ask, she said, "Union. Now be quiet. Anyway, at the time it was blamed on the South—an easy mistake, considering. But later on, somebody figured out that it hadn't been a war crime at all, and tracked it back to none other than our very own Horace Hogg."

"Who figured it out?" interrupted Grady. "When?"

Maggie sighed. "This is the short version, remember? Anyway, they couldn't pin it on him, because the gold had disappeared into thin air. Poof. And Horace had gone to Washington—"

"To find fame and fortune deforesting the Great Northwest," Grady cut in.

"Exactly," said Maggie. "Except he left his wife and daughter behind. They were watched closely, as was Horace, but there wasn't any overspending. No trips abroad. No fancy carriages, not even any elaborate parties. Eventually the case faded into the background. The Pinkertons decided maybe they'd been wrong."

"The Pinkertons had this case? Way back then?"

Maggie stared at him. She held up one hand and wiggled the fingers. "The government," she said. She held up the other. "The Pinkertons." She clasped her hands, interlacing the fingers. "Get the idea?"

Grady nodded, and sneaked another bite of chicken.

"So a couple of years go by, and Harriet and her mother set out to join Horace. Nobody thinks anything about it, except that about a month later, somebody down in records, somebody working on an unrelated case, finds that an enormous amount of gold has been systematically—and rather stealthily—converted into diamonds, first by way of—"

"I thought this was the short version," Grady broke in between mouthfuls.

Maggie gave him an annoyed look, which bothered him not one bit. He helped himself to another slice of bread and began buttering it, one-handed.

"All right," she said. "So now it's diamonds, through a very interesting set of trades, which I won't bother you with."

"Thank you. Harriet, we hold our knives this way." He put his bread down and demonstrated, saying, "Go on, Mags."

"Are you even *interested* in how we—that is, Harriet—came to lose one point three million dollars in diamonds?"

Grady returned Harriet's knife and sat back in his chair. "Good Lord! That much, was it?"

"Oh, Grady, sometimes I could just murder you!"

"Sorry, Mags. I'm listening."

"Well, *anyway,* Mrs. Hogg must have had them in the house somewhere, because when Horace sent the doll, it was clean. They used to check all the parcels before they were delivered. So sometime in there, after Harriet 'lost' it, Mama

Hogg got out her little needle and thread and went to work like a good wife. Then they started for the West Coast, with the doll in the strongbox.''

"Why the doll?" Grady asked. "Why not just carry them loose in the box?"

Maggie shrugged. "The doll looks innocent enough. If they were stopped, nobody'd steal a doll. And she could say that she put it away to punish Harriet. I'm just supposing, here."

"So the Indians attacked them," said Grady, picking up his fork, "and Mama thought 'oops!' and panicked, and sent little Harriet to hide the goodies, which she did. Except that Mama met an untimely end, and the Indians carted off Harriet. End of story. Until the Pinkertons got wind that Horace had died and you were off after Harriet." He took another bite of chicken, then picked up his bread.

Maggie's brow furrowed. "Did Agent Caulder tell you this already? On the trip back to town?"

He paused, the bread in midair. "Not at all. The man was positively tight-lipped."

"Pass chicken," Harriet said.

"Please," said Grady, picking up the platter. "*Please* pass the chicken."

"Please," said Harriet, and took another leg.

"Good," said Grady.

Maggie wadded her napkin and smacked it down beside her plate. "If I'm boring you, I'll leave the table."

"Not at all, Maggie. Harriet and I are fascinated." He looked over at Harriet, two-fistedly devouring the chicken. "Well, I am, anyway."

"All right. Agents Caulder and Trimble were dispatched along with several others, but they were ordered to follow me and keep a low profile. They also knew about Corcoran—"

"Who was he, anyway?"

"A private investigator," Maggie sniffed disdainfully. "Not one with very high standards, I must say. It's men like him who give a bad name to—"

"Go on," Grady urged, hoping to avoid a diatribe. "What else?"

"Well. They knew about most of the others, too. Not Evil

Eye Garrett, but about the others, and some we didn't come across, most of which they picked up. Altogether, Ralph Scaggs had promised one hundred and fifteen percent of the inheritance.''

"Which, of course, was a small price to pay," Grady said thoughtfully.

"Exactly," said Maggie, nodding. "Considering the pot at the end of the rainbow. And considering he most likely planned to hop the first ship bound for Europe and short everyone in a most profound way. Of course, he didn't count on a wild card like Biscuit Pete. Well, who would have? So the diamonds go back to the government. The Pinkertons probably get a nice juicy reward. Oh, I've been promised a share, but I'm not holding my breath."

Grady picked up his fork again. "The Agency must think highly of us. I mean, you. If they were just supposed to follow you, that is."

"I don't know whether they respect my work, or if they just figured they'd let me take the knocks for them. I know they have a file on me. Cora Trimble remarked on it. Though by the way I bungled this job, I don't see why they'd care."

Grady studied her face for a moment, then said softly, "Mags, what on earth makes you believe—"

"I should have known!" she said. "I should have at least figured out that Kid Concho business—I mean, it was so obvious!"

"You weren't there to figure out Kid Concho, Maggie."

"Well, I should have, that's all. I might have saved his life. Well, not saved it, exactly, but prevented his death. If I'd figured out Biscuit Pete."

"If, if, if," Grady said. He'd best get her out of this mood before it took hold, or it would be weeks before she was her old self again. "My dear Maggie, you found Harriet, and you kept her safe—well, reasonably safe," he added, remembering that romp in the mountains. Correction, foothills. "You found her and protected her. That was what the job was. It was what you were hired for. And in addition, you recovered more than a million dollars in diamonds. I'd say that's cause for celebration, not soul-searching. And what happened to Sopsucher just happened, that's all. You couldn't have prevented it. If it wasn't Pete, it would have been somebody else from his past, sooner or later.''

"There's still Harriet,'' she said, her head propped in her hands. " 'Of sound mind and will, untouched by liquor or spirits, and unblemished by savage hands,' '' she quoted. "Oh, I'm batting a thousand, all right. How am I ever going to get her past Quincy?''

Grady buttered another slice of bread. He was beginning to get the hang of it. "Oh, I don't think you'll have that much trouble. For one thing, Quincy's soft on you.''

"He is not!''

"And she's sober. And she's learning, aren't you, Harriet?''

The girl looked up, a chicken wing in her fist. "Learn fast.''

"You see, Mags?''

"But she had a couple of—I'll tell you about that part later. All I can say is you'd better work a miracle, Grady. You really think he's soft on me?''

He winked at her. "You'd have to be blind not to see it.''

She actually blushed! Well, that was a shocker. She was soft on Quincy, too! She looked up, suddenly smiling. Well, sort of a smile. "I took care of Mr. Tom Festing. The sheriff here said he'd have the U.S. marshal investigate. I'll bet they turn up all sorts of goodies. Still, I wish . . .''

He put his good hand on her arm. "Mags,'' he said softly.

She sighed, then brightened. It was artificial, but it was a start. She said, "I'll just be glad to get home to Otto and Ozzie.''

This time it was his turn to sigh. "How much you want to bet Otto's got my telephone in pieces? I can just see it now, laid out all over the desk. . . .''

"How's your arm?''

"Better than my telephone, no doubt. I'll live.'' When she arched a brow, he added, "Oh, I know, I should be crabbing to beat the band. But frankly, the thought of a nice cozy train ride with San Francisco at the end of it is a marvelous pain-killer. That slug of laudanum the doctor gave me didn't hurt, either.'' He turned his head. Harriet was having cutlery problems again. "Harriet, don't hold your spoon like you're going to stab someone with it. Here, like this . . ."

Grady took Harriet's spoon and handed it back, folding it into her hand correctly. "By the way, I found something while I was emptying my pockets for the laundry." He made a show of patting his chest, then his pants. "Now where did I put it? Ah, yes. Here it is."

He pulled a handkerchief, the ends twisted, from his front pocket. Laying it on the table, he slowly unwrapped the three stones he'd found. "Our fee," he said. "What do you say, old darling? One set of earrings for you, one stickpin for me?"

Maggie, aghast, looked at the handkerchief's contents. "You didn't."

His hand over his heart, he said, "I found them on the desert, Maggie. They'd be lying there into the next century if I hadn't picked them up!"

"You have to take them back."

"But Maggie!"

"Take them back."

He sighed, and tried his best to look like a wounded kitten. "Mags?"

"Back."

POSTSCRIPT

TWO WEEKS LATER

>━┤━◆━◯━◆━┤━<

WHILE QUINCY CHECKED WITH THE *MAÎTRE D'*, Maggie took a moment to tug at the neckline of the infamous blue silk dress. She wished she'd stuck something into her cleavage. A scarf, perhaps, or a handkerchief. Maybe a cocker spaniel.

It wasn't nearly as scandalous as many of the other dresses she saw in the nightclub—a glittery, high-ceilinged affair, full of red-upholstered furnishings and waiters with towels over their arms and diamond-encrusted clientele and a small, tuxedo-clad orchestra that, at the moment, was playing a waltz. Still, she'd spent too many days buttoned up to the throat to feel comfortable in anything even slightly plunging. She felt that any moment her breasts would pop all the way out and wave at someone across the room. Probably someone she knew, who would rehash the story at dinner parties for years.

"My dear?" said Quincy Applegate, breathtakingly handsome as usual. He offered his arm. "You're blushing," he said, as they started the walk to the table. "Anything wrong?"

Dear gorgeous, never-a-wrong-foot Quincy. How could she explain that she had just pictured one of her bosoms signing autographs for the couple in the far corner? A change of subject was in order, and just then her gaze landed on the perfect one.

She said, "Isn't that Grady over there?"

"Ah." Quincy brightened, then frowned. "He's not going to join us, is he? I want you all to myself tonight, Magdalena."

She gripped his arm tighter. Quin always knew just the right

thing to say to give her butterflies. She said, "Let's just say
hello, shall we?"

Grady saw them approaching, and stood up, one arm still
in a sling, the other waving over the heads of the other diners.
He fit in here. Everything was loud and merry. The men
looked wealthy and carefree, the women were the epitome of
stylish, monied San Francisco upper crust. In fact, the room
was San Francisco—one generation removed from the grimy,
free-for-all mining camps, and another generation, she supposed, before it was scolded into shape by back-East morals.
It was a good time to be alive.

Unless you got shanghaied, or unless you were Chinese or
Mexican or just plain born poor, or unless you—

"Mags!" Grady enthused, breaking into her reverie, which
was a good thing, since it was going downhill fast. She wanted
tonight to be merry.

"Hello, you charmer," she said, brushing a kiss over his
cheek and plucking a cat hair off his lapel.

"Maggie!" he whispered, glancing down toward her cleavage and wiggling his eyebrows. "My God! You're a woman!"

As she turned, she clipped his shin with her heel, and without comment offered a gloved hand to the blond, busty bit of
fluff sitting beside him. "You must be Miriam." She made a
mental note not to get too close, lest one of Miriam's breasts
put her eye out.

"Charmed, I'm sure," said Miriam, who mustered a little
more enthusiasm for Quincy's hello. Actually, a lot more. He
was looking a tad uncomfortable.

"Ah, champagne!" said Grady, still hopping on one foot
and doing his best not to be obvious about it. He said, "Won't
you join us, Applegate?" and gave Maggie a look that said,
"Won't you leave as soon as possible? Preferably at a run?"

Maggie moved out of the waiter's way but remained standing. "Sorry, but Quin and I—"

"Grady was just telling me about his exploits," Miriam
broke in. "How he saved your life and got mortally wounded
and all."

Maggie looked toward Grady and hoisted her brows. "Was
he?" she said, and sat down. Quincy sat next to her, resign-

edly. "Did he also tell you that the minute we walked into the office he ran to his telephone and wept?"

Miriam said, "Beg pardon?"

"Only because I'd been counting on it to bring me closer to you, dear Miriam," Grady said, glaring at Maggie.

"It was broken," Maggie explained, smiling. "Someone had taken it apart."

Quincy grinned. "Otto been at work again?"

Grady reached for the champagne, grumbling, "It went back together. Thank God."

"And in only a day and a half," Maggie said brightly.

Grady's lips twisted. "At least I didn't bring a horse home with me."

"Nickel had nowhere else to go," she replied indignantly, as he lifted the champagne bottle. "You wouldn't want him to go to the glue factory, would you?"

"Oh, no, by all means, save him. I enjoy writing the board checks. Keeps my penmanship in shape."

"You two!" said Quincy with a laugh, then, "Just one glass." As Grady poured, he added apologetically, "We haven't eaten yet."

Miriam giggled behind her hand and said, "Who needs food?"

Champagne was poured and glasses were passed, and then Miriam said, "Let's make a toast," obviously thinking it would be to some facet of her beauty. Girls like Miriam, Maggie thought somewhat nastily, always expected toasts.

So Maggie said, "To Harriet," and raised her glass.

"To Harriet," said Quincy.

Grady said, "Hear, hear."

Miriam looked puzzled, but went along.

"How's she doing?" Grady asked after the toast had been drunk.

"Splendidly," Quincy replied. "Mrs. Russell, her father's nurse, has brought her along swimmingly. She's progressing well with her studies. I must say, you people made a spectacular job of getting her back in one piece." He patted Maggie's hand. "She's certainly told some stories."

Maggie felt heat traveling up her neck. "Stories?"

"Living with the Indians. Then that relocation camp. Then working on the dreary farm in Arizona, then the granary, before she migrated to Nevada and took shelter in the convent."

Maggie looked at Grady. Grady said, "Convent? Farm?"

"The hog farm," said Quincy, picking up a breadstick. "Surely she said something about it."

"I don't recall," muttered Maggie, still looking toward Grady. She elbowed a spoon off the table, and both she and Grady dived for it. "Couldn't she have come up with something better than *that*?" she hissed beneath the tablecloth. She picked a cat hair off of his cuff. "I thought you two settled on the story about the Mormon family that took her in. I don't even know that there *is* a convent in Nevada! And a pig farm?"

"Just be grateful she came up with anything at all," Grady whispered. "And stop plucking me!" He grabbed the spoon and sat up. "Amazing girl," he announced brightly. "Another round, everyone?"

"This toast should be to the Pinkertons, I think." Quincy lifted his glass again, and Grady obligingly filled it.

"The Pinkertons?" asked Maggie, brows raised. It was turning out to be a depressing evening. At least Grady was doing his best to get Quincy drunk. Maybe he wouldn't remember.

Quincy dug into an inside pocket, pulled out an envelope, and handed it to her with a flourish. "For you, Magdalena."

Maggie clinked her glass with the others halfheartedly and downed the contents in one gulp. "What is it?" she asked, eyeing the return address suspiciously, and then opening it. Inside was a bank draft, in the amount of five hundred dollars. At one corner was the memo *Hogg/Reward*.

She stuck it back in the envelope and said, "Hit me again, Grady."

He picked up the bottle. "Mags, think of tomorrow."

"I don't care. Hit me."

"Harriet's been doing a little investing, too," Quincy went on. "I believe I'd like another glass while you're at it, Grady."

"Investing?" said Grady. He emptied the bottle into

Quincy's champagne flute and signaled the waiter for another bottle.

"Of course, we have to give permission. Western Mutual Specialties controls the trust. But so far, she's chosen very well. Bought a little concern that manufactures paper products. Paper boxes, cardboard shoes, and the like. Dovetails nicely with the family lumber business. And today she bought a distillery."

Maggie choked on her champagne, and Quincy and Grady both patted her on the back.

"I'm fine, I'm fine," she said. And then, afraid of the answer but utterly unable to keep silent, she asked, "A distillery?"

Quincy looked at the ceiling for a moment, thinking. "Old Backwash, I believe. Nasty name. I tried to talk her into changing it, but the only name she could come up with was, oh, what was it? Something Cougar. Or maybe puma?"

"Tall Cougar," said Maggie.

"Yes. How on earth did you know?"

"Wild guess," said Maggie.

He continued, "Well, we're better off with Old Backwash, if you ask me."

Miriam, apparently weary of being ignored, tugged Quincy's sleeve. "Dance with me," she said with a pout, shooting Grady a nasty look, and practically pulled Quincy to his feet.

Maggie waved them away. "Go, Quincy," she said. "Dance."

Wearing a pained expression, he allowed himself to be dragged away.

"Another toast," said Maggie. She held out her glass. Grady filled it, then lifted his, waiting. "To Alvin Sopsucher, the late, great Kid Concho," she said.

"Hear, hear. Kid Concho," Grady said. "May he live forever in legend." They both drained their glasses, then sat, silently. After a moment, Grady asked, "So what's in the envelope?"

"What? Oh. A bank draft."

He brightened.

"For five hundred dollars."

His face fell again. "That's it? That's the reward for finding more than a million in diamonds?"

"That's it," she grumbled, raking a small furrow in the tablecloth with the nail of her index finger. "Makes me wish you'd kept those three stones you found on the desert."

He gazed up at the ceiling and started to whistle.

She looked at him, her mouth spreading into a grin. "Grady! You didn't!"

He reached into his coat pocket and produced a small, blue velvet box, which he handed to her.

She opened it. A pair of diamond earrings glittered within. They looked much more impressive set in gold than they had loose, in his hand, back in Nevada—and they had been impressive enough then. Mouth hanging open, she looked up.

"Well, I, for one, am glad that's finally out in the open," he said, grinning. He reached into his pocket again and withdrew yet another box. "Now I can wear my new stickpin!"

And then, smiling like the cat who swallowed the canary, he reached for the bottle. "Champagne, Mags?"